# FALSE SECURITY

DEATH BEFORE DRAGONS
BOOK FIVE

LINDSAY BUROKER

*False Security: Death Before Dragons Book 5*
Copyright © 2020 Lindsay Buroker. All rights reserved.

www.lindsayburoker.com

No part of this book may be reproduced, scanned, or distributed in any printed or electronic form without permission. Please do not participate in or encourage piracy of copyrighted materials in violation of the author's rights. Thank you for respecting the hard work of this author.

This is a work of fiction. Names, characters, places and incidents are either the product of the author's imagination or used fictitiously. No reference to any real person, living or dead, should be inferred.

Edited by Shelley Holloway
Cover and interior design by Gene Mollica Studio, LLC.

ISBN: 978-1-951367-08-4

# FALSE SECURITY

# Acknowledgments

Thank you for following along with my Death Before Dragons series. These characters have been a lot of fun to write, and Zav has come a long way (I think you'll agree when you reach the plunger scene).

Before you continue with the adventure, please allow me to thank those who help me put these books together. Thanks to my editor, Shelley Holloway, my beta readers, Sarah Engelke, Rue Silver, and Cindy Wilkinson, and my cover designer, Gene Mollica. Also thank you to Vivienne Leheny for narrating this series for the audiobooks.

I hope you enjoy the new story!

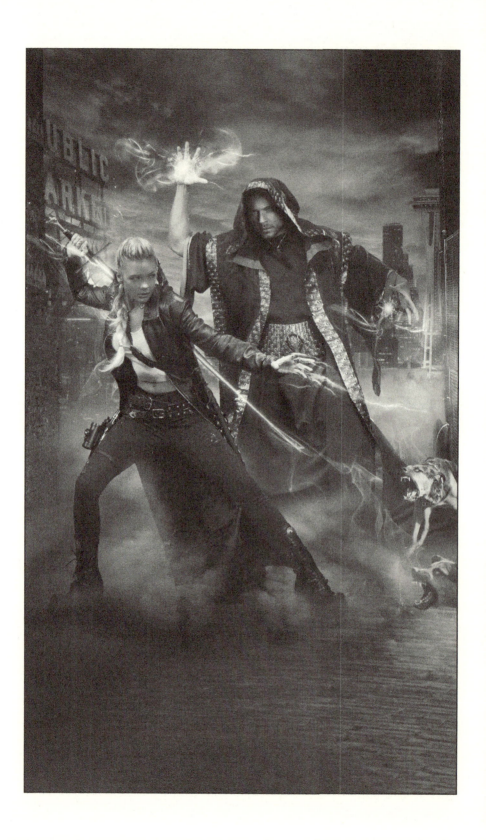

# Chapter 1

"Here it is." Nin smiled and spread an arm toward the front of the four-story, solid gray apartment building, her enthusiastic flourish making her purple pigtails bounce.

"Uh." I'm sure there were better words to describe my first reaction to the monolithic poured-concrete structure, but they eluded me. The sign above the double glass doors read *Paradise Cove*. Hah. "You said your *friend* owns this?"

"And will give you a good deal on the rent, yes. He promised."

"How good of a friend is it? And did he pick it up at the same time as he purchased matching gulag barracks in Russia?"

Nin's brow creased. Maybe gulag hadn't come up on her word-of-the-day apps when she'd been learning English. But as usual, she pieced together the meaning behind my sarcasm. "You do not like the style? I believe it is called brutalism. Is that not perfect for an assassin who brutalizes people for a living?" Her smile returned.

"I'm a half-elf assassin. That means I like trees and leaves and nature and junk." There wasn't a single tree lining the busy street behind us, and the cars honking and buses rumbling past assaulted my sensitive ears. "Didn't you say this is supposed to have a water view?"

I turned to face a gas station across the street. Lake Union was in that direction, but I couldn't see it through the blocks of intervening buildings.

"Or was your friend referring to the pond-sized puddle that was blocking the exit of the alley where we illegally parked?" I shook off my still-damp boot.

This was supposed to be my day off, and my therapist Mary had made me promise to relax. Hunting for an apartment in the overpriced Seattle area was possibly not the most relaxing thing I could have chosen. Just finding a parking spot around here was stressful. But I didn't really know how to relax. Mary had suggested I get a massage but had been nonplussed when I'd asked if I had to take my weapons off for that.

"Perhaps the lake is visible from the upper levels." Nin reached up to pat my shoulder, avoiding the sword scabbard strapped to my back, Chopper's hilt poking up behind my head. Since she was a quarter gnome, she could see the weapon. To most mundane humans, it was invisible unless I took it off. "Let us go inside," she added.

"That's not necessary. Thanks, Nin, but this isn't quite my style."

"But it is only two blocks away from Dimitri's coffee shop. Now that you are a partial owner, it will be good for you to be close so you can keep an eye on everything. His soft opening is this week, remember."

"I remember. But my apartment in Ballard isn't that far away." The apartment my landlord had strongly suggested I leave, due to everyone from dark elves to orcs to government agents coming by this summer to ransack my unit. He didn't even know my now-frequent visitor Zav—or Lord Zavryd'nokquetal, as his fellow dragons called him—was the one responsible for crushing the outdoor chairs on the rooftop deck on a regular basis. As Zav had informed me often, dragons landed where they wished.

"Did you not say the rent is being increased?"

"Yeah, and mine is going up a lot more than anyone else's. The landlord wants me gone."

"I do not think it is legal to single out specific tenants to pay higher rent than others. Come, we have a meeting with Mr. Jeong, the superintendent."

Reluctantly, I followed her through the front door.

Mr. Jeong, a thin man with white wispy hair ringing his bald pate, was as short as Nin. I felt like an ogre towering over them in the small, stark lobby. My senses told me that he didn't have any magical blood, so he couldn't see Chopper or Fezzik, the compact submachine pistol in my thigh holster.

## False Security

Even on days off, I rarely went anywhere without my weapons. In theory, there shouldn't be anyone after me right now—we'd cleared the dark elves out of Mt. Rainier, and Zav's sister and all the dragons who hated me for killing one of their kind had left Earth—but I had irked plenty of magical beings over my career, so I always felt like a walking target.

Mr. Jeong greeted us politely and led us off on a tour of the building.

"This is the recreation room." He pointed through an open door to two Ping-Pong tables, a stained mustard-yellow couch, and a wood-framed tube TV that was as old as the building. "And the laundry room." It featured dirty white coin-operated washers and dryers from the '80s. One was shaking and rattling like a paint mixer as it crept away from the outlet restraining it by its power-cord leash.

"And now I will show you to the available unit."

"Can't wait," I muttered.

Nin frowned as she swiped a finger across a layer of dust covering a wall-mounted vending machine offering generic boxes of detergent for two dollars apiece. When she walked out, her shoe made a sticking noise as she passed over a suspicious dark spot on the cement floor. Maybe Paradise Cove wouldn't meet her standards after all.

Mr. Jeong led us through a fire door and into a cement stairwell more suited to a parking garage than a residence.

"No elevator?" I asked.

"No need. There are only four floors. You will get excellent exercise."

I shot Nin a dirty look as we climbed, imagining ascending with laundry baskets and arms full of groceries.

"Perhaps if you got some roommates, you could afford to rent a house," she suggested. "That is what I do. You have seen my house in Queen Anne. There is a fenced yard and a washing machine and dryer on the covered porch. It is very nice."

"I can't have three roommates. I have to have privacy for my dragon visitor."

Mr. Jeong frowned back at us as he headed down a whitewashed hallway on the third floor.

"I did not think he stayed over." Nin raised her eyebrows. "But perhaps you could put a whiteboard on your door to leave messages or have a do-not-disturb magnet to alert your roommates."

"How very college dormitory."

Besides, Zav did not *stay over*. He visited to pick me up to go hunt villains out of town when he deemed my Jeep—my human conveyance—too slow. A couple of times, we'd hung out on the couch and I'd shown him the delights of *Deadliest Catch* and *Ice Road Truckers*, but he'd been clear that we couldn't be romantically involved until I learned enough magic to protect myself from enemies who liked to compel me to attack him.

Mr. Jeong unlocked a door and took us into a single room that served as the kitchen, living room, and dining room. "Here we are. The rent is very affordable. Only sixteen hundred dollars a month. No credit check required if you pay first and last months' rent today."

"Is that not less than you pay for your current place?" Nin asked.

"It's the same, and my current place is a lot nicer." Maybe not orders of magnitude nicer, but it was in a modern building with a parking garage and had a small balcony with room for a little table and two chairs. I walked to the window to see what kind of view there was. It looked out into the alley, right down onto the pond-puddle, my Jeep, and a giant trash bin overflowing with cardboard boxes. "Is there parking?"

"There is street parking," Mr. Jeong said.

"*Legal* street parking?" I opened the window and poked my head out to make sure there wasn't a ticket distributor in sight.

"Many of our residents save money by not owning a car and using public transportation."

"That's not going to work for me. I travel for work."

"We were told that there's a water view," Nin said to Mr. Jeong.

"Yes. You can see the lake from the roof."

"Oh, is there a deck up there?"

"No."

I rolled my eyes. "Nin, I've seen enough. I'm going to pass."

"We should at least check out the bedroom. Maybe there is a better view from there." Nin looked around the apartment for a door leading to a bedroom.

"It's right here." Mr. Jeong stepped forward to what I'd guessed were double doors to a closet and pulled down a Murphy bed. The previous renter had left the sheets. How thoughtful.

"You're right, Nin. The view from the bedroom is fabulous. It looks right at the refrigerator. Maybe I can stick some nice art on the freezer door."

# False Security

Nin spread her arms. "The options in your price range are limited. The cost of housing is very high in Seattle. I know this because I am still saving to buy a home and bring my family over from Bangkok. I read an article that said the booming tech industry is responsible and that people are calling this the next San Francisco. This is problematic for anyone who is not in the tech industry."

"Tell me about it."

I sensed someone with magical blood walking through the alley below and looked out the window again to check. My hand strayed to Fezzik as I anticipated some threat.

But it was a thin older woman packing a purse instead of a gun. Admittedly, the purse was large enough to *carry* a gun—and twenty boxes of ammo—but I doubted she was dangerous. She wore a slouch hat and a white T-shirt with a giant tarot card in the front. The orcs who liked to attack me usually favored black leather and metal.

"Can you not take on more freelance work?" Nin asked. "Your duties for Colonel Willard do not take up all of your time, do they?"

"Most of it. And helping Zav takes up the rest."

"Does he pay you to help?"

"Dragons don't have money."

Mr. Jeong was still in the room, and his eyebrows climbed at this second mention of dragons.

"Val," Nin said sternly. "That is unacceptable."

"I can't help it. Zav isn't in the tech industry either." Besides, he'd promised he would soon take me through a portal to the elven home world to help me find someone to teach me magic. I could do pro bono work for a while if it led to me learning how to more thoroughly defend myself. "What is that woman doing?"

Tarot Lady had stopped to cup her hands around her eyes and peer in the window of my Jeep. I'd left it partway down because it was a sunny August day, but she would need a coat hanger to unlock the door. Given the size of her purse, it was possible she had one.

But what could she want? I hadn't left my weapons or anything valuable in the Jeep. My camping and climbing gear were still in the back from my trip to Mt. Rainier, but they were twenty-year-old army surplus items, not hoity-toity REI finds that people might want to steal.

My keys were in my pocket, so there was no way the woman could drive off with the Jeep, but I patted it to double-check. The government had lent me the vehicle. I could *not* let it be stolen.

"Val?" Nin came over, but before I could point out the suspicious visitor, Tarot Lady opened the car door.

"What the hell. I locked that!"

I tried to open the window, tempted to take a shortcut down to the alley, but it wasn't designed to open. Another checkmark against brutalism.

Snarling, I sprinted for the door, nearly mowing over Mr. Jeong on the way out. If I lost that Jeep, I was screwed.

# Chapter 2

As I burst out the front door of the apartment building and sprinted up the sidewalk, I sensed Tarot Lady with her magical blood take off up the alley. On foot and not in my Jeep, I hoped. With the traffic zipping past on the busy street, I wouldn't have been able to pick up the sound of the engine. Either way, she was moving fast. Had she sensed me?

"Not how I imagined my day off," I grumbled, running faster.

When I raced around the corner, the Jeep came into view, still where I'd parked it behind the trash bin, but with the driver's side and rear door wide open. The woman was sprinting up the alley, holding her slouch hat to her head as her big purse banged against her hip. I paused long enough to slam the doors shut—my camping gear had been rummaged through but was still there—and tore after her.

Tarot Lady disappeared around a corner and onto the next block, and then I sensed her traveling upward. What was she doing? Climbing a building?

Even though I could sense partial- and full-blooded magical beings, I couldn't detect normal people, and when I charged around the corner, I almost ran into a woman walking her Doberman. The dog barked at me, and I veered abruptly to go around. My target was halfway up the side of a brick building, her large purse dangling as she climbed. Her hat and her pumps were in danger of falling off.

The dog walker was staring at her, and I almost stopped and did the same. Tarot Lady had to be in her fifties and didn't look remotely athletic. Was that elven blood flowing through her veins? She reminded me more of Nin, who was a quarter gnome.

I'd climbed numerous buildings in my life, and I started up after her, using window frames and divots and cracks in the old brick facade for handholds. The dog walker pulled her phone out as she alternated gaping at me and at Tarot Lady.

Who was she going to report us to? The police? The owner of the building? Cirque du Soleil?

Tarot Lady reached the top and vaulted acrobatically onto the roof. Her hat tumbled off and fell toward me. I snatched it out of the air as she disappeared from view and stuffed it in my waistband.

My fingers found holds that most people's wouldn't, and I reached the top of the three-story building seconds after my prey. She'd taken off toward a fire-escape door that should have been locked, but she waved her hand, and it opened before she reached it.

Growling, I sprinted faster and caught her before she could descend more than a couple of steps into the interior.

"Let go!" she cried, swinging her purse at me.

I caught it before it could batter me—a good thing since it had the heft of a wrecking ball.

"Not until you tell me who you are and explain why you were snooping in my Jeep."

I glared at her, then glared at the purse, though I was already starting to feel like a bully. Tarot Lady could have joined Mr. Jeong and Nin in the shorties club, and I could have picked her up and tossed her over my shoulder, purse included, without much trouble.

"I'm Janice Lindberg, and because you're one of his weird *gang* members." She wrinkled her snub nose at me and tried to pull away.

"What?" I'd been accused of a lot of things in my life. Running with a gang wasn't one of them. "I think you've got me mistaken for someone else."

"No way." She—Janice—tried to pull away again, but I easily restrained her. "You've been at that supposed coffee shop all the time, and I've seen you carrying in boxes."

Coffee shop? Was this about Dimitri's new business? His coffee-stand-slash-yard-art-slash-alchemy-lotion shop?

"At Dimitri's?" Even if I possibly knew what she was talking about, I was puzzled. "The only boxes I carried in there were loaded with the parts for his new espresso machine."

Technically, it was a new-used espresso machine refurbished by Gondo, Willard's new assistant who, like all goblins, fancied himself a tinkerer.

"I'm *sure* that's just a front. I work in the building next door, and I've *seen* the night-time deliveries."

I eyed her tarot-card shirt and returned her hat to her. "Are you the psychic?"

"I run Star and Moon House, yes."

This time, when she tried to pull out of my grip, I let her.

"I was working late last night, and my daughter came by. She was attacked right out front by a *vampire*." Janice pronged two fingers into the side of her neck. "Don't pretend you don't know anything about it. You people are getting deliveries from a vampire. I can *sense* the potions in those boxes. That kid who rented the place is trouble. I could tell the day he walked into the building."

I rubbed the back of my neck. At six-and-a-half feet tall and with the build of a refrigerator, Dimitri did look like trouble, but he was a lot less likely to beat someone up than I was. He wouldn't hurt anyone. Zoltan, his vampire alchemist partner, wasn't exactly menacing either, but he did drink blood, as all vampires did.

Had he been foolish enough to attack someone outside the shop? I'd always assumed Zoltan was subtle with his blood-sucking, slipping into his neighbors' houses when they were sleeping and leaving them none-the-wiser, but I didn't truly know him that well.

Janice pointed a finger at my nose. "I'm going to get to the bottom of what's going on over there, one way or another. I'll not have a vampire attacking my children or clients or anyone else in the neighborhood, and I don't want all those dirty goblins and orcs next door to my established, respectable business either."

I clamped my lips shut on an urge to point out that her bead curtains and window ledges lined with crystals and other woo woo knickknacks didn't strike me as overly respectable. Dimitri didn't need his friends picking fights with his neighbors.

Janice waved her finger. "Watch out. If you're involved, I'll find out about it, and I'm not afraid to call the police. If I have to, I'll call that special army facility that assassinates magical criminals in the city."

I almost laughed, since I worked for that facility and *was* the assassin, but if the woman's daughter truly had been attacked, I didn't want to make light of it. If Zoltan had been responsible, I'd clobber him myself.

"Is your daughter okay?" I asked.

She squinted at me, as if suspicious of the inquiry.

"I took her to the ER. Her neck was cut up, and she broke her wrist when she tried to fight him off. If I hadn't come out there with Boomer, it could have been a lot worse."

"Boomer? A gun?"

"My softball bat. I about took that jerk's head off. Don't judge me for being small. I had thirty-four home runs last year on our team."

"Did you get a good look at the guy? Are you sure it was a vampire?"

"I saw his fangs, and I sensed him. I know a vampire when I see one, the filthy scum."

"What did he look like? Besides the fangs?"

"He had a ski cap on that covered his face. I didn't see anything except a flash of blood-stained fangs. Fangs stained with my *daughter's* blood."

Did Zoltan own a ski cap? He usually answered his laboratory door in an old-fashioned suit and bow tie, so it was hard to imagine him flirting with active wear. But how did I know he didn't have a stash of ski masks for going out in search of his meals?

"What time was it last night?" I asked. "Do you remember?"

"Ten. Like I said, I stayed late for a client, and she'd just left." Her tone turned anguished as she added, "My daughter was bringing me a frittata. She's a chef at Bella e Buona."

"I'll look into it. I'm sure Dimitri had nothing to do with it. He's a good guy."

Janice was shaking her head before I finished the sentence. "Tell him to keep his grubby gang members away from my building." She backed down the stairwell.

I let her go but couldn't help but call after her, "I'll tell him that if you stay out of my Jeep. My *locked* Jeep. I don't keep vampire paraphernalia in there, I promise."

She turned and fled.

Sighing, I leaned against the doorjamb. Maybe investing in Dimitri's new shop hadn't been a good idea. I'd only opted in because Nin had gotten involved and she had a proven track record for starting businesses. But she also had never hired or partnered with any vampires before.

As I was debating whether to follow Janice down the stairwell or go back the way I'd come, my phone buzzed. Dimitri's name popped up.

"Are your ears burning?" I answered.

"What?" Clangs and the noise of a dozen conversations made it difficult to understand him.

"Never mind. We need to talk. Are you at the coffee shop?"

"I'm at the *yard-art* store, yes. But Val, we need to talk." He either hadn't heard me, or he agreed emphatically. "I've got a problem."

"According to your neighbor, you *are* the problem."

"What?" he asked again, raising his voice.

"I'll explain later."

"I need your help. My barista and I may be in danger." A crash sounded in the background, and Dimitri groaned. "At the least, my *art* is in danger. You're my security expert. Are you coming?"

"I'm coming." I hung up and shook my head. What had happened to my day off?

# Chapter 3

Hoping we wouldn't run into Janice Lindberg again, I parked the Jeep near Dimitri's new business. Nin came with me instead of going back for the lunch rush at her food truck. When I'd relayed the neighbor's story and Dimitri's call, she'd been concerned.

"There are so many magical beings here," Nin whispered as we walked up to the old yellow house that had long ago been converted to a commercial property.

It didn't have official signage yet—the last I'd heard, Zoltan and Dimitri and Nin were arguing over names—but a piece of paper in the window proclaimed it was the soft opening for Fremont's newest and best source for YARD ART AND HEALING TINCTURES (that was in all caps and on the top) and coffee (that was scrawled in tiny writing at the bottom).

"It is somewhat alarming." I'd sensed the numerous magical beings before we'd gotten out of the Jeep, the auras of at least two dozen goblins, shifters, ogres, trolls, and kobolds. It reminded me of walking into the now-closed Rupert's bar on Capitol Hill. I hoped there wouldn't be axe-throwing inside here, though that would have explained the crash I heard over Dimitri's phone.

Nin and I paused at the bottom of the steps leading to the front door. The ogres I'd sensed were visible through the recently cleaned window, their broad shoulders and shaggy yellow-haired heads surrounding the espresso cart. They had better not be harassing the young woman Dimitri had hired to make coffee.

A thump sounded inside, followed by raised voices.

"Put that down!" Dimitri ordered.

"Perhaps we should call for backup," Nin said. "I did not bring any weapons."

"Do you *have* backup?"

"Usually, you. But you know a dragon. Can you call Lord Zavryd?"

"I was working late with *Lord Zavryd* last night to capture three orcs who had the bright idea of blowing up a country bridge and ambushing cars full of people after they tumbled into a ravine. The orcs claimed they only needed money, but they happened to be killing people with their scheme. Apparently, this wasn't the first world where they'd done this. Zav insisted that we catch them in the act, so he could be sure they were the orcs on his list, which involved me pretending to stumble into their trap and fall into the ravine myself. Here's a tip for you. You can't *pretend* to fall into a ravine without *actually* falling into it. Luckily, I landed in a creek full of wet boulders that softened my fall." I rubbed the lingering bruises on my backside, glad for my body's faster-than-average healing ability. "After getting back late, I told Zav I was taking today off and didn't want to deal with bad guys or dragons."

Nin gazed blandly at me as I relayed this story. "So, you *cannot* call Lord Zavryd?"

"No. It's not like he has a cell phone anyway."

Another crash came from inside, followed by swearing.

"Then we will have to be diplomatic." Nin lifted her chin. "I will go first."

"Good idea. You know how I handle diplomacy." I loosened Fezzik in my thigh holster and followed right behind her in case her tongue wasn't as smooth as she thought.

We stepped into the front room of the shop and found it much more crowded than expected considering we hadn't done any advertising yet. All of the visitors were magical, either full-blooded or half-blooded. Dimitri, with his one-quarter dwarven blood, had the least noticeable aura of anyone inside.

There were only four tables, all up front and near the espresso stand, and they were all taken. Elsewhere, ogres, trolls, and shifters sat on display cases or lounged against curio cases full of Dimitri's up-cycled decor and Zoltan's alchemical tinctures. Several shelves and pieces of yard art and housewares had been knocked to the floor. Dimitri was running around with a dustpan and a broom that he was using like a halberd to push customers away. They all had coffee mugs or paper cups in hand, so they *had* to be customers.

"Val!" Dimitri blurted when he spotted me, then raised his voice to address the room. "The Ruin Bringer is here!"

I groaned as more than two dozen sets of eyes swiveled toward me.

"If you fight," Nin said, "lure them outside so they do not damage the premises."

"I thought we were going to be diplomatic."

"I will be diplomatic with the ones who don't attack you. We will know those are the reasonable customers and worth keeping."

Why did everyone want to use me as bait?

Nin stepped out of the way as chairs scraped on the battered hardwood floors and magical beings rose to their feet. A nearby shifter lifted his face and sniffed the air in my direction—I was pretty sure I recognized him as a werewolf from Gregor's Gang and wondered what had brought him all the way from West Seattle.

"It is true," the werewolf said, lifting his hands toward the rest of the gathering, a gathering that was now poised to spring in my direction. "I'd heard rumors, but I didn't believe them."

I'd been about to dart outside, as Nin requested, but I paused on the threshold and raised my eyebrows.

"She is marked," the werewolf said. "She has been claimed by the dragon that has been flying around Seattle."

I groaned as more sets of nostrils lifted into the air, sniffing. Others simply nodded.

"You can sense his aura on her."

"Everyone, sit down," the werewolf said. "It would be suicidal to attack the mate of a dragon."

Just as I was thinking that I'd be able to walk in without a fight, an ogre with a coffee mug in one big hand and a half-eaten king-size Hershey bar in the other plunked down his snacks and stepped toward me. "Trogg is not afraid of a dragon. Trogg would have much status among his people if he slew the Mythic Murderer."

His head almost brushed the ceiling, and his sleeveless hide vest revealed bulging shoulders like boulders as he looked me up and down.

He pulled a spiked club out of a sling on his back and hefted it like a cartoon character from the *Flintstones*.

"Trogg might be made *chief*."

"Trogg might find out if ogre corpses fit in the city morgue," a goblin seated at a table with his kin said with a snicker. There were three other goblins with him and no fewer than twelve espresso cups between them. Gondo had mentioned that his people enjoyed coffee.

The ogre curled a lip to sneer at the goblins, but he took another step toward me. Though tempted to draw Fezzik, I didn't want to shoot up the business I was a partial owner in.

"Did he pay for his coffee?" I asked Dimitri, wondering if this guy was an actual customer or a thief who had been wrecking his art and bullying the help into giving him food.

Dimitri glanced at the wide-eyed barista. She nodded.

Hell, I didn't want to eviscerate paying customers.

Trogg lumbered toward me with his club raised and scraping the ceiling tiles. A few of them crashed down behind him, and Dimitri groaned.

I jumped out of the doorway and down the stairs, landing in a crouch on the walkway, with Chopper in hand. Movement to my left caught my eye. Janice was walking up the sidewalk and gaping at me. Oh, fabulous.

Trogg rushed down the stairs, swinging his club, and I had to focus on defending myself.

More than a dozen of the other patrons ran out to watch—and make bets. Money changed hands faster than tickers updating on the stock exchange.

The ogre feinted at me a few times with his club before committing to a massive downward swing at my head. I sprang to the side before he could nail me into the pavement, then swept Chopper back toward my opponent. The magical blade flared blue and sliced through the club with only the slightest sensation of impact.

I darted past the startled ogre and kicked him in the back of the knee. His leg bent, and he stumbled forward, not quite face-planting. The second kick went to his butt and caused him to topple.

A familiar aura came within range of my senses—I almost missed it due to the auras of so many magical beings nearby, but this was a very powerful and very distinct aura. Zav.

# False Security

Trogg staggered to his feet.

I pointed my sword at him. "Dimitri's is a *peaceful* gathering place." We needed to come up with a better name for the shop. "If you can't keep your weapons holstered, you can stay out of here."

Trogg growled, clenched the remains of his club, and crouched like he would spring. A shadow fell over the sidewalk, a great winged shadow. Several of the magical beings who'd been watching scattered, leaving their beverages behind to flee. Others gaped up at the huge black dragon soaring into view, their eyes mesmerized.

Inside the doorway, Nin gave Dimitri a high-five. Nin appeared ecstatic at this development. Dimitri watched Zav's landing dubiously.

As he dropped down beside me, Zav shifted into his human form, his black robe, trimmed beard and mustache, and short dark hair impeccable, as always. He slipped an arm around my waist and gazed at Trogg, who'd frozen in his crouch as he gaped at us.

"I am Lord Zavryd'nokquetal, and this is my female." Zav's voice rang out as if he had an amplifier. His power crackled over me, and as always, I had to resist the urge to stare at him, as mesmerized as the onlookers. "You *dare* lift a weapon in her presence?"

"I'm handling it," I whispered to Zav. "Why don't you go inside and get a coffee?"

But Zav was focused on the ogre, his eyes flaring with violet light, indignation on his handsome but oh-so-haughty face. His muscled arm was tight and possessive around me. As much as I appreciated having him as an ally, this was entirely unnecessary. I'd been handling the situation.

Trogg looked at his stump of a club and tossed it aside. Zav used magic to knock him off his feet.

The ogre pitched forward to his hands and knees and stammered, "Trogg sorry, Lord Dragon. Trogg didn't know."

"You're sorry, Lord *Zavryd'nokquetal*."

I swatted Zav on the chest. "I told you. Nobody can pronounce that."

Occasionally, Zav let out a hint of his sense of humor, such as it was, but this wasn't one of those times.

"How did you not know, ogre? My mark on her is clear. You are not fit to speak to the mate of a dragon, and if you ever raise a weapon to her again, I will punish you until you wish you were dead."

"Trogg won't." He tried to get to his feet, but Zav's magic held him prostrate.

"Don't be a bully." I elbowed him in the ribs. "Let him go."

Zav turned his glowing-eyed gaze on me, but I refused to look away or be intimidated.

*None shall raise a hand against you,* he spoke silently into my mind, *unless they want me as an enemy. My mark tells them this. The ogre sensed it, but he chose to ignore it. Do you deny this?*

*No, I don't, but he's an idiot, and I was handling it. Let him go. I'll buy you a coffee.*

If the goblins hadn't consumed it all.

Zav's eyes narrowed. Was he going to ignore me and magically beat the snot out of the ogre? How did I convince him that I could take care of myself and didn't need an overprotective boyfriend around? Especially since we weren't even having a romantic relationship, aside from a few wayward kisses that we'd both agreed were a bad idea.

Funny how I forgot just how bad of an idea they were when he was standing next to me, his body pressed against mine and his electric power tingling all along my nerves. Even if I could take care of myself, there was a tiny part of me that was thrilled that Zav wanted to protect me.

*You are unharmed?* he finally asked.

*Yes.*

*And you do not wish him punished for his presumptuousness?*

*No, I don't.*

*Very well.* Zav twitched an eyebrow, and the magic pinning Trogg to the ground disappeared.

The ogre sprinted away without looking back. About a dozen onlookers remained, staring at Zav and me.

*You can also let me go,* I added.

He was gazing down at me with a look that suggested he had something besides coffee in mind. I remembered it well from the hot tub, but even if I'd been in the mood to test his resolve about not having a relationship with me right now, I wouldn't have done it in front of a crowd.

*Or does vanquishing my attackers get you randy?* I cocked an eyebrow, figuring sarcasm was the way to dissipate amorous feelings. It had always worked with my human boyfriends.

*Holding you and having your soft parts pressed against me makes me randy.* He looked down at my chest.

A part of me was titillated that he felt that way, but...

*Then we should probably avoid such compromising positions.*

*Yes.* Zav took a deep breath and his arm loosened around me, but he let his fingers drag as he slowly withdrew, and a tingle of magic flowed from the tips. That ignited my nerves even more than the powerful magic of his aura, and I almost forgot about my resolve not to engage in a make-out session in front of a crowd.

"If you're going to use your magic on me like that," I murmured, "we better find an elf to teach me how to defend myself soon."

His eyes flared again. "Yes. I have apprehended many of the criminals hiding here on your world and turned them over to the Dragon Justice Court." He lifted his chin. "Soon I will take you to Veleshna Var to see your father, and we will find an elf who will instruct you on your inherent powers."

I bit my lip, far more pleased by his willingness to take me to meet my father than any of his posturing toward my enemies. "Good. Thank you." I stepped away from him, so neither of us would be further tempted toward hanky-panky, and gestured toward the front door. "Coffee?"

"What is coffee?"

"A beverage. Lots of people love it."

"Do you?"

"No. It tastes like burnt water to me, but I'm told I'm weird."

He gazed at me, and the first hint of humor entered his eyes. "Yes. This is true."

# Chapter 4

Dimitri had already cleaned up a lot of the broken housewares, so the shop wasn't too much of a mess inside, other than abandoned mugs and napkins left on tables, shelves, and display cases. But there was a weird scent in the air that I couldn't blame on the espresso maker.

"Did something spill?" I wrinkled my nose and looked at Dimitri. "Something toxic?"

"Several of Zoltan's products were knocked off shelves." Scowling, Dimitri stalked toward a back corner with his broom and dustpan.

"That's probably a yes, then." My nostrils twitched, and I hoped the spilled potions didn't set off my sensitive lungs. It was my day off. I wasn't supposed to need to use my inhaler on my day off. My lungs were relaxing, just like I was.

"They're not toxic." Dimitri bent and picked up a lid with a beige smear of goop under it; it was all that remained of a ceramic jar. "This is a healing lotion for your face. It's supposed to make those dark circles under your eyes go away."

"I've heard sleeping straight through the night does that too, but I wouldn't know."

"Tam." Dimitri turned toward the barista. "Can you get a mop?"

The barista had been staring at Zav, who'd trailed me into the shop, with wide eyes. She scurried into the back, appearing relieved at the order to leave the room.

Tam worked for Nin in the afternoons and evenings and had a hint of magical blood, so she must have met some of Nin's magical clientele—those who purchased her weapons rather than her food-truck fare—but a dragon was above and beyond the norm.

"What happened, Dimitri?" Nin peered around, her gaze pausing on the single table that hadn't been vacated. The four goblins were still there, and a new one had come in. Gondo. "Why did all those magical beings come here and make a mess?"

"I don't know. I just opened yesterday, and this week is supposed to be a trial run. Other than putting out a sign, I've hardly told anyone about it. I thought it would be a challenge to get business, but they all showed up early this morning and have been coming for hours." Dimitri shook his head as he swept. "Coming for coffee, I should say. None of them wanted Zoltan's tinctures or my housewares. That was the whole point of us opening this business. I don't even know how they found out about this place."

My gaze shifted back to Gondo. "I may have an idea."

Dimitri was sweeping up broken ceramic and didn't hear me. "Can you come by a few times a day to loom threateningly with your sword, Val? Now that you kicked that ogre's butt—literally—the others should know to leave you alone. Especially if you smell like dragon."

Zav had been silent, either ignoring the exchange or deeming it unworthy of his participation, but his chin rose at this. "Neither a dragon's aura nor mark *smell*. It is a magical emanation that those with attuned senses can detect."

"Don't be offended by Dimitri," I told Zav. "He's not very smooth. He just told me I have bags under my eyes."

I headed over to the chattering goblins. One was standing on his seat, which almost made his head level with mine, and speaking in his native language while gesticulating expansively to his buddies.

Goblins were always expansive and perky, but this fellow was extra amped up. The others were bouncing and jittering too as they listened raptly, one thumping a wrench on his thigh. Another was building what looked like a rubber-band ball during the discussion. Gondo was sipping from a mug, relatively calm compared to the others, but he'd only just arrived and was on his first cup.

"Willard doesn't have any work for you today, Gondo?" I didn't bother to activate my translation charm, not particularly wanting to solve the mystery of what goblins discussed with each other while amped up on coffee.

"She said I've already done all I need to do for her today and that I should go out into the community and gather intelligence for her. She also forbade me from touching her paper shredder again, even though I added power to the motor and *quadrupled* its capacity to shred."

"She didn't like that?"

"It's a little noisier than it was before. I believe it disturbed her phone call in the other room."

"Are you the reason all these interesting beings came to visit today?" I waved toward where the ogres, trolls, and others had been.

Only Zav was in that area now. He was examining some of Dimitri's housewares, but there was a bored glaze to his eyes. I assumed he hadn't flown in solely to protect me from posturing ogres and was surprised he hadn't yet stated what he wanted. Being circumspect, polite, and patient wasn't his way.

"I may have mentioned to a few people that I refurbished the espresso maker for a new establishment that would be friendly to magical beings." Gondo tilted his head, his thick white hair in a tousled nest. "Didn't you wish me to spread the word?"

One of the jittery goblins bobbed his head and sipped from a mug with a grin and a wink.

"Not to ogres and trolls and werewolves." I glanced at Nin, who'd come over to listen.

"Why not?" Gondo asked. "They consume a great deal of food and beverages. You should add sandwiches to the snack bar there. Ogres like giant triple-decker sandwiches with big piles of meat and bacon and rosemary."

"Rosemary?"

"It's an ogre favorite."

Nin took out her phone. My first thought was that she meant to call the police, but she started tapping notes into a text app.

"What are you doing?" I whispered.

"Making sure we stock the inventory our customers want."

"I'm positive that Dimitri doesn't want his customers to be ogres."

"The magical community needs a place to congregate now that

Rupert's is closed," one of Gondo's buddies said.

I shook my head. "Unless ogres need tinctures for their under-eye bags—"

Nin stopped me with a hand on my forearm. "We should discuss this with the other owners before ruling out who we want as clients."

"I doubt Zoltan is going to agree to huge brutes who smash his wares, and he's the only owner who isn't here right now."

Nin pointed to a tip jar full of dollars on the espresso cart. "If they pay and can be convinced not to destroy anything, we will accommodate them. I believe this morning's problems are due to a narrowness of aisles between display cases and shelves."

Before I could reply, Zav strode up to us, looming behind Nin. Almost everyone loomed in comparison to Nin, but his approach unnerved all of the goblins except for Gondo. They scattered, leaving their partially consumed coffees behind. Gondo merely scooted his chair back.

"I will speak with you," Zav told me.

Apparently, his period of standing politely to the side and waiting for me to finish was over.

"I told you last night that this is a day off for me, and I'm not going to do any research for you or come along to be bait for an ambush. You and Willard have been running me ragged for two weeks straight. Besides, I need to speak with Dimitri about a vampire issue." I plucked one of the almost-full coffee mugs off the table and placed it in Zav's hands. "Here, try this."

His nostrils twitched as he stared down at the dark liquid. I squeezed past and caught Dimitri on his way to empty a dustpan.

"Hey, was Zoltan here last night?" I glanced out the front window. The psychic's shop wasn't visible from here, but *she* was visible, standing out on the sidewalk and speaking into her phone.

Even though our dubious customers had dispersed, Janice didn't look happy. If Dimitri's shop truly did end up as a hangout for the magical, he would have to figure out how to put an illusion of some kind over it to hide it from the non-magical. Unfortunately, that would mean regular people wouldn't notice it or come in to buy his wares, but this was too busy an area for mundane people not to notice all the strange beings through the windows.

"Zoltan doesn't come here." Dimitri emptied the dustpan in a trash bin and frowned. "But he's started putting barcodes on all of his stock to track it, so he's going to find out stuff was destroyed today."

"Are you *sure* he doesn't come here and wasn't visiting around ten last night?"

Dimitri stopped to face me. "He doesn't leave his carriage house except to feed, and he prefers local blood." His lip twitched in distaste. "He had a delivery sent last night, but he pays someone to pick up his shipments."

"I ask because your psychic neighbor got in a skirmish last night with a vampire in a ski mask. Her daughter was bitten and had to go to the ER."

"A ski mask? That's not Zoltan's style."

"You don't think he would *adjust* his style if he had a mission that was important to him?"

"Mauling a girl in Fremont also isn't his style. You can't trust anything Lindberg says. She's a flake. She believes all that psychic stuff and tries to sell it to people at ridiculous prices. She wanted to read my palm for ninety-nine dollars."

"She talks to you? She thinks you run a gang."

"*Now* maybe. She came over a few times when I was first moving stuff in and cleaning this place out. She wanted to put brochures for her business by my cash register. It wasn't until our first customers started showing up that she stopped talking to me."

"Have you had any trouble with her?" I waved toward the window, though Janice was no longer in view. "Anything you've told Zoltan about that he might have taken into his own hands?"

Dimitri shook his head. "You've got the wrong vampire, Val."

"If that's the case, we may have a problem."

How well would Dimitri's business fare if the word got out that a vampire was attacking people on the sidewalk out front?

"That's what I've been trying to tell you. Though now it sounds like we've got *two* problems. Ogres like bulls in a china shop and a proliferation of vampires." His gaze shifted past my shoulder, and he lowered his voice to mutter, "Maybe three problems."

I sensed Zav behind me before I turned. Dimitri mumbled something about taking out the trash and disappeared into the back.

"This is loathsome." Zav held up the coffee mug.

"I agree. I don't get the appeal." As I looked down at the mug—interestingly, he'd consumed half of it before reaching his decision—I noticed he wasn't wearing his usual slippers. His tidily trimmed toenails were on display in a pair of double-strap Birkenstock sandals. "You're experimenting with footwear again?"

"A sign at a local mercantile proclaimed that these were comfortable, unlike the boots, and that my feet would not grow unpleasantly warm, as they did in the high-tops. The merchant assured me that they are not gay."

"I'm not entirely positive that's true." I rubbed my face. I couldn't believe Zav was still worried about his slippers. It had been weeks since that dummy at the ice cream shop had snubbed them. "But now, you're more likely to be mistaken for a cultural studies professor at the U."

"I am well-educated and could teach on any number of subjects. I know much about the cultures of lesser beings throughout the Cosmic Realms."

"I guess those could be right for you then. I can't promise they won't get as many comments as the slippers."

"Only a fool dares make derogatory comments about a dragon's attire." Despite the words, Zav looked down as if considering the choice anew.

Dimitri returned from the back and would have slipped past, but I caught his arm and pointed to Zav's feet. "We're having a debate. Are these something a modern, uhm, masculine guy would wear?"

"Well, those aren't feminine, and ugly-chic is in again, so I guess." Dimitri glanced at Zav's face and hurried past.

"*Ugly*-chic?" Zav squinted suspiciously at Dimitri's retreating back.

I grinned at Zav and patted him on the arm.

He returned his focus to me, glancing down at my hand on his sleeve. At first, I thought he would object to me presuming to touch him, but he laid his hand on mine, fingers stroking my skin and making me forget all about sandal fashion. Maybe menacing my enemies *did* make him randy.

"Can you sense any vampires in the area?" I changed the subject since this wasn't the appropriate place for randiness.

"I did not come here to discuss vampires or footwear."

"Is that a no?" I knew one wouldn't be out in daylight, but the fanged ski-mask wearer could be holed up in a nearby basement.

"I do not sense a vampire. Val, I am pleased that you have assisted me with capturing several criminals and returning them to the Dragon Justice Court for punishment and rehabilitation." His eyelids drooped, so that he was gazing at me through his lashes. "You vexed those orcs very much. And you know it pleases me when you vex my enemies."

"Yes. You've told me that before. I have to admit, I like it that you like it."

"I must check in with my family today, but tomorrow, I will take you to the elven home world of Veleshna Var."

"You'll what?"

"Did you think I would not fulfill my promise?"

"No, but I figured it would be after you'd collected all of your criminals."

"I have caught up with my brother, so I can take a short break." His eyes narrowed, and he lifted his hand to the side of my face, fingers sliding through my hair. The power of his aura—of *him*—wrapped around me, and a buzz of energy raised gooseflesh all over my body. "Also, I do not want to wait until I have completed my entire assignment to *tysliir* with you."

"My translation charm isn't active," I murmured.

My gaze caught on his mouth, a mouth not that far from mine, and the urge to lean into him came over me. A vague notion that we were in full view of the rest of the shop kept me from doing exactly that while asking for more details.

"I want you in all ways that a dragon takes a mate." He shifted closer, his chest close to mine, and the power of his aura made my knees weak. "Your kin will teach you how to defend your mind in the elven way, and then I will claim you with more than magic."

"I'm agreeable to that, but in a bedroom, not a coffee shop." I rested a hand on his chest, intending to push him away, since I was sure the others were watching us, but Zav leaned in closer and kissed me. It was a smoldering kiss that made me forget about pushing him away—and forget there were witnesses—and I found myself crushed against his hard body as his other arm wrapped around my back.

*I will claim you where I wish,* he informed me telepathically as his mouth slid against mine, his power flooding my body with heat and desire. *And you will find it too pleasing to object.*

*You better wish it in a bedroom,* I replied in my mind, my lips too busy for talking, *because we've both learned that assassins lurk in public places.*

He broke the kiss, and I regretted the words. I knew his history and how real a threat assassins were to him and his family.

*Assassins can also lurk in bedrooms,* he informed me.

*I know. I'm sorry. But there won't be any in one we share. I'll have Sindari stand guard outside to make sure.* I could imagine how delighted Sindari would be with that task, but I didn't take back the words. Zav had still never delved into my thoughts—never scoured them as other dragons had—to learn what I was truly thinking, but he seemed to trust me now. I didn't want to do anything to change that or make him doubt me.

*Good. If the tiger is wise, he will ensure nothing interrupts our first mating. Or the thousands that will follow.*

*Thousands, huh?*

*Thousands.* His smile was cocky as he gazed into my eyes, but as he slid his hand from around my back, his fingers trailing across the thin material of my shirt, he teased me with his magic again, magic that lit up my every nerve. *We will battle by day and mate by night. This is how it will be.*

Our kiss hadn't lasted that long, but I was breathless as he walked away. I groped to fight off the disappointment of his touch, magical and otherwise, leaving me.

*Tomorrow,* he spoke into my mind as he walked out the door, *we will go to see your people.*

*Thank you.*

Nin, Dimitri, and Gondo were watching from the espresso stand, the very witnesses I'd expected. As Gondo sipped his coffee and smiled, I remembered that he was Willard's informant now. News of the public kissing display would probably get back to her. Oh, well. She was rooting for a half-elf–dragon wedding, anyway.

"I can tell this is going to be my most interesting business," Nin said.

My phone buzzed. My daughter's name showed on the display along with a text.

*Are we still on for sword-fighting lessons?*

I winced because it was later than I'd realized. I'd either been caught up in the new vampire problem—all of Dimitri's problems—or that kiss had gone on longer than I'd realized.

*Yes. I'll be right there.*

# CHAPTER 5

We met at Yost Park, not far from Thad's house in Edmonds. It was close enough that Amber could ride her bike over—though she complained vehemently about the hills along the way—so I wouldn't have to pick her up. As far as I knew, Thad was still dating Shauna, AKA "the girlfriend," a woman who had made it clear she found me loathsome and a threat, so I didn't want to show up at their house or interact with Thad in any way that might make her jealous. I didn't think she was a good match for him and hoped he dumped her of his own accord, but I wouldn't do anything to prompt that.

"Wooden swords?" Amber eyed the practice weapons I carted out of the Jeep. "I was hoping to poke you with something sharper."

"And were you hoping I poked you with something sharper too?"

"No. You could have a wooden one, and I could have a steel one. That would even the odds, don't you think?" She smirked at me.

Her blonde hair was back in a ponytail, and I fancied we looked similar—exactly like the mother and daughter we were—but she would have objected to the comparison. I was in my usual jeans, combat boots, and tank top—it was warm enough that I left my duster in the Jeep—and she wore far girlier attire: teal printed leggings and a loose pink terrycloth hoodie that left her midriff on display. A few teenage boys in the swimming pool area watched her as we headed for the pickleball courts. They weren't in use, so I planned to claim one as a flat practice area.

"For your first few lessons, we'll mostly go over footwork. There won't be much poking."

"That's disappointing. I'd really like to learn to poke people. Especially dragons." Amber grimaced.

She hadn't told me exactly what happened when Zav's sister, Zondia, had shown up at the house to question her about me. All I knew was that it had bothered her enough that she'd asked Thad if she could learn how to use a weapon. Having me be her sword-fighting instructor had been his idea, not Amber's, and I didn't think she was excited to spend time with me. I wouldn't get cheesy and emotional and say that *I* was excited to spend time with her.

"You don't want to try that unless you get a magical sword," I said.

"Will that happen? When I'm good enough?" Amber picked up one of the wooden swords. "I want to be able to take care of myself if any dragons show up and pin me down and hurt me."

"I want you to be able to do that too." My heart ached at the knowledge that she'd been hurt by dragons, not once but twice. And both times were because I'd made the mistake of inserting myself into her life. It was possible Zondia would have found out about her even if I hadn't encountered Thad and Amber at the lake earlier that summer—Zondia had been thorough in her research—but I still blamed myself for all this. I would do my best to teach Amber.

We worked out for about an hour, and I tolerated a lot more lippiness than my combat instructors had ever taken from me, but she was a civilian as well as my daughter. I'd been in the army when I'd been learning this stuff. I remembered my mouth getting me in trouble and doing a lot of push-ups in between rounds.

During a break, with sweat streaming down her face, Amber lifted her hands. "When do we get to the part with the swords?"

"Soon."

"You said that *hours* ago."

"We've only been practicing footwork for—" I checked my phone, "—fifty-two minutes. Your swim team practices are longer than that."

"We get to rest between sets. You're barely giving me any breaks. These are different muscles than I use for swimming." She waved at her thighs.

"Just be glad I haven't made you paint a house or wax cars."

Her forehead furrowed. "What?"

"I thought you watched movies from the eighties. Classics, right?" I'd been aggrieved when she'd called *The Princess Bride* a classic. How could movies I'd grown up watching be lumped in with those hokey black-and-white flicks from the dawn of television time? "You never saw *The Karate Kid*?"

She wrinkled her nose. "I don't like sports movies. Or Jackie Chan."

I almost corrected her on Jackie Chan, then remembered that there had been a remake I hadn't seen. "What kinds of movies do you like?"

She shrugged. "Stuff about high school kids."

That sounded about as scintillating as watching paint peel. I groped for another topic to discuss while she rested, but I doubted we'd seen any of the same movies or listened to the same music. Thad had said she liked dresses and was into fashion, but as my wardrobe attested, I was not.

"Your father said you're interested in beauty pageants," I remembered. "Did you see *Miss Congeniality*?"

Amber hadn't been born yet when that came out, but maybe it was another *classic* that she'd watched.

"Yeah." Her eyes widened at some realization. "Oh man, Val. You're *just* like the girl that Sandra Bullock played."

"I'm not that bad."

"Yes, you are." She grinned. "Did you ever beat up a bully in grade school to save a wimpy kid? And then get rejected by the wimpy kid? And then punch him?"

"No. Your grandmother homeschooled me. I didn't get any opportunities to beat up anyone at school until I was fifteen."

"Maybe that's why you're so weird. And dress like Rambo."

What did that mean? That homeschooling had shaped me or that a lack of kids to beat up had?

Did normal parents find things their children said mystifying, or would I be more in tune with her if I'd been around her whole life? Probably the latter.

I was about to put her back to work when my phone buzzed. I half-expected it to be Willard—she'd said she wouldn't have a new assignment for me until next week, but it was possible Gondo had reported in and she wanted to goad me about the dragon kiss. But it was an unfamiliar number.

"Yeah?"

"Is this Val-mey-jar Thorvald?" a woman asked.

"It's Val. Who's this?"

"I'm Tanya Drake, the executive assistant for Mr. Bernard Weber. Mr. Weber is interested in hiring you."

"To do what?" I hadn't heard of a Bernard Weber and would look him up after I got off the call. My number was in the digital rolodexes of some locals with the means and need to hire an assassin with my unique skillset, but I'd heard of most of those people. "I'm pretty booked right now."

Booked to go to Elf Land with Zav and learn wizarding skills.

"Mr. Weber needs you to drop your other clients and come work for him."

"We don't all get what we want."

"He's willing to pay you two thousand dollars a day for the next two weeks and will include combat bonuses if it comes to that."

"Two thousand dollars a day?" I mouthed but didn't say out loud. It was gauche for an assassin to be impressed by some rich guy's offer of payment. "To do what?"

The executive assistant—I wonder if Willard called Gondo her *executive assistant* when she talked about him—had avoided mentioning that.

"To be his bodyguard while he's in town and go to some events with him. He also wants you to take a look at the security on his estate. He's had some trouble with corporate spies using magic and wants a *professional* assessment of some new items he's installed."

I thought of Dimitri's bear-holding-fish statue that shot darts at intruders and wondered if those were the kinds of items this Weber guy had installed. For his *estate*. I smirked as I imagined Dimitri's tacky yard-art defenses lining the mile-long driveway of some business mogul's property.

"Are you interested, Ms. Thorvald? Mr. Weber heard you're the best and only hires the best."

"Oh, I'm sure." I wanted to go with Zav tomorrow, but the idea of depositing a check for twenty-eight thousand dollars was appealing. With that much, I could finally pay off the auto loan I was still getting charged for, despite the loss of the vehicle at the beginning of the summer. "When would this gig start? Like I said, my schedule is full."

"Mr. Weber wants to meet with you tonight to finalize the details. He's in a bit of a bind and would like you to start immediately."

If I accepted, there would be no trip to Elf Land, at least not for a couple of weeks. Would Zav mind delaying? It sounded like his horny bits would, but it wasn't like I would instantly learn how to use my elven powers as soon as I showed up in their world. This would be a long process. Two weeks couldn't make that much of a difference. Zav could hunt down a few more criminals while I was on this mission, and then we could go.

"What happened to Weber's *last* bodyguard?" I asked.

"*Mr.* Weber hasn't had one before. He travels in civilized society, not among hoodlums. His current problem is a recent development."

"I guess it wouldn't hurt to meet with him."

"Excellent. I'm texting you the address. Do you have a dress?"

I'd been about to hang up and almost stuttered at the last question. "A *dress?*"

Amber had flopped down dramatically on the pickleball court, but she lifted her head at this mention of her favorite article of clothing.

"What would I need a dress for?" I asked.

Amber rolled her eyes and shook her head. I was questioning needing a dress for a mission, not specifically owning one, though as it happened, I didn't own one either.

"Mr. Weber doesn't want people to know he's hiring a bodyguard. You'll act as his date at events and in public venues."

Ugh, Zav wasn't going to like this. Well, he could get over it. I needed him to figure out that I didn't want a jealous boyfriend looming at my side whenever I spoke to a man. Maybe this would give me an opportunity to work on that with him. Or maybe I'd tell him I'd heard some of his criminals were in China and that he should clear out of the state for two weeks. That seemed simpler.

"As long as I can pack my gun," I said.

That earned another eye roll from Amber.

"So long as it's hidden," was all Tanya said.

She hung up and sent the address.

"Laurelhurst. Right on the water. That's about what I figured."

At least it wasn't that far from where I lived. Just separated by a few socioeconomic strata.

Amber sat up, her brows perking. "So, you're going dress shopping?"

"I'll see how the meeting goes first." I wasn't buying anything unless I was positive I would take the job and had money in my hand. Mr. Weber had better be prepared to give me a retainer.

"Do you even know where to go?"

"To buy a dress?" I shrugged and thought of the closest shopping center. "Alderwood Mall?"

"Oh, Val." She said it like I was the kid in math class who couldn't figure out how to carry the one. "To go work for some guy in Laurelhurst? You've got to go to The Shops at the Bravern." At my blank look, she added, "In Bellevue."

"Great. I not only need a dress, but I have to fight traffic to get one." And why did I have visions of Julia Roberts in *Pretty Woman* waltzing through my mind? There was another *classic* that Amber probably hadn't seen.

"If the job is ongoing for a rich client, you'll need a few. Black tie, cocktail, business casual, country club casual... Do you have a simple skater dress?"

I envisioned kids at a skate park rolling down the ramps and doing jumps in dresses.

I was positive Amber didn't have enough magical blood to read minds, but my facial expression prompted another eye roll.

"You need help, Val."

"I have an appointment with my therapist later this week."

"With your *wardrobe*."

"Are you offering?" I tried not to make my smile too hopeful so she wouldn't read it as desperate. Even if the idea of dress-shopping horrified me, I wouldn't mind spending time with Amber. Maybe she would be less lippy if sweat weren't streaming down her face.

"Uh, will you buy me something?"

This seemed a tad manipulative, but one couldn't expect altruism from a teenager, right? Besides, taking me dress-shopping would probably be a lot of work. People deserved to be paid for work.

"A skater dress?" I offered.

"You don't know what that is, do you?"

"I'm hoping it's an item of clothing that doesn't cost more than fifty dollars."

"At Goodwill, maybe."

"Is Goodwill an option?"

"*No.*"

As I headed back to the Jeep, I decided to ask this guy for three thousand a day. Only an amateur didn't negotiate on salary. An amateur who didn't have a teenage daughter with expensive tastes.

# Chapter 6

*I hope you have called me forth to do battle, not simply to ride around in your cramped conveyance,* Sindari said from the back of the Jeep.

"I thought you could fit back there okay with the seats down." I glanced over my shoulder. "I even rolled down the windows. It's August. There are laws about making sure your pets don't overheat in the car."

His big silver head had been pressed up against the ceiling, but he lowered it to more effectively glare at me with his green eyes. *We have discussed the danger of having your limbs gnawed off if you refer to me as a pet.*

"I thought it was only my feet that were in danger from that. I was only letting you know about our laws referring to dogs and such, not Del'nothian tiger ambassadors."

*I care little about Earth pets.*

"But I bet you're appreciating the air flow back there." The sun was low over the Olympics now, so it wasn't that warm, but I assumed someone covered in fur would prefer it be as cool as possible.

*I am sitting on lumpy metal and canvas.*

"Sorry." I turned off Sand Point Way and into Weber's neighborhood. "I forgot to take my camping gear out. Dimitri's psychic neighbor decided to break in this morning and rummage through everything."

*Perhaps you could have returned the items to their containers to ensure the relative comfort of your passengers.*

"You're in a grouchy mood this evening. Did I interrupt a hunt?"

*No, but there is a stick trying to insert itself in a tender area.*

"I think that's one of my ice axes."

*Is its proper place not in a glacier?*

"Hanging in my closet next to the vacuum cleaner, actually."

*Your vehicle smells more offensive than usual, even with the windows down.*

"That's because I took it through the car wash, and they gave me an air freshener." I waved at the cardboard pine tree hanging from the rearview mirror. It was strong, but maybe the scent would keep strangers from snooping in my Jeep.

*It's loathsome. It's wilting my whiskers and searing my nostril hair.*

"We're almost there. I may have a new gig as a bodyguard for the next couple of weeks."

*What will my gig be?*

"Helping me if bad guys try to assassinate my charge—some guy who's apparently having problems with magical beings."

*Apparently? You did not research him?*

"I did, but there wasn't anything about him having ties to the magical community one way or another. He's a tech guy. He sold a cybernetics company a few years ago for a hundred million dollars. Since then, he's dabbled in a couple of start-ups, and he just invested in an online dating platform, but that may be due to personal rather than business interests. He's single and looking, according to his recent appearance on Seattle's Most Eligible Bachelors list."

I made another turn. The houses were getting progressively larger and nicer, so I knew I was heading in the right direction.

*Why does he need a bodyguard?*

"We're about to find out. I thought you'd like to come to the meeting. Tigers are classy, and you can help me look like an exotic professional instead of a schlub with a gun."

Sindari lowered his head to gaze at me again, and I expected an indignant comment about him being rolled out as my arm candy. Or would it be hip candy for a tiger?

*I am classy,* he said.

I snorted. "Yes, you are. I also would like your senses when we meet him. Let me know if there's anything magical or strange about his house or the grounds. I'm not sure how this guy got my number or why he's being targeted by someone from the community. His assistant spoke of magical corporate espionage."

As the street curved and dipped down a hill, Lake Washington came into view, sailboats and kayaks dotting the water on the lazy summer evening. There was something odd about my life that my day off involved an interview for a bodyguard assignment rather than hanging out at the lake. My therapist, I was sure, would agree.

I turned onto the final street, a dead end paralleling the shoreline, with houses along the water and trees and a slope full of ivy above it, the foliage barely restrained by a retaining wall. Several signs informed me that parking was for specific addresses only, and I spotted more than one security camera mounted on brick walls separating houses from the street. Weber's place was the last one at the end, blocked off by a closed gate with a speaker mounted next to it.

*Will you seek to court this new client?* Sindari asked.

"What?"

*You pointed out that he is an eligible bachelor.*

*No. I saw his picture, and he's not my type.* I switched to telepathic communication, since I was pulling up to the speaker, and I didn't want anyone to hear me explain why I wasn't interested in their boss. *Besides, it's never a good idea to get involved with your boss.*

*It is also not a good idea to get involved with dragons.*

*I'm not going to argue against that.*

*And yet, you are spending a great deal of time with Lord Zavryd.*

*We're just working together to catch criminals. That reminds me, have you sniffed out any vampires in the neighborhood where Dimitri's thus-far-unnamed coffee shop is?*

*I have not, but you have not had me out there often.*

*We may change that later tonight.* If this meeting didn't take too long, I could head back to the shop and stake it out for a few hours after dark.

*The woman in the shop next to Dimitri's does have some magical artifacts that I have sensed.*

*The psychic? I think she's half gnome.* I didn't see a button to press, so I waved at the speaker. "Hello? Val Thorvald here. Assassin and, for the right pay, potentially a bodyguard."

*I concur.*

*If she has something valuable, that might explain an attack that otherwise seems random. Maybe we'll pay her a visit. Too bad she won't want to see me.*

*Why is that?* Sindari asked.

*I chased her onto a rooftop. It was her fault. She was the one rooting around in my car.*

*Perhaps she will allow you in if you have me with you. As you observed, I am classy.*

*I'm not sure classy is what's needed to visit a psychic. But we can pretend to want her services. Or actually pay for her services, I suppose.* Paying to have my fortune told sounded even more ludicrous than paying for dresses, but it would probably be cheaper.

Nobody answered over the speaker, but the gate swung open. I drove forward slowly toward a couple of expensive sports cars that I was even less likely to be able to identify than fashion brands. They looked like something out of a science-fiction movie, and I would be disappointed if they didn't fly.

*What services does she offer?* Sindari asked.

*According to the sign on her door, clairvoyant guidance, energy transformation, and intuitive advising for individuals, groups, and couples.*

*I do not know what any of that means.*

*I think it means you give her your paw and some tea leaves, and she reads your fortune.* I stopped the Jeep well away from the expensive cars, doubting Weber would appreciate it if I pronged any of them with the winch on my fender.

The modern two-story house wasn't as ostentatious as I'd expected, though it was easily ten thousand square feet on a private acre lot screened in by foliage. The slope rose sharply behind the large driveway, and the neighbor's house on the ridge above wasn't visible through the trees. A small, immaculately kept green lawn stretched to one side of the driveway where a marble fountain gurgled, faux lily pads floating in the pool. The grassy area wrapped around the home and extended toward a bunch of patios and decks overlooking the lake. I could just make out a boat—or would that be considered a yacht?—at a private dock.

*I do sense magical items here,* Sindari said as we headed for the front door. He looked at a couple of cement gargoyles with magical signatures that were mounted to either side of the walkway.

*More refined versions of the kinds of pieces Dimitri creates?* I guessed.

*Will he be offended if you call his work unrefined?*

*I don't think he has any delusions about the rusty chains and bicycle wheels he recycles for his art.*

# False Security

The gargoyles didn't exude any magical power to impede us, but a security camera rotated to watch as we climbed the steps.

As I rang the doorbell, Sindari stood regally—and classily—next to me. When the door opened, I was surprised to be face to face with Weber himself. I'd expected a butler or the executive assistant or some such person, though I wasn't sure if anyone in Seattle actually employed butlers. It seemed more of an Old Money than a New Money thing.

Also unexpected was the fact that Weber had a black eye along with a swollen nose and puffy lip. He had pale skin to match his red-blond hair, so the bruises were noticeable, but he managed an affable smile. He reminded me of a young Alan Tudyk.

"Mr. Weber?" I stuck out my hand. "I'm Val. And this is Sindari."

Weber accepted the hand clasp with a firm grip, then looked at my tiger ally. "Does he shake too?"

"No, he causes others to shake. As in the sense of quivering in their boots."

*Don't tell him that,* Sindari spoke into my mind. *He'll think I'm a monster.*

*I've heard your roar. It's monstrous.*

"That's impressive. Is he likely to eat my dog?" Weber waved into the house, where a yappy dog was barking upstairs somewhere.

"No," I said.

*It depends,* Sindari said. *How* annoying *is the dog?*

*It doesn't matter,* I replied silently. *You can't eat clients' house pets.*

Sindari made a noise somewhere between a grunt and a snore.

"He agrees," I said. "No danger to the dog."

Sindari lifted his gaze to mine, then gave my foot a pointed look.

I ignored him. Weber was already looking at me like I was weird. Maybe my tiger wasn't as classy as I thought.

"Where's the meeting?" I asked.

"This way."

Weber led me across marble floors and through halls I was positive had been decorated by an interior designer rather than a tech nerd. Earlier, I'd thought about calling Thad and seeing if he knew anything about this guy, but I decided it was unlikely their paths had crossed. Thad's tastes ran toward decorating with science-fiction movie posters and the legions of fantasy-game miniatures he'd painted over the years. When we'd been married, he'd installed a toilet paper holder in the guest bathroom that was a knight in armor holding the roll between his gauntleted hands. I wagered he still had it.

Magic plucked at my senses, and I didn't need Sindari to tell me that there were artifacts inside as well as outside. Weber even wore some magic on his wrists. Long sleeves hid whatever it was from view, but I assumed he had items similar to the charms on my neck thong.

Such trinkets were rare and valuable here on Earth. I'd won all except one of mine through battles and quests, but I was aware of a black market where they could be bought and sold. The last I'd heard, something like my cloaking charm went for more than a hundred thousand dollars. Chump change for Weber.

*This places reeks of a canine,* Sindari stated.

*You're supposed to be scoping out magic, not pet odors.*

*It's impossible to miss.*

*Just don't leave your scent on top of the dog's. This isn't our house, and it's not your territory.*

*I am a supreme being. All that I survey is my domain.*

The dog was still yapping from whatever upstairs bedroom it had been left in. Maybe it, like Maggie the cat, could detect Sindari from afar and was affronted by his presence.

*Not the client's house,* I told him. *If you scent-mark anything, I'll find a bottle of odor eliminator and spray you down.*

*You would not dare.*

*I would dare. And after I spray you, I'll tie the car air freshener to your tail.*

*I don't know why I help you.*

*Because you like going into battle, and I get in fights* all *the time.*

*That must be it. It's not your charm.* Sindari sashayed close to a pedestal holding a fancy antique violin and rubbed against it, leaving his scent all over it, I was sure.

I shot him a glare, but Weber turned into a bookcase-filled office before I could again threaten Sindari with the air freshener. The shelves were full of pretentious classics instead of quality reading like Harry Potter and The Belgariad.

Weber gestured for me to sit in one of two leather chairs opposite his.

"I'll stand. Thanks." I took a position where my back wasn't to the door or a window. Part of his monitor was visible, a screensaver showing the logo of some business, a newspaper with a dollar sign coming out of it.

"Is standing a tough-gal assassin thing?"

"No. It's a pain in the ass to remove my weapons."

He looked me up and down. I didn't sense a hint of magical blood in him, so he wouldn't be able to see Fezzik and Chopper as long as they were on my person. To alleviate his confusion, and because he might pay me more if he saw my cool gear, I drew Chopper and laid the naked blade on his desk. When I removed my hand, it came into view for him, and he jumped.

"Huh," he said, then smirked and arched his eyebrows. "There are others?"

"Yes." I returned the sword to its scabbard. "Who's been beating you up, Weber, and is that why you need a bodyguard?" I waved to his battered face.

"I believe they were werewolves, though they didn't get furry in front of me. They called themselves the Brute Squad. They hit hard."

"And they're after you why?"

Weber pulled opened envelopes out of a drawer. "I'm working on an app for the police. It was supposed to be a part-time thing on the side for a friend, but there's been a lot of interest. Its purpose is to facilitate tracking magical beings, ideally to help find those who partake in criminal actions. It scours the social media platforms for up-to-the-minute information and triangulates locations. It's smart enough to suss out lies and false rumors and dismiss those. It's still in beta, and random people can't download it, but I guess the word got out anyway. I'd been getting threatening letters from magical beings who don't want to be tracked. I handed a couple of the letters over to the police, but I've mostly been ignoring them, other than beefing up my home security. I didn't quite realize there were so many ways magical people can thwart home security."

I skimmed through the handwritten letters. The blue cursive writing all appeared to have been penned by the same person, someone whose grasp of English was tenuous. I thought of Trogg, though it wasn't quite that bad. The author never referred to himself in third person.

"You didn't think it would be a good idea to stop working on the app?" I couldn't imagine the police offering to pay anywhere close to what this guy could make from projects in the private sector. I would ask Willard if she knew anything about Weber or his work. This app seemed like something she would be aware of.

Weber stood straight. "I won't let someone threaten me into stopping a project. I *will* take precautions. Such as hiring a bodyguard. The final app should be complete and ready to distribute to the police force and other government agencies around the world in the next couple of weeks. I only need you on a short-term basis. I've heard you're good and that you've even taken out some shifters lately."

"Among other things, yes. My fee is three thousand a day, more if you want me to sleep here, propped outside your bedroom door."

His eyebrows twitched. "My assistant should have told you I'm offering two thousand a day. I believe I've suitably fortified my modest home with protective artifacts and won't have to worry about brutes busting into my bedroom, so you don't need to sleep outside my door."

"As I told your assistant, I'm already booked. For me to shift my plans around, you'll have to pay more than I'm already being paid. And I'm going to be honest with you. I prefer to hunt and attack rather than defend. Jumping in front of people to take a bullet for them doesn't excite me that much. If you'd prefer to just put a bounty on the werewolves who attacked you, I could find them in the next couple of days."

"They are only one of the groups who are angry with me. Killing them would change little. There are a lot of bitter magical beings who don't want to be tracked."

"If so, keeping you alive will be a full-time job. It is, however, one I'm capable of doing. I'm very familiar with the magical community—they've been trying to kill me for years. I can keep you alive, but not for less than three thousand a day." I spread a hand. "It's not that I'm that greedy, Mr. Weber. But your assistant said I'd have to get all manner of dresses to walk around on your arm. *This* is my usual wardrobe." I waved down at my tank top and jeans. "And I've been told that dresses from Goodwill won't cut it for whatever hoity-toity places you go to."

Weber looked me up and down without any apparent male interest. Maybe I didn't meet the standards of one of Seattle's Most Eligible Bachelors.

His gaze returned to my face. "I will meet you in the middle and pay twenty-five hundred a day for the next two weeks. I'm going to a charity dinner tomorrow evening at the yacht club, and I'll need you with me. Preferably in a dress, yes. Or something otherwise feminine and formal. There's a dress code. If you agree to the terms, I'll get you the first four days' worth of money now."

"Agreed." That left me time to go dress shopping with Amber in the morning, if she was free.

Weber rounded his desk and started for the door but paused.

"I believe there's a no-pets-allowed policy at the yacht club. Unless he counts as a service animal?" He eyed Sindari, as if looking for something like Rocket's search-and-rescue vest.

Sindari growled low in his throat.

"He's neither pet nor service animal, but I won't bring him." Silently, I added to Sindari, *Trust me. You'd be bored out of your fur at a dinner event that I'm sure is more about networking and currying favor than donating to any charity.*

*Will you not also be bored?* Sindari asked.

*Oh, I'm sure of it. But things will perk up if someone attacks Weber. Then I'll bring you out.*

*You had better.*

"Good." Weber headed out the door. "I'll be right back."

*What do you think of all the magical gizmos around the house?* I asked Sindari. *Are they just for protection? Or is this guy dabbling in dark-elf pleasure orbs or other more nefarious magic?*

*I thought all those orbs were destroyed.*

*Willard's office tried to find them all, but I wouldn't be surprised if there are still some around. And I highly doubt all the dark elves were killed when we invaded their glacier base.*

*I do not sense anything like that. What is here seems to largely be for protection.*

My phone buzzed.

A text from Dimitri read: *Zoltan is missing.*

*How do you know?* I replied. *Was he supposed to come to the shop tonight?*

*No. But a delivery was supposed to come. When it didn't arrive, I called Zoltan and didn't get an answer. I'm over at his place now. He's not here, and a whole bunch of stuff in his lab is broken. Someone drove a spear through the giant mechanical guard spider and it's not working. Can you come take a look?*

*I can come look tonight, but I just accepted a new gig, so I can't spend the week searching for vampires.*

*I'll search for him by myself if I need to.*

I shook my head, worried Dimitri would get himself in trouble. *If he ran afoul of someone, it's not any of our business.*

*He's my business partner. That makes his business my business.*

*Only the stuff related to the coffee shop.*

*He pays the lease on that building, you know. And he's... my friend. Val, we have to find him.*

I sighed. *I'll be there as soon as I can.*

# Chapter 7

Weber returned with an envelope and handed it to me. I opened it to count the stack of hundreds inside.

"I'm good for it," he said dryly.

"In my business, you don't trust anyone until they've proven themselves to you." It was all there. I folded the envelope and stuffed it in a pocket.

"And what does one have to do to prove himself to you?"

"Sindari bites my enemies in the butts and refrains from gnawing off my foot when I tease him."

Weber didn't look like he knew if that was a joke or not. Nope, he was definitely not my type. Fortunately, I didn't seem to be his type either. That would make everything simpler. The last time I'd worked as a bodyguard for a guy, he'd thought bedroom services should be included.

"Be here tomorrow at six," Weber said.

"In a dress. Got it. I'll see myself out."

I wasn't surprised when he followed me to the front door. He probably thought I would grab his antique violin on the way out and sell it on eBay. Our date at the yacht club would be a blast; I could tell.

Before I reached the Jeep, I sensed Zav approaching and stifled a groan. It was going to be hard to explain the two-week delay to him.

As I turned to face west, the direction he was approaching from, I realized Weber was standing out on the porch. I hoped he wasn't the type to get uptight about a dragon landing in his yard. The sun had set, but landscaping lights had come on all over the property, so it wasn't like Weber would miss it.

*It is likely his arrival will set off the magical wards placed around the house,* Sindari observed.

*Zav, can you hear me?* I had yet to learn telepathy, but I did my best to project my thoughts toward the distant black figure soaring toward us. Maybe he would be focused on me.

*Certainly.*

*This yard has magical wards and alarms.*

*I sense them.* He kept coming, wings flapping a few times as he adjusted direction. *They are puny and insignificant to a dragon.*

*Can you land without setting them off?*

I'd hoped Weber would get bored of watching me, but instead, he turned to look in the direction I was looking. Since he didn't have magical blood, he shouldn't be able to sense or see Zav. Unless Zav *wanted* to be seen. I hoped not.

Weber squinted at me, no doubt wondering why I was loitering in the driveway instead of leaving.

"I saw some bats." I waved at the sky, then hopped in the Jeep.

Maybe I had time to get off the property before Zav came in. But dragons are fast, and he landed in front of me on the driveway before I'd done more than turn around. Just as my headlamps highlighted the sleek black scales of his legs, the magical alarms went off.

Colored lights burst from statues poised all around the driveway, and incendiary rounds streaked toward Zav. Alarms bonged, not audibly but in my mind. Something squealed from the rooftop of the house.

"What's going on?" Weber yelled.

All the projectiles targeting Zav burst into flames before reaching him, setting up a massive fireworks show in front of my Jeep.

*No, I cannot land without setting them off.* Zav sounded amused.

*You could have landed outside the gate.*

*You were not outside the gate.*

*I was heading that way.* I got out of the Jeep.

Weber was still on the porch, but he was gaping at Zav now as the fireworks died down. I had a feeling Zav had made himself visible.

"Sorry," I called. "It's an acquaintance of mine. I wasn't expecting him."

"An acquaintance?" Weber mouthed. "Is that a *dragon*? A *real* dragon?"

Zav pulled in his wings and shifted into his human form. He was still wearing his Birkenstocks. Maybe they'd been a hit at the Dragon Justice Court.

"It doesn't change anything." I waved again to Weber, trying to convey with the motion that he should go inside. "I'll be back at six tomorrow."

Zav folded his arms over his chest as he looked from me to Weber.

"I wasn't expecting you to be back until the morning," I murmured, walking up to Zav.

"You will not see that human at six tomorrow," Zav stated. "You will be with me."

"Actually, I'm going to have to delay that. I just accepted a new gig." I lowered my voice. "It's a lot of money and could get me out of debt. I can still go with you to visit the elves. It'll just have to wait a couple of weeks."

Even if this new assignment hadn't come up, I would have felt guilty leaving town—leaving the *planet*—when something was up with Zoltan and a vampire was stalking the neighborhood around Dimitri's shop.

Zav narrowed his eyes, and I grew aware of his powerful aura radiating from him and crackling over my senses, reminding me that he could force the issue if he wished.

But he wouldn't. We were allies now—*more* than allies—right?

Zav opened his mouth, but instead of responding to me, he looked at Weber and boomed, "Leave us."

A heavy magical compulsion laced the words, and my legs wanted to scurry away even though it wasn't directed at me. I expected Weber to fling himself inside, slam the door shut, and hide under the nearest bed. Surprisingly—no, *shockingly*—he crossed his arms over his chest, mirroring Zav's gesture, and stood his ground.

How the hell? Had one of his artifacts or charms allowed him to resist that? That had to be it.

If that was true, I wondered if he would sell it to me. Or pay me with it instead of with money. I'd happily work for two weeks of no pay for something that would solve one of my biggest problems without requiring months of elven-magic training.

"Nobody orders me around, Dragon. This is my property, and you will remove yourself from it."

Zav's eyes flared with violet light. "You will call me Lord Zavryd'nokquetal if you speak to me at all, vermin."

*Another Earth denizen,* Sindari murmured into my mind, *too foolish to know that dragons must be treated with respect, if not skirted around and avoided altogether.*

"I could destroy your property with a thought," Zav said.

"You will find that my *property* is well protected."

"Okay, okay." I raised my hands and patted the air. "Let's stop comparing penises, fellas. Weber, go inside, please, and I'll see you tomorrow." Being conciliatory wasn't my strength, but I gave him my best smile, and then I turned it on Zav. "And, Zav, let's go out that gate and discuss this. There's no need to destroy anything."

The two men—two males—kept glaring at each other and didn't seem to hear me.

*Think I could hoist him over my shoulder and carry him through the gate?* I asked Sindari.

*I would suggest not doing anything that impinges on his authority.*

*So, I guess you're not interested in biting him in the butt.*

*I am not.*

*Darn.*

Zav scoffed. "Your meager defenses have insufficient power to inconvenience a dragon."

"We'll see about that," Weber said, though he glanced at me, a little uncertain. If he'd gotten most of his magical gadgets recently and hadn't tested them against more than werewolves, his beliefs about what they could do might be wildly inaccurate. Especially if some numbnuts had told him they would work against dragons.

I shook my head, hoping he would take me as a neutral third party.

While they continued to glare at each other, I got back in the Jeep, waving for Sindari to join me. It occurred to me that the best way to get Zav to leave was to leave myself. I highly doubted he wanted to stick around and bathe in the fountain.

Zav blinked as I drove around him and toward the gate. Fortunately, it opened for me. I drove out slowly in case I was wrong and needed to hurry back to rescue Weber—it was against bodyguard rules to leave one's charge to be mauled by an irate dragon—but Zav shifted back into his dragon form and flew over the fence after me. With a few beats of his great wings, he passed over the Jeep and landed in the street, breaking the branches of nearby trees as he descended.

The rear-view mirror showed the gate to Weber's property closing. Hopefully, the magical defenses could be reset and Zav hadn't broken any of them. I didn't want to get an angry message from my new boss later.

Zav, not changing out of his dragon form, lowered his head so that his gaze pinned me through the windshield. *You will come out and speak with me.*

He sounded more pompous and arrogant than ever. Since I felt bad about postponing our trip—a trip he was only planning in order to help me—I kept myself from making a snarky retort.

"I'll be happy to speak with you when you're not blocking traffic in and out of the neighborhood." Fortunately, the dead-end street only had a few houses on it, and nobody had tried to drive down it yet, but that didn't make my statement untrue. "Come join me, and we'll grab something to eat on the way over to Zoltan's. I'll pay."

His violet eyes continued to stare through the windshield at me. I was starting to wish I'd taken a few negotiation and mediation classes in college. This wasn't my strong suit.

"Zoltan's missing. I need your help. How do you feel about chicken strips?"

Zav's head rose, disappearing from view, and I envisioned him stomping on the Jeep Godzilla-style in a fit of peevishness, but he shifted into his human form and walked to the passenger side.

"I have explained why it is not a good idea for me to allow you to feed me." He sat beside me and closed the door.

"They come out the window in a bag. You can feed yourself." I headed out of the neighborhood and back toward Sand Point Way.

Zav gazed over at me. He seemed more disappointed than angry, but maybe I was reading too much into his silence.

"I was looking forward to uniting you with your *real* elven kin—" that had to be a dig about Anyasha-sulin, the elf who'd called herself Lirena and pretended to be my cousin, "—and assisting you with finding a tutor."

"I know, and I really appreciate that. Will you still be willing to do it in a couple of weeks? Maybe you can hunt down a few more criminals while I'm busy guarding that guy." I tilted my thumb back in the direction of the house.

"I do not like *that guy*."

"You don't like any guys."

"He was not properly respectful. Death will befall him if a less tolerant dragon ever visits him."

"Please tell me there aren't any less tolerant dragons on Earth right now." I looked over at him. "Your sister isn't back, is she? Or any of Dob's relatives?"

"My mother gave my sister an assignment, so she is not here. I am unaware of other dragons presently on this world."

"That's a relief." I pulled into the drive-thru of a fast-food restaurant. "How hungry are you?"

"I am not hungry. *That guy* also had an inordinate number of magical artifacts in and around his residence that could not have originated on this world. It is likely they are stolen."

"That's probably true, but I'm sure Weber wasn't the one to do it. He probably doesn't know much about magic and just bought all that stuff to protect himself. He hired me because werewolves have been picking on him. He's paying me a *lot* to be his bodyguard." I pulled up to the speaker and lowered my voice when I added, "Like I said, this gig would get me out of debt. Then maybe I could take time off to go with you to visit elves and research my sword and do all the things I want to do."

"How can I help you?" a female voice came out of the speaker.

"Mate with me," Zav said, presumably responding to me and not the worker taking orders.

"I'm sorry," the puzzled voice said. "Can you repeat that?"

I pressed a hand over Zav's mouth. "I'd like eight orders of chicken strips."

"Did you say *eight*?"

"Make it ten. And we want all the dipping sauces."

"All right. I'll have your total for you at the window."

I lowered my hand and moved the Jeep forward. Fortunately, Zav didn't appear irked at my presumptuousness.

"Yeah, mating with you is on my wish list. Even if you are a pompous pain in the ass."

"Excellent. You are a disrespectful sharp-tongued mongrel, but mating with you is also on my *wish list*." He said the term carefully, probably his first time using it.

"It's clear we're meant for each other."

Sindari let out a long sigh from the back of the Jeep. *Have you forgotten that I'm here?*

"No. Did you want some chicken strips too?"

"I do not believe you should trust this Weber," Zav said, ignoring Sindari, though I was positive he heard him. "Knowingly buying stolen artifacts is not any more legal than stealing them personally. That is the law in the Cosmic Realms."

"Is it a law that's only enforced if the artifacts were stolen from dragons?"

He gave me a flat look. "It is only enforced by dragons if the artifacts were stolen from dragons. Lesser species enforce the law among themselves."

"I'll keep an eye on him and won't trust him implicitly, all right?" I had a feeling Zav's objections wouldn't be nearly as strong if Weber were a woman.

"He should be more thoroughly inspected before you agree to work for him," Zav said as we pulled up to the window. "Take me to his house with you tomorrow, and I will investigate his magical acquisitions more thoroughly."

"I'm sure Weber would adore that."

"What he adores is irrelevant."

"As long as he's paying me, his adorations are relevant."

"As my *Tlavar'vareous sha*, only *my* adorations should be relevant to you."

The girl leaned out with two big bags, her brow furrowed as she caught part of the conversation. Given that marijuana was legal in Washington, I refused to believe this was the weirdest discussion she'd heard at this job. It probably wasn't even the weirdest discussion that night.

I paid and set the bags of food in Zav's lap. Despite his assertion that he wasn't hungry, he sniffed and poked into them with interest.

The girl peered across me toward him, then smirked and gave me a thumbs-up as I drove off. Maybe she'd caught that bit about mating after all.

One of the paper bags rustled, the scent of fried chicken filling the Jeep. "Make sure to leave a couple for me."

Zav pulled out napkins, tossed them to the floor at his feet, then lifted some of the containers of dipping sauces. He removed the lids and sniffed them. He wrinkled his nose, put the lids back on, and tossed them down with the napkins. Finally, he withdrew a chicken strip and examined it from all angles.

Despite the late hour, the traffic was heavy, so I had to pay attention to it instead of his continued examination of the food, but it amused me nonetheless. At a light, I texted Dimitri to see if anything had changed.

"There is something stuck to this meat," Zav announced.

"It's the breading. It's deep-fried. You'll love it. Everyone loves deep-fried food."

*I found blood on the floor,* Dimitri replied.

*Human blood or vampire blood?*

*What's the difference?*

*Every vampire I've beheaded had sludgy, congealed blackish blood.*

*Ew. How many vampires have you beheaded?*

*Enough that Zoltan should avoid billing me as much as he does.*

*The blood was bright red and fresh. I need Sindari to come track whoever left it.*

*Be there in twenty minutes.*

The light turned, and I put the phone away. Zav was tossing more things onto the floor.

"Why are you making a mess?"

"Dragons do not eat *breading*." He scraped more off and dropped it at his feet, then stuffed an entire strip into his mouth and chomped. "Much better."

"I'll look for an all-carnivore fast-food place next time."

"Excellent. It pleases me when you seek to accommodate me."

"I'm so glad." I shook my head. I'd never had to deal with a date like this. Who would have thought a dragon would be a picky eater?

The next light was under a bright streetlamp, which illuminated the utter mess of napkins, condiments, and a huge pile of breading on the floor between Zav's feet.

"Is it considered disrespectful to ask a dragon to clean up after himself?" I asked.

Zav gazed over at me as he chewed on a denuded chicken strip.

He looked contented rather than irked, and I remembered that food made dragons randy. He flicked a finger, and a burst of flame came from the floor. I jerked in surprise, but the flame went out quickly, leaving only smoke and the scent of charred food. He'd incinerated the trash, including the condiments. I guessed I wasn't getting any honey mustard with my strips.

"It's going to be a long night, isn't it?"

Zav chomped down on another chicken strip.

# Chapter 8

The root-cellar door behind the carriage house was open. Zav, Sindari, and I walked down into Zoltan's lair and encountered Dimitri in the hallway outside the lab door, a couple of camp lanterns illuminating the area. He was kneeling in front of the mechanical guard spider that he'd helped Zoltan assemble and animate. A toolbox rested at his side, and a long pole arm lay in the middle of the hall. A big hole in the spider's mechanical skull looked like it had been made by the weapon.

"Did it short out?" I waved for Sindari to pass us. *Will you go in and sniff around to see if you can identify the blood?*

*Certainly.*

Zav also passed us, though I didn't know if he meant to sniff around or look for more food. He'd consumed all except three chicken strips, which he'd politely set in my hand as we'd gotten out of the Jeep. Thoughtfully, he'd removed and incinerated the breading for me. There'd been no sign of honey mustard anywhere.

"I think so," Dimitri said, "and there's damage to its CPU. I'm going to have to order replacement parts."

"Where does one order parts for a giant robotic guard spider?"

"You can find anything on the internet." Dimitri rose to his feet. "Whatever happened, it couldn't have been too long ago." He led me into the lab and pointed at boxes of bottles and jars that had been carefully packed and set next to the door. "Around eight, the guy who does Zoltan's pick-ups called and let me know the shipment wasn't out by the mailbox in the usual spot."

"When was the last time you talked to Zoltan?"

"I called earlier this evening to let him know about the inventory the ogres damaged, and he answered then and didn't say anything was wrong."

Even though the packed boxes hadn't been disturbed, a lot of other things had been. Zoltan's alchemy equipment had been swept off the counters, and broken glass littered the floor. Numerous substances were spilled, noxious odors wafting up from some of them, and I had the urge to rush outside and breathe fresh air.

Sindari and Zav were examining a few blood spatters on the cement floor near a drain. It was too small an amount for me to tell if there was any magic in the blood. Leaving the scent-work for them, I went to Zoltan's computer and video equipment.

"Did you already check this stuff, Dimitri?"

"No. He's never given me permission to look at any of that."

"Well, he's not here, so I'm giving myself permission."

When I prodded the mouse and all three flat-screen displays came to life, I expected to be blocked by a password prompt, but I wasn't. Maybe Zoltan considered his guard spider sufficient for security purposes.

I scanned through recent emails and comments on his YouTube channel that were asking why his daily alchemy video wasn't up yet. One person was requesting a recipe she could use to poison her boss.

An email with the subject "You're the bestest!!!" popped up a giant image of a young woman taking a selfie of her bare chest. She *might* have been of legal age, but I didn't spend a lot of time trying to guess. The majority of his emails were from what seemed to be raving fans of his channel. A lot of them hadn't been opened. It didn't look like he replied to any of them or had correspondence with anyone at all. The handful that had been opened were requests for potions and academic discourse on alchemical ingredients.

"No death threats that I can see," I said. "Though I suppose it's possible that jealous boyfriends of some of these girls found out about their obsession with Zoltan and decided to hunt him down."

"The blood belongs to an orc," Zav said. "An orc that smells freshly of Daknok-tor."

"Probably not a jealous boyfriend then."

"What's Daknok-tor?" Dimitri asked.

"The orc home world," Zav said.

"So, someone who came recently to Earth?" I asked.

"Very recently."

*There were three or four of them in here. I'll track the trail as far as I can and let you know if I reach the edge of my range.* Sindari trotted into the hallway.

"Thank you," I called after him.

Zav moved to the counters and poked into a glass cabinet full of books that emanated magic. He pulled out a few journals, flipped through them, and returned them to the shelves.

Dimitri watched the investigation with his hands in his pockets, a glum expression on his face. I wasn't sure what else to do to help either. It wasn't as if we could call in a forensics team, not without creating a lot of questions from the people who'd moved into the main house. We'd used magical stealth to sneak into the back yard, but police cars full of investigators would be harder to hide.

"It looks like someone made a deliberate mess," Zav said, "but his journals and the more valuable items in his collection are all here."

"I don't think anything was taken. Except Zoltan. Why would orcs want a vampire?" Dimitri gave me a puzzled look.

"There are a lot of orc thugs for hire," I said. "Someone may have paid them to kidnap Zoltan."

"But to what end?"

"Your guess is as good as mine."

"What should I do?" Dimitri pushed a hand through his hair.

"Get some sleep. I'll go to Willard's office in the morning and see if she—or her prime informant Gondo—has heard anything." I wanted to ask her about Weber and his app project too.

"It seems wrong to go to sleep when your business partner is missing."

"Maybe you'll get a ransom note in the morning that gives you some hints."

"That's not funny," Dimitri said.

"I was being serious."

His expression grew bleaker.

"I would suggest going to Rupert's and asking around if it was still open," I said. "I'm not sure where magical beings are congregating now. Unless your coffee shop is the new hangout."

"It's a housewares and lotion store," he mumbled, though none of his usual indignation was in the objection. "But... maybe I should *let* it become the new hangout. And listen as the customers gossip. Maybe someone will reveal something over coffee."

"Get that liquor license we were talking about. People would be even more likely to reveal secrets over booze."

*The orcs went to the street,* Sindari informed me, *where they were picked up in a vehicle. I am unable to track them further.*

*I was afraid of that.*

*What next? I cannot stay much longer in this realm today.*

*Go home and rest. I'll figure something out.* What exactly, I didn't know. I glowered down at the floor.

Zav walked over to me and put his arm around my shoulders.

The gesture startled me, since he'd never done it before. "What are you doing?"

"I am comforting you."

Dimitri was across the lab, but he raised his eyebrows.

"Oh. Thank you. I didn't know dragons did that." I leaned against his side.

"Dragons are not emotionally fragile and do not engage in physical gestures of commiseration. But as I have learned in the past, elves often touch each other to convey feelings and comfort each other. And you are half elven."

"I appreciate your gesture, but I think Dimitri is in more need of comforting right now than I am."

Zav looked at Dimitri. "I am uninterested in touching a human male."

Dimitri backed up until his back bumped a counter. "And I'm uninterested in being touched by a dragon male."

"Are you sure?" I smiled, hoping to lighten his mood. "I thought you were into guys."

"Not that guy, no."

"Is it the sandals?"

Zav looked down and studied his bare toes.

"No." Dimitri shook his head without humor. "I just need to find Zoltan."

## False Security

"I don't think there's anything else we can do tonight." I patted Zav's stomach and headed out, crossing my fingers that Willard would have some intel for me in the morning.

# Chapter 9

The next morning, my phone buzzed as I pulled into the parking lot outside of Willard's building. It was Mary. I debated whether or not to answer it. When I'd gotten home the night before, I'd left a message to cancel my therapy appointment. Between Zoltan being missing and preparing for my new gig, I doubted I would have time for it.

"Hello?" I answered.

"Hi, Val. I got your message about canceling last night—at 12:03 am." Was that judgment in her calm and usually neutral tone? For the late hour or for the cancellation? "I wanted to make sure you're okay and see if you want to reschedule."

"Things got busy yesterday." I climbed out of the Jeep. "And the next couple of weeks may be busy too."

"Wasn't yesterday your day off?"

"Yes. I don't think I did it right."

"Did you get a massage?"

"No. I took a new job and a friend was kidnapped."

"That's awful, Val."

"The kidnapping, I assume."

"Well, yes, but neither are acceptable activities for a day off. As soon as you're able, you need to take some real time to relax and work on your relationships."

"I know. I will. I'm still looking at things I can do to relax that won't put other people at risk." I imagined somebody giving me a massage in one of those little rooms as a grenade sailed through the door.

"Have you looked into meditation yet? I know I've mentioned it a few times. You can meditate from the safety of your own home."

"Not yet, but I will." I nodded to one of Willard's soldiers as we crossed paths—he was heading for the coffee shop on the corner. "Thanks for checking up on me. I need to go. Meeting with my boss."

"I hope you're feeling better and that your life settles down and becomes less fraught."

"Thanks," I said, though I couldn't imagine what a *settled* life would look like. Would dragons denuding chicken strips in my Jeep still be allowed?

When I walked into Willard's building, Gondo and the young elven intern Freysha were in her outer office, arguing over a set of blueprints spread on the desk. It looked more complicated than the siege engine they'd built out of office equipment. Maybe I should let Weber know that some magical engineers were available if he wanted to add fortifications to his house.

Willard's door was open, so I headed straight toward it, but Gondo jumped onto the chair and picked up the phone.

"I will let the colonel know that you have arrived," he said.

Willard was looking through the door at me from her desk, her cell phone to her ear as she ordered supplies from someone.

"I think she knows. Colonels are clairvoyant."

"There is a protocol, as I've been informed. I will call." Gondo pushed buttons.

"You only need to call me if I'm in here with someone and the door is shut," Willard's voice floated out as she ignored the office phone flashing on her desk in favor of finishing her other conversation.

"Oh." Gondo put the phone down.

Freysha smiled at me. Her blonde hair was down, save for a few thin braids held in place by green beads that matched her bright eyes. "Greetings, Val. You have not been to this office for several days. Have you been helping Lord Zavryd'nokquetal catch villains?"

"You can *pronounce* his name?"

"I study linguistics and know several languages."

"Oh, that's right. You were going over translations for Willard."

"Yes. I am seeking ways to be useful so that she will hire me as more than an intern. Did you know Zavryd'nokquetal means Noble Son Soaring in the dragon tongue? Will you tell me more about the work you are doing with him someday? Do you wish to have lunch? I have learned that humans often discuss work over the midday meal."

"Uh, sure, kid. The next time I have a day off." I had a few thousand questions, none that involved lunching with teenage linguists, so I continued to Willard's office.

But I halted on the threshold as an idea slammed into me. Freysha wasn't *truly* teenage—she just looked it. She'd said she was thirty-seven. Young for an elf who would live centuries, but was it old enough to have learned some elven magic? And if so, was it old enough to teach that magic to others?

"Freysha." I turned slowly around. "You've studied linguistics, but have you also studied magic?"

"Yes, I have studied forest magic, but I am a long ways from being a master."

What was *forest* magic? It didn't sound promising for getting dragons to leave one alone.

"I will return to my magical studies one day, but I am taking a leave of absence while I am learning engineering in this world."

"Leave of absence? I thought you were a refugee who'd fled some trouble back home." Though now that I thought about it, I didn't think Freysha had ever said that. I'd assumed that because that was what brought almost every other magical being to Earth. And, the last I'd heard, she was living under a bridge and bathing in a fountain.

Freysha tilted her head. "I came here to study from your metallurgy and engineering masters."

"Like Gondo?"

Gondo smiled and thumped himself on the chest.

"Yes," Freysha said politely, "and also some professors at your university. Colonel Willard is letting me use a computer here to take an online class."

"Can you make a portal and go back home any time?"

"I cannot leave whenever I wish, no."

"Hm." So no portals. But what about what I needed? "Do you know how to defend against mental attacks? And magical compulsions?"

"Yes, of course. All students must learn such things."

"Magical compulsions applied by dragons?"

"Those are difficult to resist. You can learn the basics and practice them, but a great deal depends on your inherent power and natural talent."

Maybe I'd be better off trying to get that charm from Weber. "Would you show me the basics?"

"It is not permitted for any but a master to teach magic."

"I'll pay you."

"I cannot go against the laws of our people, even here in this somewhat lawless world. I am sorry."

Damn.

"But I could give you some tips for tapping into your natural aptitude." Freysha touched her temple.

"I'll take it." Anything was better than nothing. "And I'll pay you."

"That's not necessary."

"Are you sure?"

Gondo hopped onto the desk and bumped her shoulder, then whispered into her pointed ear. I debated whether I wanted to activate my translation charm. Judging by the way Freysha lifted her eyes heavenward—it wasn't quite a good old human eye roll, but it was in the ballpark—she wasn't going to implement whatever scheme he was suggesting.

"You don't need to pay me," Freysha told me with a quelling glance at Gondo.

Gondo refused to be quelled. "But if you want to donate to our cause in exchange for my assistant's extremely valuable time, we would be honored to allow that."

"What cause, and how did Freysha become your assistant?"

"We're building a steam lorry to facilitate trade between goblins and other magical communities. Your gasoline is expensive, and we have trees we could use in our sanctuary, so a steam-powered vehicle is best."

"Trees in your sanctuary in the national forest? You're not supposed to cut those down."

Gondo waved dismissively. "As for the rest, I'm an informant on the payroll here. She's an intern. That means I outrank her, and she assists me."

"Get in here, Thorvald." Willard had finished her call.

"Lunch as soon as I can get free." I pointed to Freysha.

I'd almost said today, but I had to pick up Amber and go dress shopping. Maybe I should have told Mary I planned to do that. She might consider shopping a sign that I was relaxing. Retail therapy was a thing, right?

"Hey, Willard." I kicked the door shut, removed my weapons, and plopped down in her guest chair. It wasn't as posh as Weber's, but I slung my leg over the arm to take a stab at being comfortable. "Do you actually pay Gondo?"

Willard frowned at my dangling leg. "Ten dollars a day and all the sodas he wants out of the vending machine."

"That's not minimum wage."

"Trust me, it is. Goblin bladders must be amazing."

"Magical even. Got anything for me?" The night before, I'd texted her about Zoltan and asked her to gather information on Weber and his app.

"Yes." Willard pulled a printout from a drawer. "I came in two hours early this morning so I could gather data for you for this posh assignment you've gotten that has nothing to do with this office and should by no means rely on its resources or require work from its personnel."

"Does that mean I should thank you profusely?"

"I'll also accept gifts. You offered to take my intern to lunch, but all you ever want from me is money."

"I'm terribly sorry. I would have brought you some leftover chicken strips from last night, but Zav ate them all."

"Your diet is deplorable. It's no wonder you have health issues."

"I'm actually fasting currently since the only chicken strips left for me looked rather unappetizing after the breading had been incinerated."

"I'm not going to ask." She pointed to the printout. "The summary is that Weber has never done anything illegal. He started a couple of software businesses before shifting focus and getting into cybernetics and biomechatronics. He got very rich turning people into cyborgs for a living."

"Pardon?" I envisioned movies featuring half-robot super soldiers taking over the galaxy.

"Creating computer bits to put into people to address health problems. He had some top-notch scientists and engineers on his team and patented a bunch of stuff, some proven and some still in development. There's an artificial pancreas for Type 1 diabetics that's in testing right now. It's been a couple of years since he sold the company, but he'll get a lot of credit for good work if even a fraction of it turns out to be viable in the real world."

"Are you saying he's one of the good guys?" I'd expected her to dig up some dirt, but maybe Zav's suspicion of Weber had colored my thoughts.

"It's not like he was doing research for charity, but as far as corporations go, his had a noble purpose."

"What about the app he told me about?"

Willard leaned back in her chair. "I couldn't find anything about that."

"He said it's not public yet."

"I called the Seattle PD and also talked to my military contacts. Nobody knows anything about an app for tracking magical beings."

"Nobody except the werewolves who beat him up?"

Willard spread a hand. "It's your mission. You'll have to solve some of the mysteries yourself. But you're welcome for the work I did do. When you bring me a lunch, I want my chicken to be free-range, organic, and non-breathed-on-by-dragons."

"You're what they call high maintenance, Willard." I rose to my feet. "But you're my favorite boss, so I'll bring you a giant salad from Whole Foods with meat so fresh it's still running."

"Why don't you grocery shop while you're there, so you don't have to feed your dragon substandard fast food?"

I almost said I didn't make enough to shop there, but given the wad of cash I'd been given the night before, that wasn't entirely true. Not at the moment. "I'll keep your advice in mind. He would be a fan of the raw steaks counter."

"Before you go—" Willard lifted a hand, "—have you heard about a vampire attack?"

"In Fremont? Yeah."

She frowned. "In Lake City. A car dealership was broken into and an employee was found dead with fang marks in his neck."

"Dead? I thought vampires usually take what they need and leave their victims alive."

"Not this time."

"When did this happen?"

"Last night."

"It could be the same vampire that attacked the psychic's daughter in Fremont." I summed up what I'd learned from Dimitri's neighbor.

"I sent an agent out to look at the body at the dealership, so hopefully, I'll have more information soon. I was going to send *you* out until you said you have this new gig."

"I may end up involved in the vampire case anyway if it has something to do with Zoltan's disappearance."

"Are you working around the clock for Weber?"

"I'm not sure yet. I'm accompanying him to the yacht club tonight." I grimaced. "In a dress."

"A dress? Do you know how to put one on?"

"Is it complicated? How many holes are there?"

"It's the straps you have to worry about." Willard waved me to the door. "Let me know if your dragon wants a job hunting down vampires. I assume he's not going with you to the yacht club."

"I didn't invite him. He doesn't like my new employer."

"Because he's jealous of another man spending time with you?"

"Because he doesn't like anyone."

"Except you."

"I feed him fast food. What's not to adore?"

# Chapter 10

As I drove across town with Amber, I worried I should be investigating the car dealership murder or questioning people in the magical community about Zoltan rather than going shopping. Maybe this had been a mistake.

That feeling intensified when I pulled into the parking garage for the fancy mall Amber had recommended. As soon as I saw signs for Neiman Marcus, Gucci, and Louis Vuitton, I knew I was out of my element and nothing good would come out of this trip. But we were here, and I needed at least one dress. I'd get in and out quickly and return to work.

We bypassed the valet to self-park among the BMWs, Mercedes, and Land Rovers filling the stalls. I pulled in next to a spotless black Hummer taking up two spaces in the back of the garage—it had probably never been on a street with potholes, much less taken off-road.

"Thank God." Amber flung open the door and slid out. "That was horrible."

"What, you didn't like my music?"

"Eighties metal by guys with hair longer than mine is horrific, but I meant the lack of AC."

"The air-conditioning was on."

"If you say so. Dad's car lets you set the temp for your own zone. And has butt coolers."

"Butt coolers?" I'd heard of butt warmers, but butt coolers were new to me. As we headed for the shops, I imagined how surprised Zav would be if either came on while he was sitting in a car.

"You know, modern tech. From this century. I'm surprised you have automatic windows."

"They're easier for my tiger to roll down that way. Pets riding in the back seat had a rough life back in ye olden days." Since Sindari wasn't around, I didn't worry about offending him by lumping him with *pets*.

"Don't talk about your tiger in the store, please. That's weird."

"Can I talk about dragons?"

"*No.*"

"The girl at the drive-thru last night was impressed by Zav."

The look Amber gave me promised she was already having second thoughts about appearing in public with me, so I refrained from further comments.

She squinted at me. "Are you kickin' it with him, or what?"

The first thing that came to mind was playing soccer with Zav. That probably wasn't what she was asking.

"Does that mean hanging out? Or having sex?"

"Sex, Val." Her squint turned into an eye roll. Amazing how she could do both at the same time.

"We're not kickin' it, no. We've just been working on some assignments together."

"At the drive-thru?"

"Dragons get hungry."

We'd reached the front doors of a boutique shop Amber had angled us toward, and two women walked out in time to hear that. They gave me a who-let-the-riff-raff-in look and hustled away with their shopping bags.

Amber flung her hand dramatically up to cover her face as I held the door open for her. With her cheeks visibly pink, she led me inside, veering quickly off the main aisle and toward dresses in the back.

I lifted a hand, wanting to drag a salesperson over to get this taken care of as quickly as possible, but Amber hurried back and grabbed my arm.

"They're on commission," she whispered. "You can't trust them. That's why you've got me."

I had a feeling Amber didn't trust anyone over eighteen, but I let her steer me to the back where she went to work with the methodical precision of a soldier disassembling her firearm for a cleaning.

As she held up dresses and compared them to matching accessories—ugh, I hadn't budgeted for accessories—I poked at flimsy material and fingered straps, imagining how quickly the garments would be destroyed in a fight. If I had to tussle with werewolves at the yacht club, I'd end up naked save for my undies and weapons. What would the dress-code police think of that?

Someone with a magical aura came into my range, and my head came up like that of a zebra on the Serengeti. It was a shifter, and it—*she*—had come in through a side door.

I spotted her right away, a buxom raven-haired woman in slinky clothing that had come off the racks here. A frequent client? An employee? She was looking right at me with dark brown eyes that reminded me more of an animal than a person, and there was a feral curl to her lips. She wasn't a werewolf though. A bear? Her aura had a faint ursine tinge, but I didn't run into many bear shifters, especially not in the middle of the city, so I wasn't positive.

"What do you think of this?" Amber held up a dress, silk scarf, and some shoes she'd paired with them.

Keeping my gaze on the shifter, I barely looked. "Is there a slit in the leg?"

The woman strolled past the two employees—they didn't bat an eye, so maybe the shifter *did* work here—and weaved through the displays toward us.

"No. You're not even looking." Amber frowned at me. "Why do you need a slit?"

"So I can reach my gun without hiking up my skirt and showing the entire yacht club my underwear." I didn't bother to lower my voice. Let the shifter know I had weapons. She could probably see them anyway—the magical usually could.

"That's next-level cringe, Val." Still frowning, Amber turned toward the newcomer. She opened her mouth, probably to tell me that guns—along with tigers and dragons—shouldn't be discussed in public, but maybe she could sense the shifter's magic, for she closed her mouth again.

The shifter stopped in front of me, eyeing my sword hilt poking over my shoulder. The other two women stopped their conversation and looked over.

"We're not interested in your business," the shifter said.

"Because you don't think I can pay or because my boots don't match my belt?" I asked.

"Because you're the Ruin Bringer."

"Her belt is gauche too," one of the saleswomen said.

Her colleague elbowed her.

Amber flicked her fingers toward the shifter. "Run along, or we're going to Neiman Marcus."

"If you're the one hunting vampires," the shifter said, not acknowledging Amber, "you'll find a lot of impediments to your shopping trip." Her eyes hardened. "*And* your life."

"You're tight with vampires, are you?"

"Don't make a scene," Amber whispered, trying to grab my arm and lead me out of the store.

But I resisted the pull and lifted a hand. This woman might know something relevant to my vampire problems.

"The magical community is tight with each other." She waved a cell phone. "I could have special security here to deal with you in seconds."

I wondered what app summoned *special* security. "What makes you think I'm hunting vampires? And what vampires are being hunted? I only know of one who's gone missing."

"Charles, Estefan, and *Zoltan* have all disappeared. Don't pretend you aren't involved in it."

"Why the anguish over Zoltan?" I hadn't thought he ever left his lab, much less had connections in the community. I made a quick note in my phone so I wouldn't forget the other two names.

"He makes my anti-aging tinctures."

"Your wrinkle cream? No wonder you're stricken."

She growled. It was a very unladylike growl but a very bear-like growl.

"I'm not the one picking on vampires," I said. "From what I've heard, at least one of them has been attacking people."

"You better check your sources. Whoever hired you to kidnap vampires lied."

"My sources can't be any worse than yours if you think I'm the one kidnapping people."

Amber poked me in the arm and pointed at two security guards that had come through the door. They weren't magical, so I doubted they were the *special* forces the shifter had mentioned, but I didn't want to start a fight in a clothing store.

"I really think Neiman Marcus is going to be more your style." Amber had put away all the selections she'd pulled out for me.

"Do they have dresses with slits there?"

"I'm positive."

"A lot of women use Zoltan's tinctures," the shifter warned me as we maneuvered toward the door. "You'll find yourself bathing in enemies once the word gets out."

How different from my usual life. "I'm not the one who took him. Try barking up an orc tree."

The next time I visited Zoltan's place, I would take a careful perusal of the neighborhood—or ask Sindari to do it. I had a hunch someone else from the magical community lived out there and had seen me coming and going. Too bad they hadn't seen the real kidnappers coming and going.

The security guards looked us over as we approached but didn't step out to prevent us from passing. I was amused that I earned a longer perusal than my teenage daughter—surely teenagers were more likely than adults to come here to shoplift. Maybe it was my gauche belt. They knew how much ammo it could hold and were envious.

"What's going on with vampires?" Amber asked as she steered me toward Neiman Marcus.

"I'm not sure exactly, but I plan to find out. An ally of mine went missing last night."

"You have a vampire ally? You're not kickin' it with *him*, are you?"

"No." I couldn't tell from her tone if this was more or less appealing than the idea of me having a relationship with a dragon. She'd shared raving comments about the *Twilight* books on her social media page a couple years back, so maybe she considered vampires sexier. "He calls me *dear robber* and sics his giant guard tarantulas on me."

"Can't you say anything that isn't weird?"

"Sorry. My life is weird. I don't even know what normal people talk about."

"No kidding."

"Maybe you should do the talking."

"Obviously." She smiled for the first time as she led me into the department store. It was kind of a pitying smile, but I'd take it.

As she picked out dresses—and purses and belts and how-the-hell-was-I-supposed-to-fight-in-those shoes—I kept scanning the area with my senses. I had no idea what special-security allies the shifter knew in the mall, but here and there, people with partial magical blood moved about, and I detected a couple more full-bloods too. So far, they were meandering about solo or in pairs and seemed more like shoppers than security, but we were close enough to the parking garage for me to detect someone with a strong aura in that direction. Another full-blood. A shifter, I thought. For the moment, he was hanging out there.

Amber didn't seem to know what to talk to me about, but she made a couple of comments about "the girlfriend," and I learned that Shauna worked as a dental hygienist and hadn't yet succeeded in getting Thad to buy her a BMW, but he did let her drive his car when he didn't need it. Apparently, her old Hyundai wasn't reliable, though Amber had never seen it break down or have any problems.

A second magical being joined the first in the parking garage. Why did I have a feeling we were going to find them waiting by the Jeep when we got back down there?

"Is there a sporting goods department here?" I asked as we checked out.

"Sporting apparel, you mean?" the cashier asked. "There are sports bras in the lingerie section and yoga pants over there."

"I meant like baseball bats."

Amber gave me another mortified look. "This isn't Big 5."

"Too bad." I mulled over my options as we finished paying and headed toward the parking garage. There were still two shifters there. Maybe more. It was also possible there were others down there wearing the equivalent of my cloaking charm. "I wanted to get you something to use in case you need to crack an enemy over the head."

"We could go back for one of those Prada purses." Amber smirked. "You buy it for me, and I'll put it to good use."

"Does Prada have more skull-cracking heft than other brands?"

"Probably." Her smirk faded as she studied me. "Are you serious? Is that woman who threatened you coming?"

"No, but she must have made a call. There's trouble waiting in the parking garage." I stopped before we reached the door. Now that we were closer, I could tell that the shifters were indeed by my Jeep. "I want you to wait out here while I take care of it, all right?"

"I can help you."

"Or you can go get a box of cupcakes from that bakery we passed and meet me back here in ten minutes." I pulled out a ten-dollar bill and held it out to her.

"A box?" Amber took the bill and waved it in the air like it was a piece of toilet paper. "The cupcakes are five dollars apiece. Plus tax."

"Five dollars for a *cupcake*?" I managed to keep from adding "What kind of *world* are we living in?" to the retort, but only because I could see another eye roll coming.

"They're amazing. There's a Samoas one. Like the Girl Scout cookies."

I added a twenty to the ten. "Get a *small* box. And take your time."

I expected her to skip away without question, but she surprised me by hesitating. "Are you sure you don't need help? I could pull the fire alarm or something."

"That's a misdemeanor."

"But beating people up in a public parking garage is okay?"

"I thought I'd have my tiger do it."

"Does he want a cupcake?"

"Probably not. Tigers are carnivorous. All cats are." Though I'd heard from Willard that her cat Maggie ate olives, cheese, and whole wheat toast, among other dubious fare.

"Right."

I waited until Amber turned a corner and was out of sight—in case she was thinking of disobeying my wishes and tagging along—before heading into the garage. I summoned Sindari and activated my cloaking charm before going in. Even though we could likely handle two shifters, I would rather surprise them. Fair fights were for chumps.

# Chapter 11

*Is it time for a battle?* Sindari asked hopefully as he materialized at my side. *Unless I can use my innate charisma to talk some shifters out of attacking me.*

*Excellent. There's no chance of that.*

*Thanks so much.*

*I know you.*

Since Sindari had his own magical stealth, we passed within a few feet of the valet without the man knowing it. The two shifters—big, burly guys in black leather and chains—weren't trying to hide. They were leaning against my Jeep and eating hot dogs that looked like they'd come off the spit at 7-11 rather than any of the upscale eateries nearby.

*I smell more enemies than those two,* Sindari informed me.

*Hidden by charms?* My own cloaking charm masked my scent when I activated it, but not all magic worked as well. *How many?*

*Two more, I believe. Female bear shifters. Those two are werewolves.*

*Who knew so many people were into Zoltan's wrinkle creams?*

*Alchemists are highly valued.*

*Apparently.* I stopped about ten steps away, debating if I could sneak past them and into the Jeep, start it, and back out without a fight. Doubtful. They would hear me even if I could avoid getting close enough for them to see through my charm. Besides, I wanted to question one for more information about the vampires. *We're taking these guys out, Sindari. Can you locate the bears?*

*Easily. I'm not an amateur. But please define taking them out. Does that or does that not involve evisceration?*

*Just knock them out if you can. I think we may be on the same side, even if they don't believe it.*

*It is difficult to knock someone out with paws.*

*Do your best. I couldn't find any baseball bats.*

*You're an odd handler.*

*Amber was just telling me that, except the word she used was weird.*

*I'm going in.*

I drew Chopper and circled to the side, hoping to sneak up on one of the werewolves to bash him in the head with the hilt. Knocking out shifters wasn't easy, but fights always went better if I could start right out cracking a skull or mangling a body part.

Unfortunately, the werewolves were expecting me. As I surged in from a few feet away, my target whirled and grabbed for my arms. With his hands up high toward my blade, I altered my plans and kicked him in the knee. Cartilage crunched, but werewolves are tougher than titanium nails. He snarled and lunged at me, his mouth morphing from human to canine, his jaws snapping as they elongated.

I dodged to the right, fangs slashing through the air an inch from the side of my face. Again, he grabbed for me, but I ducked under his arm and zipped in behind him. Turning so the Jeep was at my back, I locked an arm around his neck from behind and squeezed hard as he went completely furry. He swiped over his shoulder, trying to rake me with his claws, but I brought Chopper's hilt down hard. It slammed into the back of his head once, then twice more.

Still in human form, his buddy rushed around the hood of the Jeep and sprang at me. Without releasing the first werewolf, I turned Chopper toward my new attacker, stabbing the tip toward his face. He jerked his head to the side but not before I lopped off the top of his ear. Howling and bleeding, he stumbled back.

My captive was still struggling, and an elbow came back, finding my stomach like a jackhammer. Pain blasted me as my breath whooshed out.

The werewolf roared and lunged away from me. I let him go—I shouldn't have gotten so close to him to start with, but I'd wanted to subdue them, not kill them. Now, I just wanted to make sure I survived.

Sindari roared and a bear roared back. I glimpsed a woman walking into the parking garage with shopping bags and an ice cream cone, but she heard the noise and sprinted back out, dropping everything on the pavement.

As the werewolf spun to charge back at me, I brought my sword up between us. He paused, eyeing the glowing blue blade.

His buddy was grabbing his ear but still close enough to be a threat. He reached for something in his waistband. As his jacket slipped aside, I saw a gun.

I lunged toward him and slammed a side kick into his groin before he pulled it out. Even though he was a big guy, my adrenaline was pumping by then, and I sent him flying across the aisle and into another car.

The first werewolf thought I was distracted and leaped for me. I drove Chopper into his shoulder—it could have been his chest, but I still wanted to question one of these guys. And if I killed them, their friends would only be more convinced I was an enemy.

That didn't keep me from driving my blade in deep, his momentum causing him to skewer himself even more. A canine yelp of agony filled the parking garage. As he backed away, I lunged after him and swung Chopper again. This time, I hit him in the side of the head with the flat of the blade, willing its magic to knock him out.

A surge of power seemed to well up from deep inside me and race through the blade as if it were an electrical conduit. Blue light flashed, and the werewolf flew backward and skidded across the cement. He crashed into the side of another parked car and didn't move.

Surprised, I almost missed seeing the other werewolf pull out his gun. Before he could point it at me, I flicked Chopper and cracked his knuckles with the flat of the blade. He dropped the gun as I rushed closer, grabbing him and spinning him into the side of the Jeep. I drove my booted heel into the back of his knee, and he crumpled. I pushed him to his stomach, pulled his arms behind his back, and pinned him with my knee.

"Tell me everything you know about the missing vampires," I said.

"You took them," he hissed, his cheek smashed to the cement floor.

"That's what you believe?"

"That's what *everybody* believes. Zoltan charged you a bunch of money, you didn't want to pay, and you kidnapped him. And the others that tried to help Zoltan."

"Let's pretend it wasn't me." I hoped I could get more information out of these guys than I had from the female shifter in the store. "Who else is on your suspect list? And why would someone want vampires? It's not like you can sell their organs on the black market."

He growled and twisted, trying to bite my ankle. I calmly moved that leg away from his head and pressed Chopper's blade into his neck deep enough to draw blood.

"You go for my ankle again, and I'll tag you with the nickname Chihuahua. After I lop off your other ear."

"You're the only one who hates everyone magical and wants us all dead."

"That can't be true. And I don't hate everyone. Ask the goblins."

The wrinkled-lip glower he gave me seemed more puzzled than enlightened. So much for thinking that helping a few goblins would improve my reputation among the other races.

"Are they dead?" came Amber's wary voice from behind us. She was holding the shopping bags and a box of cupcakes and had stopped about thirty feet away. One of the bear shifters Sindari had dealt with was slumped unconscious, and the werewolf I'd knocked out hadn't stirred either.

"No. I only kill people I was hired to kill and diehard enemies who won't leave me alone."

"These, uhm, people don't qualify?"

"They'll get bumped into that category if they try to kill me again." I gave the one I'd pinned my best baleful look. "I am lenient with first-time offenders."

The roar of a bear echoed through the parking garage, followed by the louder roar of a tiger. Sindari was chasing his other target around the parking garage, heading her off and not letting her escape.

*Let her go, Sindari,* I called silently. *We only need one to question.*

And I was afraid I'd already gotten what little I could out of these guys.

My pinned werewolf tried to press his palms to the ground to rise. I leaned into him harder and reminded him of the blade pressed to his throat. His buddy groaned—he'd shifted back into human form—but he didn't try to rise.

With my free hand, I opened the back of the Jeep and pulled a coil of rope out of my camping supplies. Mundane rope wouldn't keep powerful shifters immobilized for long, but now that Amber was back, all I needed was time to get out of the parking garage.

Sindari trotted past Amber, making her jump in surprise, and came over to sit on the more alert werewolf so I could focus on tying him.

"You can't take on the whole magical community," he growled. "We protect our own. And we know where you live."

"That's good to know. I'd hate to think I needed to install a flashing neon sign outside my apartment so you could come fall on my sword." I walked over to tie the other werewolf. "But maybe you should do a little research and find out who really kidnapped the vampires. And let me know, would you? I need Zoltan back so he can stock my friend's coffee shop with breakable jars to entertain the ogres while they drink."

That earned me a confused frown.

*Did you ask them if they know the werewolves who attacked your new employer?* Sindari asked.

*No, but I will now.* "You guys know a Bernard Weber? He said some werewolves roughed him up recently."

"I don't know who that is," the werewolf said.

"What territory does your pack claim?" I assumed Weber had been attacked in the vicinity of his house, though he hadn't said. "Bellevue? You have any contacts in Seattle?"

"None of your business."

I thought about threatening to lop his ear off again, but Amber was watching all of this with wide eyes. Wide eyes that glanced from the blood on the floor under the werewolf to his mangled ear. She hadn't seen them lounging against the Jeep ready to ambush me, so I probably looked like a bully.

"Guess not." I sheathed my sword.

It was doubtful I would get anything from him anyway. There were a number of werewolf packs in the Seattle area, so it was possible he truly had no idea about who was being hunted across the water and why.

I walked up to Amber and waved for her to open the cupcake box. She gave me an are-you-crazy look but lifted the lid. There were more cupcakes than expected for the money I'd given her.

"I chipped in and got a couple for Dad."

"And Shauna?"

"She can have one of those." Amber waved at a row of plastic-wrapped cupcakes that didn't look as fresh. "I asked if they had any day-old ones. No way am I spending five dollars apiece on her."

I plucked out three of the wrapped cupcakes. "I'll pay you back."

I set them in front of the noses of each of the downed shifters. There. An overture of friendship. Maybe Amber would think her mom was a reasonable woman only acting in self-defense, not a bully pummeling helpless people.

Judging by the look I got, she mostly thought it was weird to tie people up and leave them with cupcakes.

# Chapter 12

My date was either a fast healer or he was wearing a lot of makeup.

As requested, I met him in his driveway, where I would leave my Jeep and a limo would take us to the yacht club. When the driver held the door open for us, I got close enough to Weber to see the foundation powder on his face and had my answer. Not a fast healer. Just a man with bruise-concealing makeup.

I removed Chopper so I could sit without a sword scabbard digging into my back—and without worrying about scratching the white leather upholstery. Weber, dressed in a tux for the event despite the warm muggy August evening, eyed it with bemusement when it appeared on the floor next to the black purse Amber had promised went with my emerald green dress. He hadn't presumed to sit beside me, which I appreciated. I would walk in on his arm and play the part of his date for him, but the windows were tinted, so there was no reason for the charade on the ride over.

"I ran into some werewolves today." I wasn't sure if I was supposed to chitchat with him, but I wouldn't mind getting some more information out of him.

Just because Willard's research hadn't come up with his supposed up-and-coming tracker app didn't mean it didn't exist, but her people were good at finding stuff, so I couldn't help but wonder if Weber had lied to me. And if so, why? He could have said he was doing almost anything with computers, and I wouldn't know any better.

"Sounds painful," he said.

"More so for them than me, but I do have a few bruises." My dress lacked sleeves, so I showed him a whopper on my elbow.

"I don't suppose they were the ones who beat me up?"

"I asked if they knew you, but they didn't recognize your name." I watched him for reactions as I spoke. "This was over in Bellevue though. Where were you attacked?"

"Right at home. That's what prompted me to upgrade the security system."

"You got a lot installed quickly. Judging by your split lip, the attack didn't happen that long ago."

"Is it still visible?" Weber touched his mouth. "I had the cleaning lady help me cover everything up with makeup."

"It's fine."

"Good."

"Do you always defer to your cleaning lady for makeup advice?"

"She's the only woman who comes to my house on a regular basis. Women have better advice when it comes to treating and concealing wounds. One of my male friends suggested I throw a raw steak over the eye."

"It worked for Fred Flintstone, I guess."

Weber looked out the window as we drove along the water, the evening sun still out and glittering on the surface. End of conversation? He'd deflected my probe about how quickly he'd upgraded his security. Not that I was known for being a subtle or talented interrogator. Since he was my employer for now, I decided not to press him.

"You and I have been dating for six weeks," he informed me as we rolled onto the yacht club's grounds. "That's not so long that people will think it odd that I haven't introduced you to my friends."

"Glad you've got it worked out."

"I don't have much time for dating, and everyone knows that. So we met through Tinder."

Tinder? I was vaguely aware that was a dating app and only because Nin had mentioned it once. "I don't think anyone over thirty uses stuff like that."

He blinked at me. "Are you over thirty?"

"Yeah."

"I'm thirty-two."

"I'm not."

"You don't look that old."

"My teenage daughter picked out this dress for me."

"Huh. So, you're like a cougar."

At least that term had been around long enough that I knew what it meant, though my mind first went to feline shifters. "Guess so. Watch out." I made an unconvincing cat's paw with my hand and swiped it at the air. "Rar."

Thankfully, the limo pulled to a stop before the conversation could deteriorate further. I was starting to miss my pompous dragon. Conversations with Zav weren't boring, and he didn't reference hip, happening things that I didn't know about.

I slung Chopper's scabbard across my back again and made sure I could draw Fezzik—though it had consternated Amber, I'd found my dress with the leg slit.

Weber got out first and offered me his arm. There was a bulge under his jacket. I wondered if he had a concealed-carry permit and if he knew how to use a gun or was more likely to shoot me when I was defending him. A very faint hint of magic came from the bulge—probably ammunition that he'd purchased from someone who wasn't as good at imbuing bullets as Nin.

"The organization reserved the whole place including the lawn for the event," Weber said. "We'll wander around and mingle. There will be some press people I promised to talk to, and some business networking kinds of guys, and that's all I need to be here for. We can leave early."

I eyed the grounds and the building we were walking up to, a rambling structure in a quasi-Cape Cod style with a lighthouse tower in the middle. The tower looked like a great place for a sniper to hang out.

Outside, a large grassy lawn stretched around the building with evergreens on one side and a walkway and the water on the other. That walkway led to numerous docks, some out in the open and some covered. Dozens if not hundreds of boats were nestled in the slots—more places a sniper could hide. Wonderful.

"Am I, your cougar from Tinder, supposed to say anything scintillating to your acquaintances or just smile and stick my boobs out?" The V-neck of the dress ought to facilitate that.

"Just smile and pretend to be interested in the people here."

That sounded challenging. I would rather fight bad guys. Maybe I'd get lucky and some of them would attack before dinner.

As we wandered into the building, I searched it with my senses, seeking any magical threats that might already be inside. Here and there, a quarter-blood elf or dwarf or gnome mingled among the well-dressed visitors, but I didn't detect any shifters or anyone more menacing.

Unless the journalists counted. Several of them spotted Weber and beelined toward him.

I unlinked from his arm and grazed from hors d'oeuvres trays that the waitstaff brought by. I stayed close enough to protect him if need be and to listen to the questions the journalists peppered him with, hoping to hear someone bring up the app project. But they mostly asked him about his investments, his thoughts on such-and-such tech startup, and if he could get them interviews with more prominent tech moguls in the city.

Weber answered their questions, but a hint of exasperation slipped out at the dumber ones, and I wondered if he also hoped someone would attack him soon. Or maybe he hoped a few werewolves would attack *them*.

After a half hour, Weber escaped, recaptured my arm, and led me toward an open patio door. Trusting he didn't have make-out sessions in mind, I enjoyed the opportunity to escape the crowded room. Potted plants lined the outdoor area, and the night smelled of jasmine. The sky was clear, the moon visible, and a few kayakers stroked past out in the water.

If I'd been out here on a date, it would have been romantic, but I was on duty, so I scanned the area with my eyes, ears, and my senses. Weber checked something on his phone—maybe looking for a better date on Tinder—then moved a few paces away to make a quiet call.

A few couples were out strolling along the walkway near the water, but I heard something rustling in bushes near the parking lot. I didn't sense any magical beings in that direction, but I kept an eye on the area. The bushes were in the shadows between the streetlights.

The first dangerous thing I sensed came not from the parking area but from the sky to the west. I stifled a groan. Zav.

*I can't buy you food or hang out with you tonight,* I thought as soon as I spotted his dark winged form against the starry sky. *I'm working.*

# False Security

*As am I. I am searching for the next criminal on my list. Also, your boss wishes me to see if I spot any vampires in the area.*

*And you're coming to look for them at the yacht club?* Why was I positive his appearance here wasn't a coincidence?

*I am simply flying past. Your boss said you would reward me if I found Zoltan.*

*She said I would reward you?*

*She offered me food, but I informed her that I would only accept food from you. She promised you would purchase me ribs and briskets.*

*How thoughtful of her.*

Zav soared over the yacht club and banked, circling it slowly. He wasn't just passing by.

*I already checked here,* I told him. *There are no vampires.*

*Excellent. Then I will not need to stay long.*

I thought about asking him to investigate the bushes, but I didn't want to encourage him to come down. Besides, they'd stopped rattling, and I still didn't sense any magic anywhere but from him. An amorous couple had probably been hiding in the bushes to make out.

Despite his talk of hunting criminals, Zav descended, heading straight for our patio.

"Brace yourself," I told Weber.

He'd ended his call and put away his phone and returned to my side.

"Enemies?" he asked.

"Not exactly."

Zav arrowed out of the sky and shifted into his human form at the last moment to land on the other end of the patio. Weber jumped, his hand twitching toward the bulge in his jacket. He stopped shy of reaching inside.

Zav opened his mouth to speak, but his mouth froze when he got a good look at me. His gaze traveled down my dress-clad form, apparently finding it more interesting than when it was under jeans and a duster. I shouldn't have appreciated being ogled 0by someone whose mere presence here was certain to make trouble, but I admitted to being pleased that he'd noticed.

*This is fascinating attire,* he spoke into my mind. *Is it practical for combat? Your leg appears to be free to kick a foe if necessary.* He was a few paces away, but his fingers made a stroking motion in the air as he eyed my bare thigh.

*It's lightweight and more flowing than a lot of the stuff I tried on, but I'd rather have my armor for combat.*

*I find it appealing.*

"Good evening, Zav," I said politely, aware of Weber gaping at him. "I didn't know you would be a guest here." Silently, I added, *Apparently, there are three missing vampires now, Zoltan being one of them, and I'm suspected of being responsible.*

"I'm positive he's not on the guest list," Weber said.

Zav lifted his chin. "A dragon attends whatever events a dragon wishes to attend." Telepathically, he added, *Who suspects you of this? Since I investigated his domicile with you and saw the orc blood, I can speak to your accusers and give a dragon's word that you were not involved. A dragon's word is irrefutable.*

*That's not necessary. I gave them cupcakes. I'm hoping that will be enough to put me back in their good graces.*

"Not without an invitation," Weber said.

*I do not know what* cupcakes *are, but hope is insufficient. You will tell me who threatened you, and I will ensure they won't bother you again.*

*Amber left me a couple of cupcakes,* I replied to deflect his attention. I still didn't think those shifters had truly been enemies, and I didn't want him beating them up. *I can give you one later, so you can see what they are, but they're very sweet and not meat-flavored, so I don't think you would like them.*

Zav curled a lip. *Why do you consume such things? Meat is superior to all other foods. There is nothing better than gnawing the flesh off a bone.* His head rotated toward the open door. *Is there meat here?*

It had been easier than expected to distract him from the shifters threatening me. I made a mental note about the power of meat when dealing with dragons.

*Some waiters were wandering around with pâté when we were in there. I don't think dinner is being served yet. And you're not invited.*

Weber stepped up to my side, brushing my shoulder with his. He frowned back and forth between Zav and me, and I realized we'd been staring at each other while we communicated silently. At some point, Zav had crept closer so that he was standing right in front of me.

"You are not welcome, dragon." Weber put an arm around my shoulder, and my instincts almost drove me to grab it and break a few bones, but I remembered in time that he was my employer. And that I was playing the girlfriend part tonight. Even though the patio was relatively private, people were standing just inside the open door and could look out any time. "Val and I are here on a date."

Zav's eyebrows flew up and his eyes flared with violet light. "You said this man was employing you to protect him."

*He is,* I said silently, holding up a hand, lest he was thinking of getting physical with Weber for touching his supposed mate. *Will you go away? You're going to mess up my job.*

"We're putting on an act for his buddies," I said out loud. "He doesn't want them to know he hired a bodyguard."

"I don't particularly want the *dragon* to know that either." Weber frowned at me, his arm still around my shoulders.

I extricated myself from it, though I captured his hand and patted it, hoping that would be enough for any onlookers. "He's telepathic. He knows everything."

"Actually," Zav said coolly, watching Weber's face, "I cannot read this human's thoughts. He is using some magical charm to prevent it."

"Of course I am. Magical enemies have targeted me and want my business secrets." Weber lifted his chin. "If it keeps busybody dragons out of my mind, so much the better."

"I am here to speak with Val, and I will do so." Zav's eyes flared brighter, and he looked like he was on the verge of hurling a wave of power at Weber, one that would leave him stranded on the roof with half of his bones broken.

I put a hand on Weber's chest before he could reply and pushed him away from Zav and to the other end of the patio.

"Have you ever interacted with a dragon before?" I asked him quietly.

"Just this one," he said. "I don't like him."

"Here's the thing: dragons are nearly immortal and insanely powerful, and they think humans are vermin, so they're not afraid to smash us like bugs." Admittedly, Zav was unlikely to kill someone, since he considered himself a noble upholder of law in the Cosmic Realms, but by now, I'd met other dragons who would do exactly what I'd described if Weber pissed them off.

"I'm powerful too," Weber said mulishly.

"Uh huh. He's going to be super daunted when you show him your mighty bank account."

Weber frowned at me again. "Employees are usually more circumspect about being sarcastic with their employers."

"I'm special."

"Do you spend a lot of time unemployed?"

"No. My services are in high demand."

"Your sarcastic services." He sounded skeptical. I decided I wouldn't ask him for a reference in the future.

"Yup."

I thought Zav, if he said anything at all, would point out that I also was not properly respectful of dragons, but his eyes were closed to slits as he watched this exchange.

"This inferior human is not being properly respectful of my *Tlavar'vareous sha*," he stated.

"Inferior human?" Weber's hand strayed again toward the bulge in his jacket.

"That won't work on him," I muttered, not mentioning that it probably wouldn't work on werewolves either, unless he'd gotten silver bullets. Even then, without some powerful magic imbuing them, they would be less bothersome than shotgun pellets to an elephant.

"Shooting him won't hurt?" Weber asked.

"Nope." This time, I walked across the patio and put a hand on Zav's chest. "Please return to your hunt for criminals and vampires."

He looked down at my hand, then let his gaze wander to other parts of my anatomy that were possibly more intriguing in the dress than when they were under my usual work clothes.

Silently, I added, *This job pays well and will get me out of debt for that Jeep that a certain powerful winged being destroyed. If I can keep it. Please don't mess it up for me. If you want to talk about something, we can talk at my place in the morning.*

*You will be alone?*

*Yes. Bring some tea and scones, and don't squish the rooftop deck chairs when you land, and I'll listen raptly to anything you want to say.*

His gaze shifted to my face. *You wish me to feed you?*

*Yeah, but it doesn't work the same way with humans. Don't expect me to get randy.*

*We shall see.* Zav rested his hand on mine, his aura crackling in the air around us, and his eyes seemed to promise that we'd do more than munch on scones in the morning.

Before I could decide if I wanted to object to his hungry, possessive look—at least to his doing it in front of a client—Zav released me and stepped back. He sprang into the air and shifted into his dragon form, his powerful wings flapping hard enough to rattle the branches in the nearby trees—and kick up my dress enough that I was glad I'd picked some of my classier underwear for the evening.

"Are you *sure* shooting him wouldn't work?" Weber patted his jacket.

The fact that he kept drawing attention, intentionally or not, to his hidden firearm told me he had little experience with it. If there was a fight, I'd definitely have to watch my back so he didn't accidentally shoot me.

"I've seen him incinerate bullets before they hit him." I turned to face him, glad he appeared more contemplative than truly angry or petulant about this. Even if I was sarcastic by nature, that didn't mean I didn't want this job. "I've also seen him fight another dragon. They knocked down houses and set fire to a neighborhood in Bothell. You're in enough trouble already with werewolves. Don't make an enemy of a dragon. Trust me. That never goes well."

"Very well, but I would appreciate it if you asked him not to show up again while you're working for me."

"I'm working on that. Dragons tend to do what they want and ignore the wishes of lesser beings, as they call us."

"Inferior humans."

"Yes."

"Mr. Weber?" someone called from inside. "We're starting the meal soon."

"Coming." Weber offered me his arm again. "Shall we?"

"Can't wait."

Zav had flown out of sight, and I could barely sense his aura, but he was still close enough to speak telepathically to me.

*What is a scone?* he asked.

*You have all night to find out.*

# Chapter 13

The limo wasn't waiting when we walked out to the parking lot. Weber had already called to arrange it, and he called again, asking where the driver was.

My paranoia kicked in, especially when I saw how close we were to the bushes that had been rattling earlier. And how few guests were out here milling around. Weber had opted out of the post-dinner boozing out on the yachts and hadn't cared about waiting to see if he won one of the charity things he'd bid on, so we were leaving before the rush. I still didn't sense anything magical in the foliage or anywhere around us, unless one counted the faint signature of Weber's gun, but someone could be camouflaged.

Deciding to be safe rather than sorry, I tapped my feline charm and called forth Sindari. As the mist formed beside me, the bushes rattled as if a tornado were sweeping through.

Weber cursed and dropped his phone as I spun, yanking out Fezzik. More than ten snarling hounds with shaggy black fur rushed toward us. Their eyes glowed yellow, and silver collars jangled around their necks as they ran. Flecks of slaver flew from their fangs as they issued unearthly growls that sent shivers down my spine.

They weren't werewolves, but they weren't mundane dogs either, so I didn't hesitate to step in front of Weber and fire. My bullets slammed into the chest of one of the lead hounds, and it faltered but didn't cry out in pain. I fired again and again as the pack tore toward us. The bullets found their marks, sinking in deep, and a few of the hounds slowed down, but others kept coming, their eyes flaring an even brighter yellow and their silver collars glowing. I could *see* the magic, but I still couldn't sense it.

"Go back inside," I barked, waving behind me for Weber to run away.

Sindari finished forming in time to spring into the pack, his claws slashing and fangs sinking into two enemies in the lead. The rest of the devil hounds surged around him and continued toward me. I fired a few more rounds, but then they were too close. I switched weapons, using Chopper as much as a barrier to keep them back as a means of attacking.

Snarls and eerie barks filled the night, the possessed creatures sounding nothing like real dogs. They looked like they'd been made in some mad scientist's laboratory, pieced together from spare parts and animated by magic.

At one point, I fought five at once and was forced to back up until my butt almost bumped an SUV. Even with Chopper slashing and blocking so quickly the blade left blue streaks in the air, the hounds slipped past my guard more than once. Pain lashed up my arms as fangs cut into my unprotected skin. Damn the useless dress.

At least the hounds focused on me and didn't try to run past to get to Weber. I glanced back, hoping he'd gone inside. I didn't see him. Good.

*Their controller is in the bushes,* Sindari informed me as his fangs sank into one of the hounds he faced. His powerful muscles bunched as he heaved the big creature into the air and threw it into another one fighting beside it.

*Controller?* I was panting from the exertion of defending so rapidly, whipping Chopper left, right, and down in front of me to deflect the myriad attacks. Slaver spattered my hands and face, and fangs clanged as they struck my blade.

*The one ordering them to attack with magic. I believe it is a vampire.*

*A vampire?* I sprang straight up as a hulking hound dove for my legs. It crashed into the car as I came down on the creature's back, driving Chopper's point into its spine. Bone crunched, and the hound's legs gave out.

*I do not sense him, but I smell him.*

I scrambled up onto the hood of the car so I would have the high ground—and because I couldn't fight while standing on a huge body. For a heartbeat, nothing was attacking me and I could look toward the bushes Sindari had indicated.

A cloaked and hooded figure stood beside a tree within them, a device gripped in a hand with pale white fingers. I didn't have Sindari's sense of smell but that did look a lot more like a vampire than a werewolf.

One of the hounds backed up, then took a running jump at me. Before he reached me, I leaped off the hood of the car, slicing Chopper into his flank as I went.

Another hound waited in front of the car, and I had to shift in the air, slashing my blade downward before I fell into its snapping jaws. Chopper flared bright blue, the light glinting off the creature's eyes, and sliced through its fanged snout, cutting off the end like a guillotine beheading a criminal.

A yowl tore through the night, the first sign that these things felt pain—or maybe that was anger and indignation. I twisted to land beside the hound and shifted my blade to hack through the back of its neck. It pitched sideways, legs twitching, but the fight had gone out of it.

As another one surged around the car toward me, the crack of a gun went off not far from my head.

I swore. Weber hadn't gone back inside.

The vampire jerked away from the tree, grabbing his shoulder. Weber fired twice more, bullets thudding into his target's back. They clanged off some armor under the vampire's shirt, but the first one had caught him, and he was still gripping his shoulder. It surprised me that the bullet had hurt him.

"You've made enemies of the wrong people," the vampire snarled at Weber as he stumbled away, still clenching that control device. As he spoke, the hounds continued to harry me. "There are more of us than you think, weakling human."

Weber fired again, but the vampire leaped a hedge and ran around the building.

I thought about chasing after him, but the remaining hounds hadn't given up along with their master. By the time Sindari and I finished them, leaving flesh and fur all over the parking lot, a distant splash reached our ears. The vampire swimming to the far side?

With the last of the cursed hounds dead, the parking lot fell silent, save for the hushed murmurs of people watching from the open door to the building.

"You're death to dogs." Weber looked around at the carnage. "I wish you'd gotten the vampire instead though."

"If you're going to get attacked by ten magical beings at once, maybe you should take on a couple more bodyguards."

He pointed as he counted the heads of the fallen hounds. "Eleven."

"What's the deal with the vampire? I thought it was werewolves who were pissed at you?" I removed one of the magical collars that had cloaked the hounds from my senses, thinking Willard or Nin might be able to figure out who had made it. If Zoltan hadn't been missing, I would have asked him.

"All of the magical community feel threatened by the app I'm working on."

"Apparently so." As I prowled, looking for other clues, I spotted one of the bullets that had bounced off the vampire's armor. Still surprised the first one had hurt a nearly immortal undead being, I plucked it up to examine.

The tip, flattened from striking the armor, was made from metal, but the core of it was wood, wood with a couple of ancient vampire-hunting symbols carved into it. I'd seen them before. Magic imbued the wood to give it extra strength. I doubted the bullet could have killed a vampire—it was a far cry from a long wooden stake—but it had proven it could sting.

"Funny how you came armed specifically for vampires." I held the bullet up between my fingers.

"Is it? I like to be prepared."

"Want to tell me who else is likely to attack you this week? As your bodyguard, I think I have a right to know."

"Nobody tomorrow. I'm going to stay at home." He lifted a hand as his conveniently detained limo driver pulled into the lot, and waved him over. "So I won't need your services."

"What about the day after that?"

"Likely so. Keep your phone on so I can contact you as needed."

"Whatever you say, boss."

*Do you no longer trust your employer?* Sindari sat at my side.

*I never did. You don't give trust to random strangers, even the ones dropping wads of money in your lap.* Especially *the ones dropping wads of money in your lap.*

I looked toward the water, wishing I'd thought to send Sindari off after the vampire before he'd disappeared. Maybe he could have caught him and I could have questioned him. Because I would dearly like to question a vampire right now.

# Chapter 14

The next morning, I was on the phone with Dimitri when I sensed Zav approaching my apartment. Dimitri hadn't slept. He'd checked on Zoltan's place, found him still missing, and then driven down to Beacon Hill with Gondo, hoping to get information from a vampire that supposedly lived in the basement of an abandoned building there.

"I sneaked in and poked around," Dimitri said, "but couldn't find him. I did see signs that he lived there, but the place was empty last night. I was hoping that if I could talk to some other vampires in the area, they'd know what happened to Zoltan."

"I appreciate you wanting to find your friend and business partner, but you shouldn't be sneaking into strange, potentially vampire-filled basements in the middle of the night. That's a good way to get yourself killed." I wished he'd told me about his plans. Even though I'd gotten back late from Weber's shindig, I would have joined him.

"I wore my cervical collar and had backup."

"That's not going to do anything except keep your neck warm. And *Gondo* doesn't count as backup. I'll come over to the coffee shop later to help—this might be a good time to start questioning some of the customers." I wanted to question *Weber*, who'd not only known that being attacked by a vampire was a possibility, but he'd deemed it more likely than a werewolf attack, at least judging by his bullet choice.

If I thought he would tell me the truth, I would consider doing it, even if it lost me the job, but I doubted he would. Too bad Zav couldn't read his thoughts, or I could ask *him* to question Weber.

Maybe it was time to ask Weber if he wanted me to do that security survey of his house the assistant had mentioned. That would give me an opportunity to snoop while I offered advice and played the role of loyal employee. He might be more likely to open up to a loyal employee than a sarcastic one who kept peppering him with questions. Too bad I was better at the latter role than the former.

"I don't think you're supposed to interrogate your customers," Dimitri said.

"Just slip something in their coffee to make them chatty."

"Like what?"

"Whatever you give the goblins."

"They seem to be naturally chatty."

Zav was arrowing toward the rooftop, so I wrapped up the conversation. "Just wait for me before getting into any more trouble. I'll help you. Whatever is going on with Zoltan could be linked to the rest of the missing vampires *and* my new employer."

After hanging up, I checked my messages to see if Willard had replied yet. I'd sent her a report covering the attack at the yacht club and done my best to describe the vampire. I was hoping she could identify him and had uncovered more information on what was going on with the vampires of Seattle. Nothing yet.

*I have acquired scones,* Zav spoke into my mind from the rooftop.

*Good. Did you manage to land without smashing any deck chairs?*

*A landing pad is not the appropriate location to place flimsy wooden chairs.*

*It's not a landing pad, and I'll take that for a no. I've seen you shift forms right as you alight in tight spots. What's the deal with the deck?*

*There is no deal.*

*I'm beginning to think you like the way they crunch under your butt.* Maybe it was the dragon equivalent of popping bubble wrap.

The balcony door slid open with a gust of wind that nearly tore the curtains off the rod. Zav strode inside, his robe flapping around his ankles, and the gold medallion he sometimes wore glowing on his chest.

"Making a dramatic entrance, I see."

After the curtains settled, I noticed two more things. First off, Zav was carrying a large white paper bag bulging with scones. Second, he'd refined his foot attire. He still wore the Birkenstock sandals, but now he'd added white socks. I decided not to make matters worse by telling him that look wasn't trendy.

"Dragons are dramatic by nature," Zav said.

The balcony door slid shut, seemingly by itself.

"No kidding."

"I have your baked goods." Zav lifted the bag. "Will you now agree to listen in rapt attention?"

"Yes, I will." I checked my phone one last time for updates, then flipped it to silent so I wouldn't be tempted to break my word to him. It wasn't until he handed me the bag and I set out plates for the two of us at the peninsula counter that it occurred to me to ask, "Where did you get the scones?"

I hadn't forgotten that dragons didn't have money, but it hadn't been on my mind the night before when I'd suggested that he bring food. I also hadn't truly thought he would do it. Instead, I'd expected him to say that grocery shopping was too menial an activity for dragons.

"After researching what they were and where they could be acquired, I went to a bakery and selected them, as well as fish for myself." He pointed to several pouches of smoked salmon that had also been in the bag.

Smoked salmon wasn't cheap, and I took out a pen and a pad of paper, then perched on the stool opposite him instead of beside him. Sitting side by side seemed dangerous, like it would lead to me leaning against his shoulder and having the randy thoughts I'd promised him I wouldn't have.

"Which bakery? I assume you haven't gotten a job and earned money since the last time we talked, so I need to send the owner a check, right?"

"A check?" Zav arched his eyebrows and drew a checkmark in the air, his magic making a glowing line visible for a moment.

"A check is… complicated. Let's just say I'm prepared to send the owner some money. Was there a receipt, by chance?" I peered into the bag. My stomach grumbled at the delightful sight and smell of freshly baked blueberry and raspberry scones—oh, and some of them were even frosted. I didn't see a receipt.

Zav gave me the name of the bakery and said, "There is no need to pay."

"You already paid? Or bartered something?" I couldn't imagine what he would have bartered. For that matter, where had he gotten those socks?

"I told the merchant what I wanted, and she gave the items to me."

"Because you threatened her?"

"No, because I am a dragon and *most* members of lesser species seek to please me." His narrowed eyes suggested he felt I should work harder to do that myself. Fat chance.

I tallied the number of scones and packets of salmon and made a note to check the bakery's website later to see if the prices were listed there. I also made a note not to ask Zav to bring me things anymore.

He was watching and frowned. "You are making calculations and plans for payment? This is not necessary. I assisted her with a problem, and she was very eager to give these items to me. She said they were on the house. Which I did not understand because it was not a house, nor was there anything on the roof, but she assured me I did not need to pay."

"What problem?"

"Vandalism. When I arrived, she was out front attempting to remove an uncouth graffito from her wall with an ineffective scrub brush. I incinerated the paint as well as the grime embedded in the brick. In addition, I repaired a sign that was supposed to light up but had a short-circuit."

"You know how to repair short-circuits?" I set down the pen, suspecting my honest dragon was telling the truth about this story, even if his willingness to assist someone surprised me.

"I do not. But I can make *anything* light up. I infused it with magic."

On a hunch, I typed the name of the bakery into a social media site. Freshly posted photographs greeted me, all showing a "dope new sign," as one citizen journalist reported, glowing like a sun on Market Street. When nighttime came, there might be complaints from nearby residents about the brightness of that sign. Some of the people lining up at the door were wearing sunglasses, but if that line was an indication, the sign was having its desired effect and bringing in customers.

I would still call the owner to see if I owed her anything. "Well, good. I'm glad you didn't expect her to feed you simply because you're magnificent."

"I thought you would be pleased." His eyelids drooped as he smiled at me. That was his bedroom-thoughts gaze. I wasn't sure if *he* was having bedroom thoughts, but it always put bedroom thoughts in my mind. "I *am* magnificent," he added.

"I'm sure." I tried not to look at him as I broke off the end of a blueberry scone to eat. "What did you want to talk about?"

He watched me thoughtfully for a moment before responding. "It will not please you. Perhaps you should finish your meal first."

"Are you going to tell me you don't want me to work for Weber anymore?"

"No. But I do not like him or trust him."

I thought about explaining the hounds and the vampire and admitting that I didn't trust him either. But did I want to get Zav involved? He might overreact and raze Weber's expensive mansion to the ground. Given that I didn't know if Weber was doing anything wrong, or if he was simply being secretive and evasive with me for well-founded reasons, I was reluctant to bring in the big guns.

"Then why, my magnificent dragon, did you do something to please me this morning and now you tell me that you intend to displease me?"

"It is for your own good. And for my good, because I wish to mate with you." He rested his hands on the counter and entwined his fingers. "I had erotic thoughts about you last night after seeing you in that revealing garment."

I coughed and barely managed to keep from hawking a piece of scone out of my mouth at him. It was rare for me to be speechless, but I didn't know how to handle this bluntness and needed a moment to gather my thoughts. And to swallow the scone.

"Do you have erotic thoughts about me?" Zav asked, not giving me my moment.

"If I do, they're not inspired by your socks."

He gazed at me with that I'm-too-mature-for-snarky-comments gaze that he sometimes employed. I sighed, propped my elbow on the counter, and dropped my forehead in my hand.

"I observed that the change to your clothing affected my thoughts and preoccupation with mating," Zav said. "Your garment was skimpy and made me more aware of your body. Is it similar for females? Should I wear something skimpy?"

"No," I blurted, horrified as I imagined him changing his robe into something similar to that dress. "No."

"You scrutinized me with sexual interest when I wore nothing and climbed into the water box with you," he added, prompting my imagination to picture him completely naked except for the socks and sandals.

"I thought you were too preoccupied with taking off those boots to notice that," I muttered.

"No," he said simply.

"Look, Zav." I made myself look at *him*. And be mature, not snarky. "I am attracted to you, as it seems you can tell. Even when you're in the midst of removing boots without a shoehorn. And I have had, ah, erotic dreams about you."

I couldn't remember ever admitting to a guy that I'd dreamed about him. It had happened before. I just hadn't admitted it. Were all dragons driven to honesty and bluntness around mating topics?

"Excellent. Then perhaps you will not be displeased."

"About what?" I thought about taking another bite of my scone, now that I'd managed to chew and swallow the last piece, but I might end up choking on it again.

"I am going to take you to Veleshna Var to meet your kin who will, if they know how to properly respect the wishes of a dragon, train you to develop your magical powers."

"I already know that."

"Today. After you finish eating."

I set down the scone. "We can't go today. Weber said he doesn't need me right now, but I'm still on his payroll. If he calls, I need to hurry over there and guard his body."

"I do not care if *he* needs you. Also, if he is as obnoxious to other magical beings as he is to dragons, you will get yourself killed guarding him."

"If that happens, then that's the job. It's what he's paying me for."

Zav flung his arms up in exasperation. "Currency is such a preoccupation on this world."

"Yes, it is."

"Being able to protect yourself from enemies is far more important. You will complete your meal, and I will take you to Veleshna Var."

"No," I said slowly, looking him in the eyes. "You will not. You can't force someone to do things against their wishes if you want them to love and respect you."

"It is your wish to go."

"Not *today*. I'm in the middle of a job, and I've promised to protect him."

"You will always be in the middle of a job. The mundane vermin of this world are incapable of doing anything for themselves."

I could tell he was getting hot, because he'd changed humans back to vermin. Well, I was also struggling to rein in my temper. I'd thought we were past him threatening to force me to do things.

"You're not going to compel me to go with you," I said. "*That's* not going to make me have erotic dreams and want to have sex with you."

He stood up, and my stomach flip-flopped nervously. Damn, *was* he going to do it? I wasn't even wearing Chopper to help me ward off magical compulsion. I hadn't expected to need to bring my weapons to breakfast.

"I do not have to *compel* you in order to take you somewhere. Have you completed your meal?"

"*No.*" I stuffed some scone into my mouth and regretted it because it was too large a bite, but I didn't care. I chomped angrily at it and glowered at him.

He turned toward the living room and lifted a hand. Magical energy ignited in the air and crawled over my skin like a swarm of ants. A silver portal formed in front of the couch. Was he *serious*?

Thanks to my mouthful of scone, I couldn't talk, but I thumped a fist on the counter so he would know I was pissed. My weapons, which had been lying on the coffee table where I tended to leave them, floated over to me. The uneaten scones returned to the bag and floated in the air next to them.

"Do you require anything else?" he asked calmly.

"*No.* Because I'm not going." I dashed away crumbs that tumbled out of my mouth.

"You will go. It is for your own good."

"Stop saying that. If you force me to walk out in the middle of a job I've committed to doing, I'm not going to have sex with you, no matter how good I get at keeping asshole dragons out of my mind." I folded my arms over my chest, ignoring the floating gear, and glared at him, certain my words would change his mind.

"That will be unfortunate, but I will still be pleased when you learn how to care for yourself better."

"I'm not bluffing, Zav."

My feet left the floor. I grabbed the counter, refusing to be magically tossed through a portal. "You don't even know if they'll teach me. They may resent the crap out of you for trying to arrange this."

"Many elves resent dragons. This is how it is."

Power pushed at my hands, forcing my fingers open, and I soon dangled in the air, unable to reach anything. "I can't imagine why!"

My weapons floated toward the portal, the bag of scones almost laughable as it trailed after them, and I drifted inexorably toward it. Zav walked behind me, his face determined and self-righteous. The bastard.

I almost spat out something mean, but I clamped down on it. Whether I wanted to go or not, he was going to be my only way back.

"Wait," I blurted less than a foot from the portal. "Let me at least call Dimitri and Willard to tell them I'm leaving."

I half-expected Zav to stuff me through anyway, but he halted my progression.

"Do so."

Both calls dropped to voicemail after a few rings. Damn it. I'd hoped to talk to someone and give myself time to come up with an argument to sway Zav. All I ended up doing was telling them that he was kidnapping me, that I wasn't joking, and that I wasn't sure when I'd be back.

"But I only have enough scones for a day or two," I finished with a snarl in my message to Willard.

After hanging up, I said, "I better tell Weber too."

"No." Zav thrust me through the portal.

# Chapter 15

The leaves on the trees were blue and purple. I hadn't expected that. Perhaps thanks to *Star Trek* and *Stargate SG-1*, I'd been certain leaves were green throughout the galaxy.

The grass in the clearing we arrived in was also blue, not a fake vibrant blue, but a muted blue-gray that didn't compete for vibrancy with the trees. Alien scents wafted to my nose, reminding me of the first time I'd been out in the Sonoran Desert after a rain. Even though the lush, strangely colored forest reminded me nothing of a desert, something in the area had a pungent, earthy scent similar to the creosote bush.

The sky was gray above the canopy, rain dripping from brownish-blue branches, so I had no idea if there was one sun up there or three. The portal trip had passed in a blur of streaking stars, similar to my first journey, and I had little concept of how much time had gone by. I almost pulled out my phone, but what was the point? It didn't matter what time it was in Seattle.

"They change the colors of the leaves and trees depending on what holiday approaches," Zav said, watching me from behind as I stared all around, "or if a visiting musician or artist or someone of cultural importance is arriving. Sometimes, the trees sing."

"That'll be something. Most people have to take drugs to experience that stuff."

He gazed blandly at me.

Reminded that he'd brought me against my will, I thought about giving him the cold shoulder and walking off in a random direction, but it wasn't as if I knew where to go or if there was anything out here that would kill me. Though the last thing I wanted was to have my fate dependent on him, I had little choice. Unless an elf taught me how to make my own portals, I was a prisoner here.

My weapons and the bakery bag were at my feet. I strapped on Chopper and Fezzik and picked up the scones, snorting as I imagined my mother's scathing commentary on how I didn't have three days' worth of food and water and an emergency first-aid kit. She wouldn't even go hiking with less than that.

A wave of panic washed over me as I realized I hadn't grabbed my inhaler. Whenever I left my apartment, I stuffed it in my pocket, but I hadn't *intended* to leave the apartment. Zav had asked me if I needed to take anything, and I'd been too busy being recalcitrant to realize I should pack a bag. I also didn't have a toothbrush or a clean pair of underwear.

Though disgusted with myself, I struggled for calm. If I collapsed on the ground wheezing, Zav should take me home. Assuming he could figure out what was wrong with me. At no point had I opened up to him about my asthma. Given that I was currently irked with him, I didn't feel like doing so now. Instead, I would focus on how to get in and out of here as quickly as possible, so I could go back to my life.

"What's the plan?"

*We will fly,* Zav spoke into my mind. He'd shifted into his dragon form which took up the entire clearing. *The elves protect their villages, and it is not possible to make a portal that pierces the veil and allows you to travel directly to their homes.*

"They like to keep out the riffraff, huh?" I walked to Zav's side.

*They defend their territory from would-be assassins and troublemakers, the same as many magical beings do.* He levitated me up onto his back and sprang into the air, magic assisting him in rising above the canopy before he had the room to stretch out his wings and flap them.

"Elves have to worry about that too? I thought only dragons were targeted by assassins." I bit my tongue to keep from adding, *For obvious reasons.*

Instead, as the damp misty wind swept across my face, I tried to calm my irritation with Zav. It wasn't right that he'd taken me—and it frustrated me that I would lose my gig with Weber and not be there to help Dimitri find Zoltan—but it was better to make the most of it than sulk. Besides, how many people—how many mongrel humans—got to visit other planets? And maybe I would learn something here, something to keep dragons from hoisting me off my feet and thrusting me through portals.

*If you have resources, there is always someone who wants what you have.*

"What resources do dragons have? You guys don't even hoard treasure piles of gold like everyone on Earth thinks you do."

*We claim several worlds as our own. They have prime hunting and breeding grounds.*

"What's a prime breeding ground look like?" I imagined a planet full of beds and sex toys.

Zav glanced back—an impressive feat when he was flying—and I wondered if he sometimes got a few of my stray thoughts, despite his claim that he couldn't read my mind.

*High eyries where you can see enemies coming from miles away while enjoying the view from above the trees while you engage in* xylishnar *with a female that you respect.*

I decided not to ask for a definition of that word.

"So, heights get you excited?" I was doing my best not to look down at the treetops zipping past below. He still hadn't added a harness or seat belt for me.

*Not as much as being fed meat by a desirable female.*

"All I've got is scones, but since you kidnapped me and we're not having sex, I guess it doesn't matter."

*You will experience disorientation and a nip of pain.*

"Uh, what? During the sex we're not having?"

A buzz of electricity zapped me from all sides. I gasped and flattened my belly against his back, afraid we were being attacked.

*We have passed through a defensive barrier,* Zav said as the sharp pain faded.

"I would have called that more of a blast than a nip."

*Since we are not having sex, you will never know that mating with a dragon is wondrous and unforgettable and would exceed all pleasures you've experienced previously in your life.*

"I see males are full of themselves throughout your Cosmic Realms."

Zav banked, startling a flying V of large birds that looked like red turkeys, and something that might be called a city in the trees came into view. Thatched roofs and decks were visible through the canopy. The leaves changed from the earlier blues and purples to oranges and pinks, though the species of trees didn't seem different.

My senses picked up magical beings and magical items—a *lot* of them. Far more than I'd ever encountered in one place and also more densely concentrated. It made all the artifacts in Weber's mansion seem like a few sparse trinkets in comparison.

Several elves came into view on a large platform built between and around a copse of ancient trees with massive trunks. The trunks of some of those trees were as wide as my apartment building and had windows and doors in them. They appeared to have been created by magic, making it seem that the trees had grown that way, rather than been carved out with tools.

Some of the elves carried swords or bows—the weapons as magical as everything else around them—but none of them raised them as they watched Zav's approach. As we arrowed in for a landing, I wondered if they would raise those weapons toward *me*, a half-human mongrel presuming to fly uninvited into their city.

My nerves twinged as I remembered that Zav's plan was to convince these people to teach me simply because it would please him, and lesser species should want to please dragons. It was hard for me to imagine anyone, even the father I'd never met, wanting to be forced to teach me because a dragon said so.

I wished I'd thought to bring a gift to offer the elves. Some cool piece of art from Earth. Anything that might show them I wanted to be friends and wasn't some interloper angling to get something from them. Maybe they liked scones.

The elves backed away, making room for Zav to alight on their platform.

*Note the lack of furniture impediments on elven landing pads,* he spoke into my mind.

*For the forty-seventh time, our rooftop deck is* not *a landing pad.*

All of the elves, tall lean beings with blond or pale-brown hair, wore simple clothing that reminded me of the wardrobes from the old Davy Crockett shows, though headbands made from braided twigs and vines seemed trendier than coonskin caps. The elves did something between a flowing bow and a curtsy to Zav—I'd seen Freysha make that gesture before but hadn't realized it was a gender-neutral greeting—and one stepped forward and spoke in his lilting language.

I hesitated before reaching for my translation charm, not wanting to listen to Zav be pompous or the elves call me a mongrel, but common sense overrode the hesitation. It would be foolish not to learn everything I could about what I was getting into.

"...are not welcome in our world," the elf was saying, looking not at Zav but at me.

What had been the word preceding that? Half-blood mongrels?

*I have claimed Valmeyjar Thorvald as my mate,* Zav replied telepathically. *She goes where I go, and a dragon goes where he wishes.*

For a fraction of a second, I'd been pleased that he remembered my full name, but since that was followed by him being as diplomatic as a thorn in the foot, the feeling faded.

*She is the daughter of your king and requires tutelage in the magic of your kind,* he added.

"A half-breed cannot learn the magic of our kind," the elf said, sounding affronted at the mere suggestion. "A rock could sooner learn the magic of a dragon."

Zav's eyes flared. *A rock could more likely learn the magic of a dragon than a pompous elf.*

I thumped my forehead to his scales, then slid off and raised my hands toward the elves in what I hoped was a diplomatic gesture. I was still holding the scone bag and felt silly, but I forced a warm smile and pretended being called a rock didn't hurt my feelings.

"Hey, guys. As my dragon ally here said, I'm Val, and I came to introduce myself to Eireth and to see if I'm actually related to him. And also to warn him that an elf chick is wandering around on Earth pretending to be his niece."

Zav eyed me, perhaps not approving of this detour from his straightforward approach, but he chimed in with, *Anyasha-sulin is her name.*

The elves looked at each other, but I struggled to read the expressions on their faces. It wasn't so much that they were masking their emotions as that there was an alienness to their facial gestures. Not surprisingly, they reminded me of Freysha, but back in Willard's office, she'd been the quirky weird one—she and Gondo. Here, I was the one out of place.

Even Zav seemed to fit in, as if he were far closer to being a part of their world than I was.

A female elf in the back of the group trotted through one of the doors in the tree trunk and disappeared upward, as if there were some kind of vacuum lift tube in there. Maybe there was. The tree hummed with magic, like everything else here.

"She will see if the king is home and deigns to speak with a half-blood." The one who'd anointed himself speaker seemed particularly affronted by the idea of my mixed blood standing on his platform.

Rain started to fall as we stood around, the elves managing to turn their backs to me without including Zav in the gesture. He remained in his dragon form. That surprised me. I had assumed he would change into an elven version of his human form and had been curious to see what he would look like with Spock ears.

*There is a problem,* Zav spoke into my mind, the words apparently for me alone this time. The elves didn't glance at him.

*They don't like me?*

*I am monitoring the weaker-minded ones whose thoughts I can read. King Eireth is not here. His mate the queen is here, and they believe it will cause trouble if they admit to her—or anyone who is loyal to her—that a child spawned from his loins is here.*

I curled my lip at the talk of loins spawning things. *So, let's leave a message with someone loyal to him and leave. Maybe I can get back to my job before I'm fired.*

The elves must have been communicating with each other telepathically, for one looked back and gave me a dismissive perusal, as if they were having a chat about how homely Eireth's half-human child was. Even though I had no reason to care what these people thought about me, my cheeks heated with indignation.

*No,* Zav replied. *I have come to ensure you are properly trained. If Eireth will not see to it, another elf will, an elf who values his life and does not want to be slain by a dragon.*

I rubbed my face. *Zav, nobody is going to be a good teacher if you're threatening to kill them. They'll probably get back at you—at me—by teaching me how to strangle myself with magic.*

*You will not fall for something like that. You are not unwise, even if your tongue often says unwise things.*

*Thanks, I think. But you must get my point.*

The female elf returned but did not speak aloud as she appeared to confer with the others. It was the snotty male elf who turned back to us.

"Lord Zavryd'nokquetal," he said, having no trouble pronouncing the unwieldy name, "you are welcome to stay among us for as long as you wish, but the mongrel is not." His gaze flicked toward me for only the briefest acknowledgment. "Humans, even mixed-blood humans, are not welcome among our kind."

I told myself not to be stung, that these people had no reason to care about me, but the dismissal hurt more than it should have. Maybe it was the disappointment of knowing I wouldn't even get a chance to meet my father. If he'd been here, would he have rejected me as quickly as these other elves? He must have felt something for my mother once. Wouldn't he at least be curious to meet me? Or did he consider his dalliance with her to have been a mistake, one he'd prefer to forget?

*We do not wish to stay here,* Zav boomed into my mind, and theirs too, judging by the winces. *We seek to acquire a teacher.*

"Humans can't learn elven magic, my lord. Please understand. We mean no disrespect to you, but this is simply how it is. Their lives are not long enough for mastery, nor does enough magic flow through their veins."

"Are you sure it's not arrogant haughtiness that my veins are lacking?" I demanded, giving up on diplomacy. "Because that seems to be a requirement for being an elf."

He frowned at me. "You do not know your proper place, mongrel. You will never be welcome among our kind."

"That's a shame because this is such a warm and friendly place. You guys are oozing generosity and goodwill."

He didn't seem to know what to say to that, though I took some satisfaction from the flustered look on his face as he did the bow-curtsy again to Zav, then hustled into the tree. All except one of his pointy-eared buddies hurried after him, a female elf in a thin dress that stirred in the breeze.

She smiled shyly at Zav. "My lord, please let me renew my brother's invitation. You are more than welcome to stay with us tonight. I will happily share my bed with you."

I stared at her, wondering if my translation charm had taken some liberties there. For whatever reason, I'd never imagined elves as being forward and promiscuous, but she beamed a flirtatious smile at Zav and touched her chest.

"I know how to please a dragon," she added.

*I have a mate,* Zav stated before I could recover from my surprise and decide if I wanted to punch her in the nose or something equally mature. The tip of his tail swept over and curled around my waist. *She is a great warrior. We battle together.*

I was touched by the *great warrior* comment, even if having him get possessive of me was a little weird when he was in his dragon form.

"But does she know how to honor and respect a dragon?" She looked dismissively at me. "Her tongue seems sharp."

*I trust her tongue. I will not stay with you tonight.*

"As you wish, my lord." She did the bow-curtsy and walked inside, managing an impressive hip sway for someone so slender.

Cool rain fell as Zav and I were left alone on the platform. His gaze was toward the door all the elves had disappeared into, and I wondered if he was having second thoughts about rejecting the invitation.

More likely, he was deciding who to kidnap to instruct me, but a small part of me dwelled on the woman's offer to take him to bed. Not because I truly thought he would go sleep with an elf, not after what he'd been through with one of their kind, but because it hadn't occurred to me before that he'd been telling the truth about most females being eager to have sex with a dragon. Oh, I knew he wasn't a liar, but I'd assumed he had an inflated opinion of himself in that regard and didn't truly get propositioned left and right.

"Shows what I know," I muttered.

The rain picked up, puddles rapidly forming on the platform. The day had grown darker, either due to the rain clouds or the approach of night, and I found myself noticing that some of the surrounding trees had hollows from which pairs of glowing red dots peered out. Eyes? Some sort of magical creatures seemed to live inside, but I couldn't tell if they were birds or bats or something more dangerous. Maybe they were sentries of a kind, here to protect the elves from those who weren't welcome.

Standing at Zav's side, I doubted I had to worry about being overcome by the elven equivalent of a pit bull, but all those eyes seeming to stare at me made me uneasy. The magic emanating from all around us also made me feel vulnerable.

*I will take you to a place to spend the night,* Zav told me. *Climb on my back again.*

He levitated me atop him before I had to climb anywhere, and before I knew it, we were flying back the way we'd come.

*A place to spend the night by myself? Are you planning to take the elves up on the offer of a cozy bed while I get rained on?* I would much rather go home than spend the night in an alien forest.

*I am planning to find someone to teach you.*

The painful buzz ripped across my skin again as we flew through the barrier protecting the elven city, and I grimaced. That grimace deepened when Zav dropped me off under some trees and told me to stay put.

As he flew away into the rain and the deepening night, I shivered, feeling alone and vulnerable, even though there were no magical eyes staring at me out here. Though it seemed unlikely that something would happen to him on the elven world, I couldn't help but think that if something did… I could be stuck here. Forever.

# Chapter 16

The temperature dropped, and I shivered in the rain as I sat hunkered against the base of a tree. The branches did not provide that much protection from the weather. What droplets didn't fall straight from the sky to me instead dripped from the leaves onto my head and ran in rivulets down the trunk to drench my clothing.

"Note to self: don't let anyone kidnap you, even for your own good."

Frogs or something similar were croaking in a pond nearby, but they fell silent when another creature roared in the distance. I dropped a hand to Fezzik. I was doing my best to keep the gun under my duster so the ammunition wouldn't get wet. Ditto for the scones, my only source of food. I didn't even have a bottle of water, though with the rivers dripping onto me from above, that was less of a concern.

I sensed a powerful aura in the sky, that of a dragon. It wasn't Zav.

My head thunked back against the tree as I groaned. What were the odds that lots of dragons lived on the elven world and only chance was bringing this one by?

He didn't seem familiar—at least that meant it wasn't Zav's sister or Dob's father or some other dragon that I'd pissed off. Somehow, that didn't make me less uneasy about his presence.

*Interesting,* a male voice spoke into my mind. It had to belong to the dragon.

*No, I'm really not,* I thought. *Run along.*

*You have been marked by a dragon.*

*Yes, I have. And he's not far away.*

*Lord Zavryd'nokquetal of the Stormforge Clan. Interesting. What is special about you that he chose you as a mate? Are you a supportive tail holder?*

*I vex his enemies.* I didn't appreciate this strange dragon's questions and wondered what the repercussions would be if I ignored everything else he said.

*He has many of those.*

The dragon had been on a path to fly straight over me, but he banked to circle the area. Wonderful. It didn't matter where I went; I was catnip to dragons.

*You carry weapons,* he observed. *Do you go into battle with him?*

I drew Chopper and considered bragging about how I'd stuck the blade into a few dragons, but that might get me in trouble. He might want to come down and challenge me to teach me a lesson. I settled for holding the sword and glaring defiantly up at the forest canopy. The foliage was dense enough that I couldn't see him, but I had no trouble sensing where he was as he flew in lazy circles.

*I have seen that weapon before. You must be a great warrior if you were deemed worthy enough to carry it. Fascinating.*

*Where did you see it?* My plan to ignore him vanished. Was it possible this random dragon could be a source of information?

*In battle long ago. An elf warrior queen carried it and used it to slay a dragon. I do not know its dwarven name, but my clan dubbed it Dragon Doom.*

*And what clan are you from?* I squeezed Chopper's hilt, half-expecting him to be a relative of the Silverclaw Clan—Dob's and Shaygor's family—all of whom doubtless had the dragon equivalent of a bounty out on my head.

*Starsinger Clan.*

I hadn't heard of them. Maybe that was a good thing.

*Are you an ally to the Stormforge Clan?* I asked.

*No. They're pompous and pretentious.*

*The Silverclaw Clan?*

*No. They're backstabbing schemers without honor.*

*What are the Starsingers?*

*Delights.*

I snorted. Who *was* this guy?

## False Security

*We stay out of politics if we can and hunt and seek enjoyment and make art and music.*

*Dragons make art and music?*

*Of course. We did these things long before your people existed.* A strange howling roar came from above the treetops. The foliage rattled—or maybe shuddered—in response.

Was that... a battle cry? The prelude to an attack? I tightened my grip on Chopper again as the howl-roar turned into undulations rolling across the forest.

*That is a dragon song,* he informed me when the noise died down, then his tone turned a little smug. *I sang to the mate of a Stormforge dragon.*

*Uh, and is there some significance to that?*

*I could win you away from him if I wished.* Another chorus of howl-roars floated across the forest.

*Not with those tunes. But hey, there's an elf in that village who thinks dragons are sexy.*

*Is there? Hm, maybe I will break from my hunt and visit her. I have mated with three elves at once before.*

*Good for you.*

*The lesser species are always more eager to please male dragons than female dragons are. We must please females. That is the way.*

*Thanks so much for this dragon cultural lesson.*

*I had best continue my hunt. Our queen has recently procreated and she demands tree bogrifts from this world as a snack. I will return with a great bounty, and she will be pleased with me.*

*Fantastic.* I didn't know what a bogrift was, but I was pretty sure this guy had been sent for the equivalent of pickles and ice cream. Hopefully, that meant he wasn't a threat and that I would never see him again.

*If we meet again, mate of Lord Zavryd'nokquetal, I will woo you away from him. He will be so piqued. It will be extremely delightful.* He put an image in my mind of a handsome and naked green-eyed elf taking me into his arms and kissing me.

I willed Chopper to help me push away the intrusion. It disappeared, but the dragon laughed into my thoughts, the sound lingering long after he flew out of my range.

I had no idea what to think of the encounter, but I hoped my guess was right and that we'd never cross paths again. I needed more dragons in my life like I needed nails hammered through my toes.

Grumbling, I sheathed my sword and sat down to eat a scone. When I was finishing up, Zav returned to my senses. He flew down, turning into his human form as he landed.

"You're not the only dragon on this world," I told him.

"I am aware that there are others." In the darkness, he was barely visible walking toward me, but as usual, his aura glowed to my senses.

"Are they enemies? A dragon from the Starsinger Clan sang to me and called me interesting."

"*Sang* to you? What kind of song?"

"I couldn't replicate it unless you stuck a frog in my throat."

Zav looked out toward the trees, toward the pond where the frogs had been croaking earlier. They'd fallen silent when dragons had started showing up.

"I'm joking. I'm sure I couldn't replicate it even then."

"It is not proper to sing to the *Tlavar'vareous sha* of another dragon."

"He didn't strike me as proper." I decided not to mention the talk of mating or the kiss imagery. Knowing Zav, he would take off after the dragon and try to strip him of his scales.

"No. The Starsinger Clan is full of feckless simpletons. They are *apolitical*." He said that as if it were a greater crime than being feckless or simple.

"The hippies of the dragon world, huh?" If that one hadn't been hitting on me, I might have liked him.

"What is a hippie?"

"Someone unconventional who rejects mainstream values, usually while taking hallucinogenic drugs."

"Drugs might explain the Starsingers," Zav grumbled, then sat down under the tree with me, his aura wrapping around me with its familiar tingle of electricity. It warmed me like a fire.

No, I realized. He was doing more than warming me. He used his magic to dry me and extend a barrier over us. The persistent rain stopped dripping onto my head, and even the ground under my butt dried out. His shoulder touched mine as we sat together, warmth seeping through his robe, and I reminded myself that I was irked with him for bringing me here against my wishes. I wasn't going to snuggle up to him no matter how warm he was.

Still, I admitted, "Dragons are handy."

"Yes." Zav sounded pleased that I was acknowledging this.

"I notice you didn't come back with an elf."

"No, but I made contact with one who will speak with the king and let him know you're here."

I hesitated. I'd been about to ask if he would take me home. I was worried about Dimitri. If he got himself into trouble looking for Zoltan, and I wasn't there to help him because of what turned into a fruitless quest to find a magic teacher, I would feel horrible.

But curiosity about my father reared up and distracted me. "Do you think he'll come to see me?"

"Why would he not?"

"Because I'm a mongrel and a mistake."

Zav considered his answer and applied more tact than usual. "Do not let the words of those you met here discourage you. Not all elves feel that way, and it is ludicrous for them to say that you do not have power and cannot learn their magic. I can sense your power. I believe you have as much as many full-blooded elves, which would not be surprising, since Eireth had the power to rise to prominence above many other elves."

"I don't care about power. I just…" I groped at the air, not sure how to finish that.

For my whole life, I'd believed I had no magic of my own, only what I'd found in my weapons and my charms, and I'd accepted that as the way it was. Even though it would be handy to be able to save myself from mental compulsions, I could go on living and surviving without magic of my own. What I would like was to meet my father and for him to not be an asshole.

When Lirena—Anyasha-sulin—had shown up, pretending to be my cousin, I'd been easier to fool than I should have been. Because I'd wanted to meet my father and other relatives. Even if I rarely admitted it, I'd wondered about them from time to time, wondered what it would be like not to be an only child with my mother my only living relative.

"I don't know, Zav." I leaned my head back against the tree. "I guess I just want not to be rejected by these people, or at least the ones I'm related to. It shouldn't matter. I'm too old to need a father. But it would be easier not having them exist than having them exist and knowing they want nothing to do with me."

Zav was silent. Maybe I was perplexing him. What could a dragon know of being rejected? Nobody called *him* a mongrel. Who would dare?

"Some of my relatives reject me," Zav stated. "I have a cousin who sides with the Silverclaw Clan instead of with his own family because he believes my mother will inevitably be thrust from her powerful position over the Dragon Justice Court and that we should position ourselves to land favorably when that happens. He calls me an obtuse relic from another time."

"Does his rejection sting? Or do you not care what he thinks?"

"We hunted together when we were young, so it is difficult to accept that he changed as we grew older and does not now respect me."

"Ah. Then maybe you do know what it's like to be rejected." I caught myself leaning against him, even though I'd decided I wouldn't.

"Dragons live long lives. We experience and know many things."

"Like how to kidnap women from their homes?"

"Women who are mated to dragons are supposed to go anywhere they wish at any time. You are oddly stubborn about not acceding to my wishes."

"And yet you're sitting here in the rain with me talking about rejection." I didn't point out that he could have spent the night in some elf's warm dry bed with her attending his every desire.

"You vexed that elf." Zav sounded pleased and turned his head to gaze at me.

The male, I realized. He wasn't thinking about the female.

"And you liked that? I thought you only approved when I vexed your enemies."

"He was too simple and insignificant to be an enemy, but he irritated me, so I am pleased that you vexed him." He lifted a hand to my face, fingers brushing my cheek, electricity tingling through my entire body from that simple touch.

"We're not having sex," I said, though I was reminding myself of that fact rather than informing him of anything.

"No," he agreed, his fingers trailing up to trace my ear. "You have not yet learned to defend yourself from powerful enemies."

"What happens if I never do?"

His simple touch made me intensely aware of him and of my own body, and the idea that we might never sleep together disturbed me. I didn't *want* it to disturb me and didn't *want* to be so drawn to someone so exasperating, but my body was not an obedient subject.

"You will." His mouth found mine in the darkness, and my heart pounded in my chest.

It was more of a gentle, soothing kiss than a hungry, passionate one. I wouldn't have guessed he could do that or that he would want to, and it almost brought tears to my eyes. There was probably a rule somewhere about kissing one's kidnapper, but I couldn't remember it.

*An elf is coming,* Zav informed me after a time, though his lips didn't leave mine. Somehow, I'd ended up in his lap with my arms wrapped around his shoulders.

*Do you want me to drive him away by vexing him?* I thought.

*Not unless he deserves it.*

*You don't think he will? It's rude of him to interrupt our kissing.*

*I did ask him to come.* Zav drew his mouth back, rubbing the back of my head and gazing into my eyes for a long moment before releasing me.

My legs were shaky as I shifted away from him and pushed to my feet. I rested a hand against the damp tree trunk as I gazed into the dark forest.

*Who is it?* I assumed Zav knew the elf's name if he'd requested he come. Some ally of his? Someone who might deign to teach me?

*Your father. King Eireth.*

The nerves that had been writhing in my gut off and on all day returned in full force. The elf walked—no, he was flying high above—into my range, approaching swiftly. He seemed to be alone. Were kings supposed to travel alone? I couldn't imagine our president wandering off into a dark forest without hordes of Secret Service guys trailing after him. Maybe Eireth didn't want anyone to know he was coming to see me—the mistake he didn't want his wife to know about.

Though I doubted this would go well, I squared my shoulders and walked away from Zav and the tree to face my father as he approached.

# Chapter 17

King Eireth swept out of the trees on something akin to a giant eagle wearing a saddle. It dove toward the ground, leveling out a few feet above the damp earth, and he sprang from its back to land lightly in a crouch. Without touching down, the giant bird angled back upward and flapped its wings until it could perch in a treetop.

Even though I should have focused on the silver-haired elf in green-and-brown buckskins walking toward me, I couldn't help but glance back at Zav and think, *That bird is wearing a saddle.*

He was leaning against the tree with his arms folded over his chest, and he knew exactly what I was referencing. *That bird is not a dragon.*

*Are you implying that a bird is capable of something you aren't?*

*I am implying that only a dumb bird with no dignity would allow itself to be saddled.*

*It looked dignified to me.*

*A saddle is a sign of domestication. Domestication is not dignified. No dragon would allow such a thing.*

*Are you afraid your buddies would tease you?*

*A dragon does not let buddies affect him. He can do anything he wishes. He does not wish to wear a saddle.*

*But socks with Birkenstocks aren't a problem?*

Zav's eyes flared violet in the dark. *You mock my footwear? I thought it was acceptably masculine.*

*It was borderline okay before you added the socks.*

*My toes got cold.*

"Is there a problem?" Eireth asked quietly, following my gaze toward Zav.

"We're arguing about saddles," I said before it occurred to me that I should probably bow—or prostrate myself on the ground while kissing the wet grass—to a king. And not crack jokes. But that wasn't really me, and I was disinclined to suck up. Mom was blunt and unimpressed by celebrity. He had to expect some of that from me. "I pointed out that your bird has one."

Eireth turned his fingers upward, and a floating silver globe of light appeared in the air between us before shifting over to the side. It illuminated his face and let me see his green eyes and lean, elegant features as he looked me up and down curiously. There was also wariness in his gaze, especially when it lingered on my weapons. He had to wonder what I wanted—whatever Zav had told him, I doubted it had been diplomatic—and what to expect from the Ruin Bringer.

Well, I was wary, too, after my encounter with the elf who had claimed to be my cousin. But Zav had found Eireth, and he looked exactly like the portrait Mom had of him in her house, so I was inclined to believe the person in front of me truly was my father. If he'd been human, I would have guessed him about forty—the lush silver hair appeared a natural color for elves, nothing to do with age—which was decidedly weird since I was older than that.

For the first time, I wondered what would happen if Zav and I ended up as a serious couple in a long-term relationship. Or even married, as Willard so often joked. Dragons lived for centuries if not thousands of years, so he would have to watch me grow old and die, if he stuck around that long. Would he? It hurt my head to think about anything that long-term with someone who thought nothing of claiming me without asking and kidnapping me for my own good.

"The *evinya* are not magical, so they have no way to keep their rider aboard as they swoop through the trees." Other than the bird name, Eireth spoke in English with scarcely an accent. "Most of our people have the power to keep themselves aboard, but they also don't think it seemly when their king takes untoward risks. There are dangers outside of our sanctuary walls."

"Yeah, a dragon chatted me up."

"A certain number of dragons come here to hunt in our forests each year." Eireth tilted his head, one pointed ear poking up through his straight hair. "Did he bother you?"

"Not as much as the snooty elves who said half-bloods can't stay in their quaint little tree village."

Eireth's eyebrows lifted. Maybe insulting his town wasn't the way to go. I should have brought Sindari out to advise me on proper etiquette with elves. He never had a problem advising me on dealing with dragons.

"They are the sentinels in charge of protecting our people," Eireth said. "They are sometimes overly assiduous in rejecting those with a reputation."

"A reputation as a mongrel?"

"A reputation as a half-blood assassin. News of you came to us not long ago."

"And to some chick named Anyasha-sulin too, apparently."

He winced. "I apologize for that deception. I only just learned of it. Anyasha-sulin does not live here on this world, and I do not know how she found out about you." Eireth shifted his gaze toward Zav and bent in what might have been an apologetic bow. How much had he heard about her duplicitous ways? Did he know about the events on Mt. Rainier and that she'd tricked me into attacking Zav? And if so, how?

"Lord Zavryd'nokquetal said you wish to learn the ways of your heritage. To channel the magic flowing through your veins?"

"If it's there, yeah. Your sentries called me a rock."

"As I'm sure he told you—" Eireth extended a hand toward Zav, "—you are not without power. But it does take time to learn magic and find one's natural aptitudes and choose a discipline to specialize in."

"I just want to be able to keep elves and dragons from compelling me to do things."

Eireth looked toward Zav again.

"Not that one. He kidnaps me by force instead of compelling me."

*He is not familiar with your sharp tongue and may not realize you are joking,* Zav spoke dryly into my mind.

*Who's joking?* I looked back at him. *You* did *kidnap me.*

*I brought you here for your own good, not to obtain a ransom.*

*Kidnapping is any taking by force. Ransoms don't have to be involved.*

"Are you arguing with him?" Eireth asked mildly.

I didn't know if he was able to monitor our conversation—probably not, or he wouldn't have had to ask about the arguing—or was guessing based on facial expressions.

"Yeah," I said. "We do that a lot."

"And he allows it?"

"He huffs about it, but I think he likes a woman who speaks her mind. And I get bonus points for vexing his enemies."

Zav left the shadow of the tree and came to stand by my shoulder, his eyes glowing softly in the night. I didn't *think* I'd done anything more than usual to irritate him, but it was possible he didn't appreciate me snipping at him in front of an elf king.

He laid an arm around my shoulders, his power cloaking me, as he faced Eireth. "I have claimed Val as my mate."

"Yes, I see that." Eireth's tone was carefully neutral, so I couldn't tell if he approved or disapproved. I doubted dragons asked parents for permission before dating their daughters.

"She must learn to defend herself mentally so she cannot be used against me and so she can more easily defend herself from her own enemies. I require an appropriate elf be assigned to instruct her."

"He *requests* it," I said. "Politely and with respect."

Zav's gaze shifted from Eireth to me.

I ignored it and smiled politely at Eireth. "I don't know what passes for money here, but I'm willing to find a way to pay someone for their time. Or trade something that you would value." I had no idea what, but maybe Eireth missed some Earth things. "How do you feel about scones?"

Eireth gazed at me thoughtfully, that wariness still in his eyes, and I had a feeling he didn't know what to make of me. Maybe he thought it would be dangerous to teach an assassin and potentially give me more tools to use against the magical community.

"You have met Freysha?" he eventually asked.

"Uh, yes." I hadn't expected him to know about her, much less be aware that she was hiding out on Earth.

"If you arrange accommodations for her, she will instruct you."

"I already asked her if she could teach me, and she said she wasn't experienced enough."

"She is able to teach."

"She said it's against your rules for anyone but a master to do that."

"Freysha has mastered forest magic and is capable enough to teach what you seek. She likely made an excuse because she was not certain if I would wish it. Also, she is modest about her skills. But be assured that she is powerful and talented and has learned much for someone of so few years."

"You know she's making stapler trebuchets with a goblin, right?"

Eireth's lips quirked. "She has engineering interests. That is why she wanted to go to your world. Actually, she wanted to go to the goblin home world, and she spent two years learning their culture and language in preparation."

"Then she realized we have whole schools dedicated to engineering on Earth?"

"No. I asked her to change her plans and report back to me about you."

I would have rocked back on my heels, or maybe fallen onto my butt, if Zav's arm hadn't still been around me. I don't know why I was so surprised, but... "That was the whole ruse that Anyasha-sulin gave me, that she was a cousin you sent to spy on me."

Zav had grown still at my side, his eyes narrowed as he watched Eireth. He hadn't met Freysha, and I couldn't remember if I'd even mentioned her to him. Willard and Gondo were the ones spending time with her. I'd only chatted with her the couple of times she'd been there when I'd gone to Willard's office.

"That is troubling," Eireth said, "as it implies someone in my court shared our plans with a member of the rebel faction of elves. There are not many people who knew I intended to send Freysha. I will question them carefully and find out who has betrayed me."

I wasn't sure how that helped me now, nor did I know how to feel about the admission that Eireth truly had sent someone to observe me. "So Freysha is spying on me. And that's why she asked for a job at my boss's office."

Eireth rocked his hand back and forth in what wasn't quite a familiar gesture. "I wanted to know about you. I have much to do here in my home world and couldn't leave myself, but I wanted to know what kind of person you are. Ruin Bringer." His brows rose and then his tone softened. "I am also curious... I did not tell Freysha to look for her, but

I wondered.... Is Sigrid still alive?"

"Yeah. She's retired and lives in Oregon with her dog."

"Retired," he mouthed, as if he couldn't imagine being retired yet. "Is she well?"

"She's still in good health. Oh, and you have a granddaughter too."

His eyebrows rose higher. Freysha must not have stumbled across that tidbit.

"You are..." Eireth glanced at Zav. "Married?"

"Not to him," I said.

"Val is my mate," Zav stated.

"Which is not legally binding on Earth, as far as I can tell."

"It is binding everywhere that matters," Zav said.

"Thad and I are divorced," I explained to Eireth, trusting him to have spent enough time on my world to know what that meant. "Amber is fourteen. She swims competitively, and I've just started teaching her sword fighting so she can defend herself."

I wasn't sure why I was sharing, other than he might be curious. But when I imagined him asking for more details, details that I couldn't give because I'd been an absentee mom for so long, I clammed up. It wasn't as if he could judge me for walking out on a kid, but... according to Mom, he hadn't known I existed. I'd always known about Amber.

"Val's *ex*-mate is inconsequential," Zav stated.

I thought about stepping on his sandaled foot.

Eireth looked from Zav to me and back again, then smiled slightly. What did *that* mean?

*Can you read his mind, Zav?*

*No. He is a powerful elf who can protect his thoughts. I would have to perform a* vayushnarak—*mind scouring—to gain access to them, but that is an attack, and King Eireth is currently an ally to the Dragon Justice Court.*

*So, mind-scouring him isn't cool, huh?*

*It is not. Why? Do you suspect him of nefarious intent?*

*No. I suspect him of... thinking we're odd.*

*He would not dare think a dragon odd.*

*What about me?*

*You are odd. I have informed you of this.*

I rubbed my face, not sure what it said about me that even dragons thought I was weird.

"Perhaps Freysha could meet your daughter," Eireth said. "And perhaps one day, I could slip away to do so also. Right now is not a good time. There is tension within the Dragon Ruling Council, which creates tension in the entire Crimson Realms."

"It will be resolved," Zav stated.

"With your family still in power?" Eireth asked.

"Yes."

"Hm."

"Who is Freysha to you?" I couldn't say I didn't care about dragon politics, since I kept ending up in the middle of them, but I would prefer *not* to care about them and to focus on my own more immediate concerns.

"You can trust her. If you are agreeable, I will have word sent to her that you will provide her accommodations in exchange for tutelage. I understand she's currently camping in your city. I would think nothing of her camping in the forest, but the city has dangers, even for an elf, does it not?"

"Yeah." I didn't point out that my apartment was more likely to be targeted by bad guys than whatever bridge Freysha was sleeping under, because it did seem crappy that she didn't have a place to stay. At one point, she'd been house-sitting for Willard, but since Willard was back home, I supposed that was over. "I guess she can crash on my couch, but you didn't answer my question."

"Who she is? She is my daughter."

This didn't stun me as much as the revelation about spying. Though I wouldn't have guessed it based on their personalities or looks. Mostly their personalities.

"With your elven wife the queen?"

"Yes."

"She doesn't seem..." I pictured Freysha building goofy contraptions with Gondo out of office supplies. "Regal."

The words *spoiled rich kid* had also come to mind, though I didn't know if the elves had poverty and wealth anything like we did. How much wealth could there be when you lived in a tree?

"She is young," Eireth said.

"So, she'll get regal when she gets older?"

"We'll see. Do you need anything else?" Eireth turned his palms upward.

"Do we need anything else?" I asked Zav, feeling silly for coming all the way here when the answer was in Willard's office. Though Freysha hadn't been willing to teach me before.

"I need only for you to be instructed," he said.

"I could wed you if you want," Eireth said, his tone turning dry again.

"What?" I blurted.

"In the elven way. I have the authority among our people to do so. It still wouldn't be binding on Earth, but it would be official here and show that your claim on each other is mutual." His eyebrows flicked upward. "Dragons do have a habit of simply claiming people without asking."

"Imagine that."

Zav squeezed my shoulder. "I claimed you for your own good."

"You do a lot of things for my own good."

"Because your tongue gets you in trouble and you need extra protection."

"We're not ready to get married," I told Eireth whose eyes were crinkling. Was that mirth? What did he think? That we acted like a married couple already? "Not here, not on Earth. Besides, my boss wants to come to my wedding and see me in a dress."

"In a dress?" Zav looked down at my chest. "Like that green dress? You will wear it if we marry in the elven way?"

"No. We're not getting married. You're not a citizen of Earth, and besides, we haven't even—" I broke off, aware of the near-stranger gazing at us. I refused to talk about my sex life—or current lack of one—in front of him.

"You will learn to protect yourself from enemies," Zav said, "and then we will mate often and vigorously."

"Er." I wouldn't have guessed I could be embarrassed in front of some elf I'd only just met, even if he was my father. My heated cheeks proclaimed otherwise.

"You will enjoy it *vastly*," Zav informed me.

I buried my face in my hand.

"My offer stands," Eireth said, then whistled. His saddled bird swept down from the treetops toward us. Spreading his hands palm upward again, he said, "I am pleased to have learned of your existence and that I've gotten to meet you. Please tell your mother I am also glad that she is well."

"I will." I almost told him that Mom still had a portrait of him in the living room, but he hadn't said he missed her and pined for her daily, so I kept that to myself. He was married to someone else now, and my mom's days of romance were likely at an end, since she refused to fall in love with anyone else. Sad. But maybe that was how it was when you fell in love with someone from a longer-lived species.

I looked at Zav, wondering what I was doing falling for a dragon.

"You *will* enjoy it vastly," he informed me, misreading my pensive expression. "I am not a self-absorbed dragon. I require that my mate be as pleased as I am."

"That's good to know." I patted him on the chest. "But I do insist that you learn an Earth custom. It's called Never Talk About Your Sex Life in Front of Your Girlfriend's Parents."

Zav considered this. "You are my mate, not my girlfriend."

"Same rule applies. Ditto for wives."

"Strange."

# Chapter 18

I checked my phone as soon as I popped out of Zav's portal and back into my apartment. Night had fallen, and I was surprised to realize it was still the same day. I'd only lost twelve hours. It looked like my mother had called three times shortly after I left, but she hadn't left any messages. I hoped she was all right.

There was a voicemail from Willard, but there weren't any messages from Weber. That was a relief because it meant he didn't know I'd been AWOL on his assignment. Surprisingly, there weren't any updates from Dimitri. Maybe he'd slept all day after being up the previous night searching for Zoltan. Though that seemed unlikely. Other than the part-time coffee barista, he was the only one working at the shop right now.

As the magic of the portal faded and Zav wandered around the living room as if he hadn't been there before, I called Dimitri. He didn't answer. I left a voicemail, asking for an update on Zoltan and on him. If he didn't call back tonight, I would see if Nin knew anything.

"What are you doing?" I asked Zav as I dialed Willard.

"Determining if your domicile is sufficient to house an elven princess."

"It's housing me. If my dad is a king, doesn't that make me a princess?"

"According to elven law, a mongrel cannot be a princess. Your human blood disqualifies you." Zav prodded one of the couch cushions dubiously.

"Darn, I was hoping for a killer inheritance. Maybe some of those twig headbands. I bet they go for ones of dollars on Etsy."

"Humans are overly preoccupied with money."

"Because it's hard to live here without some of it."

Willard answered. "What do you want, Thorvald? It's late, and if you're not working on my vampire problem, I'm not that interested in talking to you."

"I'm wounded. As it so happens, my gig for Weber may be linked to your problem. He was attacked last night by a vampire controlling a bunch of hounds."

"Yes, you sent me that very terse report at midnight with promises that you'd give me more details today. They didn't come. I was filled in by a reporter who was there."

"Sorry, I was distracted by Zav kidnapping me today."

Now Zav was poking into my desk drawers. He pulled out the slightly damaged poster of himself, and I rolled my eyes. I should have thrown that away after the dark elves mutilated it.

"This has been perforated," he informed me. "I will get you a new one."

"Good. I'm sure elven princesses can't sleep at night without pictures of dragons on the walls."

"What are you talking about, Thorvald?"

I didn't know if Willard referred to the kidnapping or the princess comment or both. "It's been an eventful day. Are you expecting Freysha in the office tomorrow?"

"Yes. Why?"

Zav wandered into the kitchen and opened the fridge.

"I need you to give her my address and tell her she's living here for now."

"Care to unpack that?" Willard's cat yowled in the background, probably wondering why her owner was on the phone instead of attending her every need.

"I made a deal with her father. She's going to teach me her magic in exchange for a place to stay that doesn't involve washing in a fountain with a goblin."

"There is insufficient food in this storage box for a guest," Zav said over his shoulder.

"I know. I'll go shopping."

"Who's her father?" Willard asked.

"King Eireth."

"Isn't that your father?"

"Yup. I met him today on the main elven home world."

Willard paused, though Maggie was still audible prowling and complaining somewhere in her apartment. "You better come to the office tomorrow morning too."

"I'll see what I can do. I've got to find Dimitri first." My phone beeped with another call. "That might be him now. Tell Freysha if I get there late."

Willard swore by way of a goodbye.

The incoming call wasn't Dimitri; it was Nin.

"Val, do you know where Dimitri is?" she asked.

I groaned. "I was hoping you did."

"Tam said he never came to the coffee shop today. He called her at lunchtime and asked her to do the best she could and close early if she needed to. He said he was looking for a friend and had a lead. Is it Zoltan?"

"Yeah, I think so. What lead?"

"I do not know," Nin said. "He did not answer his phone when I called."

"He hasn't answered my calls either. Do you know where he's staying?"

"Tam said his van has been parked near the shop all day. I believe he is saving money and still living in it."

Ugh. He paid to lease the building for his business. Couldn't he stay in a back room?

"I'll go check out his van," I said.

"I will meet you there."

"You don't need to come. I'll handle it. He's gotten involved with missing vampires—more than one."

"Is that worse than being involved with vampires who are present?"

"Probably."

I hung up as Zav wandered out of the bathroom holding a purple razor. "What is this? There is a blade, but it is too small to be a weapon." He turned it upside down and frowned at it.

"It's for shaving your legs."

Zav's eyebrows climbed up his forehead. "Why would you do such a thing?"

"Humans like smooth, hairless legs."

He bent forward and hiked up the hem of his robe, revealing that the white socks he'd chosen rose almost to his knees. My dragon was not a natural at fashion. Maybe I could turn him over to Amber to take to the mall someday.

Zav prodded his robustly populated dark leg hair. "This instrument seems insufficient for the task."

"It's not for you. Guys don't shave their legs. Women do. Don't ask me why. I have no idea. It's a human cultural thing." I pointed at his neatly trimmed beard. "You must shave your face, or at least trim yourself. Your beard and mustache are always the same length."

"This form that I assumed did not come with long facial hair."

"It doesn't grow?"

"No."

That explained why his haircut and beard were always perfect.

"Should it? Perhaps I could figure out how to make that happen."

"Don't. If you don't have to shave anything or cut your hair, it's a blessing. Put my razor away please." I texted Dimitri and told him that if he didn't call me immediately, I would raid his van and sell all of his quirky 80s sci-fi paraphernalia.

My phone rang, a number I didn't recognize popping up. My stomach lurched. Maybe someone had kidnapped Dimitri and was calling with a ransom request.

"Yeah?" I answered warily.

"Val?"

"Mom?"

"Of course. You don't recognize my voice?"

"I don't recognize the number. I was expecting a kidnapper demanding a ransom."

"I see your life is still odd," she said.

Zav walked out of the bathroom again, this time holding the plunger. "What does this do?"

"You have no idea, Mom." I waved for Zav to take it back into the bathroom. "It's for unplugging the toilet."

"The toilet?" he asked.

"Yes. You *must* have encountered toilets during your time here on Earth. I've seen you eat, and digestion happens for all species."

"Yes, digestion happens, but I fail to see why you would use a sanitation system that needs unplugging so frequently that there is a tool for it."

"Because we don't have magic and have to make do." Once again, I made a shooing motion. This time, he went back inside.

"I see I was correct to reserve a room at a hotel," my mother said.

"A hotel? You're traveling?"

"I'm in your city. A regular instructor canceled at a Search and Rescue conference I've attended up here before, and I was invited up to give a talk and do some demonstrations with Rocket. I thought it would be nice to see you and Amber again this summer."

The hum of my vibrating toothbrush came from the bathroom. At least I *hoped* that was the toothbrush he'd found.

"That does sound nice, Mom." I walked across the living room to rescue my things from my nosy dragon. What did my bathroom appurtenances have to do with whether my apartment was suitable for a princess anyway? "How long will you be in town? I've got a bodyguard gig right now, Zoltan the alchemist is missing, and Dimitri may be in trouble, so I'm a little busy."

"And you have a houseguest?"

Zav was indeed holding my vibrating toothbrush and examining it from all angles. I took it from him, turned it off, placed it back in the charger, and clasped his hand. Though he appeared bemused, he let me lead him back to the living room and park him on the couch.

"He isn't staying, but I am expecting someone tomorrow. Zav is helping me make sure my apartment is up to snuff."

"Zav… is the dragon? The good one?"

"The good one."

He was busy examining the coasters on the coffee table and didn't seem to hear my encomium.

"I'm at the Extended Stay in Northgate," Mom said.

"Posh."

"Do you want to meet for breakfast tomorrow?"

I was tempted to say no, but it would be rude not to see my mother when she'd driven all the way up here. And she was an early bird. She would want to eat at seven or eight. Nobody should need me that early.

"Sure, breakfast is fine."

"What's going on with Dimitri?"

"I'm going to go look for him now."

"Do you need to track him? Do you want help?"

"He was last seen in Fremont, so I don't think regular tracking skills will suffice. I've got Sindari and Zav, but I'll let you know if I need someone less magical and more earthy."

"Hm." She didn't sound like she approved of my dismissal, maybe because Dimitri had been her roommate for months before I'd ever met him.

"I'll make sure he's okay. If you see Amber, ask her for a cupcake."

"I don't eat sweets."

"Ask her for the story of how we got the cupcakes."

"That I will do."

"Good. I'll check in with you later." When I hung up, I found Zav poking through the copy of *Seattle Met* that I perused when I was painting my toenails. It had been stuck down between the frame and one of the cushions. "Are you really snooping this much because Freysha is coming or is this an excuse to root through my belongings?"

"Is it important that she learn seventy-eight ways to make the most of a Seattle summer?" He held up the article.

"If she's going to live here, it is." I was glad I didn't have any copies of *Cosmo* hanging around the apartment, or he'd be learning about his sex horoscope and games for the bedroom. "Will you come with me to look for Dimitri? Is there any chance you can snap your fingers and tell me where he is?"

I doubted that, because Zav needed me to help him research the criminals hiding here on Earth, but a girl could hope.

"Is he wearing any magical items? I could detect such things from a distance."

"I don't think so. He's probably wearing the same thing he was wearing when you walked in the coffee shop the other day. Especially if he's been living in his van." I hoped he had access to a laundromat and clean underwear.

"I do not recall that he had magical items, but I will help you seek him."

"Thank you." I hugged him. "When you're not kidnapping me, you're actually a pretty cool guy."

"Yes." He returned the hug, and I smiled, remembering when he used to flinch whenever I tried to touch him. "I shaved my leg."

"Ugh, why?" I wrinkled my lip at the thought of coarse man hair in my razor.

"Curiosity. I removed only a small stripe."

"Do you regret it?"

"Yes."

"Maybe that will teach you to stay out of a woman's bathroom."

"Yes."

# Chapter 19

It was almost ten by the time I reached the coffee shop. The lights were off and the door was locked, with no sign of vandalism or trouble, at least at the building. The ice cream shop next door had also closed for the night, and foot traffic was sparse. Surprisingly, the lights to the psychic's office were on, and I sensed Janice inside. A couple of cars were parked out front, so maybe she had a late-night customer.

Dimitri's beat-up orange camper van was around the corner. As Zav and I approached, I summoned Sindari.

*Dimitri's missing,* I told him as soon as he formed. *Can you sniff around and see if you can catch his scent or anything suspicious?*

*Yes. Is he missing in the same place that Zoltan is missing?*

*I don't know yet.*

The van was locked. That seemed to suggest that nobody had disturbed it, but I wanted to see inside in case he'd left any clues—like a notepad detailing the lead he'd mentioned to Nin.

As Sindari padded off, I rested my hand on the door and gripped my lock-picking charm. After a moment of willing the charm to do its job, the side door unlocked with a thunk, and I slid it open. I wrinkled my nose at the pot scent that wafted out, mingling with odors of laundry in need of washing.

"We've got to get this kid an apartment," I said. "Possibly a maid."

"There is very little magic in this area, other than the knickknacks Dimitri has made and houses in his shop," Zav informed me. He was gazing at the city around us, scouring the area with his senses, rather than breathing in the scents of the van.

"Can you sense any vampires?" I climbed inside. A light didn't come on, so I pulled out my phone and used the flashlight app.

"No."

"Shifters or other magical beings?"

"There is a panther shifter and a bear shifter living among numerous large but mundane animals to the north."

It took me a moment to make sense of what large but mundane animals he might be sensing. "Like at the zoo?"

"There are many types of animals there, and a lake is nearby."

"Yeah, that's the zoo." I made a note to let Willard know shifters were getting free rent there. "Just let me know if you sense any vampires, please."

The van hadn't changed much since the last time I'd ridden in it, and I didn't see any obvious clues. I poked through take-out menus stuffed down beside the seat and was about to give up but spotted writing on the back of one of them. *Longevity potion?*

I flipped the page, but there was nothing else. Maybe it was something Dimitri had intended to ask Zoltan to make for the shop. But could Zoltan actually craft such a thing? If longevity potions existed, everyone would want them. He—and Dimitri—could get rich selling them. But it sounded more like the kind of thing people *wished* existed than that did.

"Anything?" I locked the van door and hopped back out.

"Nothing."

*Sindari?* I didn't see him but sensed that he hadn't gone far.

*I detect his scent, of course, since he is often in the area, but I do not believe he has been here since early morning.*

That was when I'd spoken to him last. *You smell any orcs?*

*Yes, but also ogres, goblins, gnolls, and kobolds. Their scent trails lead in and out of the coffee shop. It is likely they were customers there today. I believe they came after Dimitri was here and left.*

*All right. Keep looking around, please.*

*It would be unfortunate to lose Dimitri. He has good hands.*

*For making things or for rubbing tiger ears?*

*Yes.*

"Let's see if the psychic has seen anything." I touched Zav's arm and pointed back toward the building. "Maybe she'd like to read your fortune."

"All lesser beings who are wise wish to be of service to dragons."

"Naturally." Before we made it to the psychic's office, my phone buzzed. "I didn't expect to hear from you again tonight, Willard."

"I'm packing."

"You're going on a trip? I just talked to you an hour ago."

"It's a recent development." She did not sound pleased. "I'm heading down to Ft. Lewis in the morning for three days of conveniently timed mandatory surprise training."

"Conveniently timed? What do you mean? Someone's trying to get you out of the city?"

"Given how quickly this came together, that may be the case. I didn't tell you, but yesterday, General Dorfman called. He's my superior who took over for Nash. He said he'd been told to pass along the message to me to leave the vampires in the city to settle their own differences."

I frowned down at a crack in the sidewalk. "The vampires who attacked a psychic, a car dealership, and my client? And are being kidnapped themselves?"

"Those are the ones. Someone thinks they're in a territorial pissing match with each other and that we should stay out of it, despite humans having been attacked and even killed. The general sounded exasperated with his superiors and didn't specifically order me off the case, so I didn't think much of it, but an hour ago, I got a call about this surprise training and that it might take all week. Major Cecil, Lieutenant Sabo, Sergeant Banderas, and I all have to go."

"That's most of your senior office staff. Who's going to be in charge? Gondo?"

"It's not quite that bad. I sent word to Freysha about moving into your place. I'll bring her by early on my way out of town."

"What do you want me to do while you're gone?" Maybe I shouldn't have offered to help, since I had to find Dimitri and protect Weber if he needed it. But I was beginning to suspect everything was tied together and I'd end up in the middle of a huge mess no matter what.

"Buy some cat food, and find the missing vampires."

"Uh, cat food?"

"You're taking my cat sitter."

"Freysha?"

"She watched Maggie when we went to Rainier. I think that was your idea. You shouldn't be surprised."

"Uh, no, but... can't you take her with you to Lewis? You know Sindari's scent is all over my apartment, right? Not to mention that there was a dragon rummaging through my bathroom earlier. Maggie won't like that."

"Why was your dragon rummaging in the bathroom? Didn't you leave an extra roll out for him?"

"He's kind of a snoop." I smiled at Zav, who'd stopped at my side and appeared to be listening to the conversation.

His brows rose. "I was determining if Val's apartment is adequate."

"I'm sure it's not," Willard said. "Val, I also want you to figure out if your new boyfriend is involved with these vampires."

"My new what?"

Zav's keen dragon hearing must have picked up Willard's comment, because his head swiveled toward me, and his eyes flared with violet light as he glowered at the phone. Hopefully, he didn't have plans to incinerate it.

"Weber," Willard said. "There's a photo of you on his arm at the yacht club in the society section."

"You read the society section? Keeping up on the weddings of the doyennes of Seattle?"

"You know my people read all the news and track everything that happens in the city." As Willard was speaking, Zav plucked the phone from my fingers.

"Val is my *Tlavar'vareous sha*," he told her. "Inform your city thus, so mistakes are not made."

"I'll be sure to get word out to Seattle right away," Willard said without missing a beat.

"Excellent. That human is weak and inferior and not worthy of a daughter of an elven king."

I took the phone back from Zav.

"You didn't go into many details about your father the king, Val. Does that make you a princess, Val?" Willard sounded highly amused.

"I'm told it does not. Half-human mongrels can't be princesses, but your cat sitter is royalty. Maggie should be honored."

"I wondered about that when you said the king was Freysha's father. I had believed she was another refugee. And she let me believe that."

"No, she's here to spy on me for the king." One of the lights in the back of the psychic's building went out. "I'll tell you more later. I've got to question someone before they leave."

"Right. Don't forget to buy cat food."

I grimaced at the phone, but she'd already hung up. "Where am I going to get cat food at ten at night?"

"I believe your employer was being sarcastic," Zav said as we headed for the psychic's door.

"You think she'll bring her own cat food? She should."

"I meant about informing the city that we are mates."

"Oh. Yeah, you're right."

"If humans were not so obtuse about observing magical marks, this fact would be self-evident."

The psychic's door opened as we were climbing the steps. Janice shrieked and jumped back inside, slamming the door closed. My first thought was that it was an extreme reaction, even though I'd chased her up a drainpipe the other day. Then I remembered she had as much magical blood as I did and would sense exactly what Zav was.

The door had a big glass window, so I could see her gaping at us from behind a curtain of vertical beads on the other side. I could also see that she had her wrecking ball of a purse on her shoulder as well as a—was that a baseball bat? No, a softball bat. She'd told me about it. Boomer.

"Don't beat up this woman, Zav." I knocked politely. "Even if she swings a bat at you."

"That would be an inappropriate way to greet a dragon."

"Once she calms down, I'll tell her about the elf bow-curtsy. And that since she's female, she should offer to sleep with you."

"That is unnecessary."

"I'm closed!" Janice glared through the door, her knuckles tight around the bat.

"We just have a few questions."

"Unless you can show me a badge, I'm not answering them." She leaned through the curtain of beads, her gaze never leaving Zav's face, and locked the door.

"What is a badge?" Zav asked.

"A sign of authority from our police."

Zav drew a heavy gold medallion out from under his robe, and it glowed like a small sun. I'd seen it a few times, describing it as Mr. T bling, but I'd never seen it glow.

"I am Lord Zavryd'nokquetal from the Dragon Justice Court, the supreme authority in the universe. You will let me in."

The woman ran deeper into the office and crouched down behind a table.

"The badge did not work." Zav tucked the medallion back under his robe and lifted his hand, as if to unlock the door—or tear it off its hinges—with magic.

I caught his arm to stop him and raised my voice. "I'm also interested in getting a reading for my friend here. I know it's late, so we'll pay double." Maybe that would entice her more than the thought of being interrogated.

Whatever her response was, it was too muffled by the table and the door to hear. Zav gently but firmly removed my fingers from his arm and flicked a glance at the entrance. The lock turned and the door opened.

Bells on the bottom of the beaded curtain tinkled and clanked, stirred by the draft. Scents of old mildewy books and at least three conflicting kinds of incense wafted out, and my nostrils twitched. Hopefully, we wouldn't be inside long enough for my lungs to react negatively.

"I'm closed," came the muffled voice from under the table. "Closed for business. I have nothing that a dragon would want. Please don't eat me."

"I don't think dragons eat lesser species." I pushed the beads aside, holding them back for Zav in case he found them perplexing.

The woman who'd climbed a building and attacked me with her purse groaned piteously in Zav's presence. "His aura is so powerful it's giving me a migraine."

"And here it just makes me tingle."

I walked in first, glancing at a computer on a desk, the only modern object in a room full of knickknacks that might have been acquired on travels around the world or scrounged from a local flea market. Probably the latter. The desk under the computer was covered in decks of tarot cards, candles, and crystals of all colors. From a nearby window ledge, ash-choked incense burners assailed my nose with their pungent fragrances.

As I moved closer, a screensaver on the monitor almost made me trip. It was a logo of a newspaper with a dollar sign coming out of the pages with the name Intelli-Ads across the top. The name didn't ring a bell, but I'd seen that logo before. At Weber's house.

"Janice? Can you come out, please?" I tapped Intelli-Ads into my phone for an internet search.

She groaned again. Was it possible she was in genuine pain from Zav's presence?

"I'll happily pay for a psychic reading for my friend, but we can leave too if that's better. I just wanted to know if you've seen Dimitri lately. He's missing."

"Maybe one of the ogres traipsing in and out of that house of ill-repute ate him."

"It's a coffee shop, not a brothel. And don't ogres like their fortunes read? Maybe you could put up some new signage to lure them over here and thus capitalize on Dimitri's interesting new clientele."

"I already have magical beings for clientele. I don't need any ogres." Janice lowered her voice, as if speaking to herself, and whispered, "Or dragons. He's *so* powerful." There was a wince in her voice.

I would have asked if Zav was poking into her mind or doing something that could hurt her, but he was lurking near the doorway, scrutinizing several strands of hanging beads in his hand.

"I guess she's not reading your fortune," I said.

Zav lowered the beads and turned his attention onto Janice. She shrank lower under the table.

"She has not seen him," Zav said after a moment. "She believes that if he is missing, it is the work of a rival gang."

"You're reading her thoughts?"

"Your method of interrogation is ineffective." Zav squinted at the woman. "She is afraid of vampires and believes your friend is in league with them."

"I know that much." I read the web entry on Intelli-Ads. It was exactly what it sounded like, at least according to the website, an advertising platform that helped small businesses get the word out on local sites and social media pages.

"She genuinely believes that dragons eat people," Zav said. "Female mongrel, you are not appetizing to my kind."

"Even if dragons did eat people, all she would have to do is slather herself in breading to become unappealing." I looked at third-party review sites and found a few for Intelli-Ads. It was a newer company and the rates were deemed fair. There weren't any complaints on the Better Business Bureau website. When I looked up the owner of the domain name, I found the information locked behind a privacy wall. "Hm. Janice?"

Her head appeared as she slowly peeked out from behind the table.

"How did you get signed up for this business?" I asked her, though she was staring at Zav, who was blandly gazing back, appearing bored by everything happening here. "Intelli-Ads?"

"Answer her," Zav said.

His voice didn't ooze magical compulsion, but Janice answered promptly anyway.

"There were brochures. Months ago. Someone stuck them under my door. The brochure promised it could show my ads to the kinds of clients who would be interested in my services. Intelli-Ads has helped me find more people who believe in and can be helped by my psychic readings."

"Do you still have the brochure?"

"I don't think so."

"Do you pay online or in person?" My digging on the internet hadn't revealed an address or even a phone number. Shouldn't a business's website have both those things?

"It's all online. They withdraw money automatically every month. It's not that expensive, and it has brought in some new clients. Mostly, uhm." Her shoulders still were hunkered down at the level of the table, but she lifted her hand enough to wave at me.

"People with magical blood?" I guessed.

"Yeah. Halflings and quarterlings. People born on Earth, not the new full-bloods."

"You think an ad might have brought that vampire to your door?"

She scowled. "I didn't ask. I was too busy driving him away and protecting my daughter."

I wondered if that was hard to do while hiding behind a table. Maybe her maternal instincts had made her braver. Or maybe vampires weren't as fearsome as dragons. She was still eyeing Zav like she expected him to bite her head off at any second. I supposed I'd gotten used to his aura. He *did* radiate a lot of power, even when he stood there looking bored.

"Have you ever heard of longevity potions?" It was a long shot—she was a psychic, not an alchemist—but I was short on alchemists at the moment.

"No."

"Seen any more vampires since the attack?"

"No."

I sighed.

"Will you go now?" she whispered hopefully.

I looked at Zav.

"There is nothing else of importance in her mind," he said. "She is thinking of pelting you with crystals if she sees you again not in my company."

Janice blanched at this proof of mind-reading and sank below the table again.

"I've had worse thrown at me, though I was hoping to see Boomer in action." I waved at the softball bat she'd left on the table when she ducked under it, then took a picture of the screensaver and walked back outside with Zav.

A soft mist had started falling. If the rain picked up, it would make tracking by scent more difficult, though I didn't know if Sindari had found anything useful even before the weather turned damp.

*Sindari? Are you still around?*

He was at the very edge of my range. What had prompted him to wander so far?

*I believe I've pinpointed Dimitri's trail from this morning. He left the area on foot. You will have to join me if we wish to see where it goes, as I am as far from the charm as I can be without being knocked from this realm.*

*Any way to be certain he went somewhere interesting and wasn't walking to pick up breakfast burritos?*

*No.*

*We'll join you.*

It was the best lead I had.

# Chapter 20

The rain glistened on the tidy green grass in front of a Victorian house a half a block from Green Lake. A streetlight showed off the home's perky green siding with white and yellow trim, as well as a second-floor turret with a spire roof. The large windows of the turret looked to have a water view, and even though I leaned toward modern architecture, I had a wistful moment as I imagined living there. The Victorian style was about a thousand times better than brutalism.

A For Rent sign was staked near the sidewalk, and my first thought was that we'd followed Dimitri's trail all the way up here because he'd been checking out a potential place to live. But Dimitri was even less likely to be able to afford a house with a water view than I was. The fact that the sign didn't list the monthly rent was telling.

"I sense magic inside," Zav stated.

I did too. Not magical beings—the windows were dark and the house appeared vacant—but something in the basement was emanating power. Or maybe something built into the foundation itself? It was hard to imagine someone leaving magical artifacts behind after moving out.

*Dimitri went inside through a back door,* Sindari informed us from the other side of the house.

Zav and I were standing in the rain and looking at the place while Sindari ghosted around the perimeter, sniffing at the lawn, garden beds, and walkways. It was a larger than typical lot for the area, and fir trees along the sides made it private other than the open view out to the street and the lake.

*Did he come out?* I assumed he had, but what if he'd encountered a vampire inside and gotten himself killed?

The bleak thought made me wince. Dimitri never would have met Zoltan or gotten involved in this world if he hadn't met me. If he was dead, it would be my fault.

*I am trying to determine that.*

"Will we enter or stand here in the rain?" Zav asked.

"The rain that isn't getting you wet because your magic is keeping it from landing on your head?"

For the most part, he was keeping me dry too, but I'd learned that if I wandered more than a few feet away, I ended up out from under his magical umbrella.

"Yes. It is damp and unpleasant out here, despite this hemisphere of your planet being tilted closer to your sun at this time."

"Despite it being summer? Yeah, Seattle can be damp any time of year. It's a thing here."

"Dragons prefer hot climates."

"You should have claimed an equatorial female for your mate."

He gazed at me thoughtfully. "Yes."

"FYI, barbecue-ribs restaurants are in shorter supply near the equator."

"I will stay here."

"I thought so."

*I do not sense Dimitri inside,* Sindari told me, *but I also cannot smell evidence that he left.*

Dread filled me at the idea of sneaking in, only to find his body. *If he's dead on the floor in there, I'm going to murder whoever did it.*

*The trail is old, so it's possible that he left and retraced his route exactly. That would have made it difficult for me to tell if he'd come and gone.*

As I padded across the lawn and around the house, I hoped that Dimitri was the kind of unimaginative guy to walk home exactly the same way he'd come. Given that we'd come over a mile to get here and turned numerous times, I wasn't sure how likely that was. I braced myself to find a body—and to have to explain to Nin that we'd lost both of our business partners in the same week. Ugh, and my mother was in town too. She wouldn't be happy to hear about Dimitri's death. And damn it, I wouldn't like it either. We didn't have a lot in common, but he was a helpful guy and didn't deserve to get killed for trying to find a missing friend.

By the time I pushed through a side gate and into a back yard full of unkempt garden beds and a drained fountain, tears were threatening to film my eyes. I firmed my chin and blinked them away. We didn't know anything yet. It was too soon to mourn anyone.

"This is a vampire's lair," Zav said as we followed the walkway.

"The house?" I halted. "Is there a vampire in there now?"

I didn't sense anyone magical inside, but my senses had been fooled before.

Sindari was waiting in front of cement steps that led down to a sunken basement door, his fur glowing a faint silver in the misty night air. *A vampire was here but is not now. I would be able to smell him if he were present.*

"The lower level of that domicile is covered with remnants of his aura." Zav waved to the door, the one Sindari was waiting patiently to enter. "*Recent* remnants."

"Lovely." It occurred to me to pull out my phone and look up the address of the house before we barged into a trap. With Zav at my side, it was unlikely anything would be able to kill me, but doing research on the property first wouldn't hurt.

The house had a Zillow listing that showed it for rent for twenty-eight hundred dollars a month. That was a lot lower than I expected, given the location, the view, and the fact that it had six bedrooms and a turret. Maybe the basement vampire lair brought down the value. Vampires weren't mentioned in the listing, but the house had been for sale for years, with numerous price drops, before being turned into a rental.

"Sounds familiar," I muttered thinking of the McMansion sharing the lot with Zoltan's haunted carriage house.

"What?" Zav asked.

"Vampires bring down property values." Nothing more than rental listings came up for the address, so I returned my phone to my pocket. "Let's check it out."

The door wasn't locked. Zav and Sindari stepped into the basement ahead of me, and I felt well-protected. Poor Dimitri would have come alone. What clue had led him here?

The small, high windows were covered with boards, not that there was any light in the back yard that would have illuminated the basement. I flipped a switch by the door, the panel set between the studs in an unfinished wall. Nothing came on.

As Sindari and Zav padded into the darkness, I drew Chopper and whispered, "*Eravekt,*" choosing that over my night-vision charm. The blade flared with gentle blue light that illuminated the low ceiling, with knob-and-tube wiring strung between the wood beams. Not far from a laundry sink and an old washer and dryer squatted a black oil-burning furnace that wouldn't be out of place in an antique shop. Judging by the pipes and vents, it was still in use as the house's heat source.

"Getting insurance on this place must be fun," I muttered, surprised some building code hadn't required a renovation long ago.

*We've found the source of the magic,* Sindari told me.

I hurried around a corner and past old wooden stairs that led up to the main level and found Zav and Sindari standing in the middle of a mess. A wooden workbench had been upended, dumping everything from nails to mallets to books on the cement floor. There was a forge in one corner, metalworking tools dangling from bars around a bed of charcoal. A huge anvil on a metal pedestal bolted to the floor was the source of the magic I'd sensed. A few wheels and barrel hoops hung on the wall among swords and axes. None of the tools or weapons were magical.

"The rental listing didn't mention a basement blacksmithing shop," I said.

*A blacksmithing shop that saw a fight.* Sindari nosed something on the floor. A phone. *This belonged to Dimitri.*

My heart sank. He wouldn't have left his phone behind willingly.

When I picked it up, alerts for missed calls and texts—several from me—appeared on the front of the cracked screen. "Now I know why he didn't call me back."

A passcode prompt came up when I tried to get in, but it didn't matter. I doubted the answers were inside. The answers were... wherever he was. Unfortunately, not here.

I peered into the corner of the basement I hadn't yet seen and jumped. A coffin lay turned over on its side, the lid open to reveal a lush blue velvet interior and a pillow.

*The vampire must sleep there during the day,* Sindari said.

"Looks like he forgot to make his bed." I rubbed the back of my head. "So, what's the deal? Dimitri and this vampire got in a fight? Or Dimitri was visiting this vampire when someone else came in and picked a fight with both of them?"

That made more sense to me. If someone was kidnapping vampires, maybe Dimitri had been in the wrong place at the wrong time and had been caught alongside this fanged blacksmith. But whoever had done the kidnapping must have realized right away that Dimitri had warm skin. Why take him?

*If he was carried out, that would explain why I struggled to detect his departure trail,* Sindari said.

"Carried out and stuffed in a van? But why? Wouldn't they have left him and taken the vampire?" I had a headache and was trying to figure out how this tied in with Weber being attacked at the yacht club. What had that vampire with the hounds said? *You've made enemies of the wrong people.* "I think... I need to visit my employer tomorrow."

Weber had to know more than he'd let on so far.

"Your boyfriend?" Zav quirked an eyebrow.

"According to the society section, he is."

"Because human society is ignorant and cannot recognize a female marked as the mate of a dragon."

"Humans can't sense magic. You can't blame them for that. We mark our mates in other ways."

"How?" He scrutinized me.

I'd been about to explain hickeys but decided against it, lest he want to experiment. "T-shirts, remember? I haven't had a chance to shop for one though. Sorry."

"A shirt would show that you are claimed?"

"Yeah, the typical ones involve pictures of the snuggling couple making lovey eyes at each other, preferably surrounded by a pink heart."

"Where can we obtain these?"

"The guy who took your photo for that poster could tell you."

Zav nodded firmly. "Excellent. I will acquire this information from him."

Maybe I should have told him about hickeys.

My phone buzzed. I tugged it out, hoping it was Dimitri. Weber's number popped up. Apparently, the fact that it was after eleven wasn't a deterrent to calling one's bodyguard.

"Yeah?"

"Ms. Thorvald?" Ah, it was his executive assistant, not Weber himself.

"Yup."

"Mr. Weber is holding a small cocktail party at his house before the theater tomorrow. He wishes you to work for both events and arrive at noon to run the security inspection that I told you about when you were hired."

"I'll be there."

"I'll let him know. Thank you."

"What are you doing tomorrow, Zav?" I put my phone in my pocket.

"T-shirt shopping."

"How would you like to put that on hold and snoop around Weber's house instead?" I would have to figure out a way to keep Weber busy and prevent all the magical alarms from going off, so Zav could do it without being detected.

"I can do both."

"It must be nice to have such an open schedule."

"I do have more criminals to find, but *you* were unwilling to help me research their locations this week."

"True. We'll get back to it once we solve my more immediate problem." I eyed the spot on the floor where Sindari had found the phone. "And find Dimitri."

# Chapter 21

When my alarm buzzed at six, it took a Herculean effort of maturity not to hurl my phone across the room. It took a slightly less but still substantial effort not to hit the snooze button. But Willard had said she would be dropping Freysha off early, and I didn't want to be drooling on my pillow when they walked in. Besides, I was meeting Mom for breakfast at eight, reporting to Weber's at noon, and… was that Zav's aura up on the rooftop?

*What are you doing here so early?* I asked silently, though it was possible he was snoozing and not monitoring my thoughts.

*I slept here.*

*On my rooftop? In the rain?*

*Yes. I thought to return to the cave I have claimed on the outskirts of the city, but I wanted to be here when your esteemed guest arrives in case she requires anything.*

*My esteemed guest? Freysha?*

*Elven Princess Freysha.*

*I didn't realize you held elven royalty in such high regard, especially since it was a princess who, ah, tried to take advantage of your ardor.*

*It is important that she find the accommodations acceptable so that she will instruct you as only another elf can. Then you will be an even* more *formidable warrior.*

I sat up in my bed, feeling bad that he'd spent the night on the roof. And that he usually slept in a cave. Even if we weren't mates in the physical sense of the word, it seemed like I should at least offer him my couch. But if he was that close every night, with his alluring dragon aura oozing down my very short hallway, would he end up *staying* on the couch? We'd both agreed that we shouldn't have a physical relationship until I could protect myself, but as far as I knew, there weren't any other dragons on Earth right now. Even his pesky sister wasn't around. Would there truly be a danger to him if we hooked up?

*You are silent,* Zav commented. *You do not agree?*

*I was thinking that I'm glad you care and want me to get good training, even if I'm pretty sure Freysha has low standards when it comes to accommodations. Her people live in trees, and she hangs out with Gondo. I don't think goblins do laundry or wash their pits.*

*She is making do since she is a visitor to this world and has not revealed her status, but it is likely she is accustomed to some luxuries. If you had been inside the trees, you would know that elves have many amenities. They even have items similar to your heated water boxes. Flower petals float on the surface, so they can perfume themselves in natural scents.*

*I've got fizzy eucalyptus bath bombs under the sink. She can knock herself out.*

The doorbell rang, and I cursed and scrambled out of bed. I'd intended to be wearing clothes and have my hair and teeth brushed when they showed up. At least my sweatpants and rumpled T-shirt weren't scandalous. I had some sexy black teddies stuck in a bottom drawer, but as long as my mate was sleeping on the rooftop, there was little reason to dig them out.

Walking past the mirror revealed my hair—why had I slept with it in a braid?—doing an impersonation of a fizzy bath bomb. Fantastic.

I sensed Freysha before I got to the door, and a peek through the peephole revealed Willard in uniform carrying a canvas grocery bag with a colorful box tucked under one arm and... yes, she had her cat carrier with her. I'd hoped that had been a joke.

As I unlocked the deadbolts, Maggie meowed loudly and plaintively, doubtless already sensing Sindari's scent in my apartment. How long had Willard said she would be gone for her training? Three days? Five? How long was that in cat-sitting years?

Bracing myself, I opened the door and smiled. "Hey, guys. Come on in."

I extended a hand toward the interior, pleased that nothing was currently on the floor. It had been weeks since the last break-in. I doubted the magical community had forgotten about me, but maybe they'd collectively agreed to attack me in parking garages instead of at home.

"Hi, Val." Freysha lifted a potted fern she was carrying and nodded toward the ceiling. "Did you know there's a dragon on your roof?"

Freysha was going to be a perky morning person. I could already tell.

"Yeah, he likes to sleep on the deck chairs after he smashes them. It's like a bed of nails. Good for the circulation."

Her puzzled look suggested she didn't know if I was joking. I didn't know either.

"Thorvald." Willard walked in after Freysha, looking me up and down from frizzy hair to bare feet. "Nice pajamas."

"Before you mock me, remember that I've seen your Garfield slippers."

"My niece gave me those."

"What about all the cartoon mugs in your cupboard?"

"Mm."

Maggie yowled loudly. I already anticipated complaints from the neighbors.

"You're coming back soon, right?" I asked as Freysha peered around curiously at everything. "Because I'm not entirely sure pets are allowed in this building."

"You have a tiger," Willard said.

"He doesn't sleep here."

"His fur is all over your couch."

"He sits on it when I do my yoga videos." I waved to the television set where I'd been working my way through the course Mary had given me. She'd reluctantly agreed, after I'd almost gotten her favorite yoga studio blown up, that home videos were best for me.

"He watches?" Willard set the grocery bag—it turned out to be full of cat food—on the kitchen counter and the colorful box on the coffee table. It was a giant LEGO castle appropriate for, according to the front, ages seven to twelve.

"I summon him to stand guard in case bad guys want to take advantage of me being wrapped up in a pretzel on the floor with my legs behind my head."

"I'd think your dragon would be more likely to take advantage of that." It wasn't until Willard flashed a wicked grin that I realized that was a sex joke.

"It's hard for him to do that from the roof."

"You should invite him down sometime."

"I see you're still trying to play matchmaker."

"I haven't been to a good wedding in ages."

"Are the LEGOs for Freysha or Maggie?" I asked as Freysha wandered into the bathroom to look around. I hoped she didn't bring the plunger out and ask what it was for. If she was spending her days in Willard's office, she ought to know about human bathrooms.

"Freysha and Gondo."

"Gondo? He's not here, is he?" I hadn't sensed any goblins in the hallway, but I also hadn't tried to find any.

"Not now, but I'm sure he'll be by. They're practically twinsies."

"You told him where I live?"

"I hate to break it to you, Thorvald, but the entire magical community knows where you live."

"It's definitely time to move."

Maggie yowled. Freysha hurried out sans plunger and rested her hand on the door of the cat carrier.

"She's distressed because the apartment smells of predators." After a pause, Freysha added, "A specific predator that she's familiar with. I wouldn't think a mundane animal could sense a dragon from afar, but…"

"It's not Zav. She hates my magical tiger, Sindari. Have you met him?"

"I have not." Freysha opened the door to the cat carrier.

Willard blurted a startled curse and lunged to make sure the door to the hallway was fully closed. "She's an escape artist. That balcony door isn't open, is it? Or any windows without screens?"

"No," I said. "Even if all my enemies know where I live, I don't leave the entrances open in invitation."

Despite Willard's warning, Maggie did not try to escape. The brown-and-tan Siamese mix climbed out of her carrier and into Freysha's arms, and the yowls faded into soft mews of uncertainty. Freysha stroked her and murmured elven words. As Maggie settled, the mews also faded, and soon her tail swished against Freysha's arms, the movements appearing more contented than disturbed.

"I am letting her know I will protect her from the tiger," Freysha said.

"She speaks elven?" I asked.

"We communicate telepathically. Most animals do not have languages as complex as ours, but they have thoughts that are easy to understand with practice." Freysha smiled at me. "You can learn to do this too, Val."

"Read Maggie's mind? Let's make that Lesson Two." Or two hundred. I already had a good idea what Maggie was ranting about when she yowled. "And prioritize protecting my mind from being taken over by dragons."

"Certainly."

A car honked in the street outside, and Willard glanced at her watch. She crooked a finger and led me into the kitchen. Since it was open to the living/dining room, it wasn't truly private, but Freysha was busy crooning to the cat.

"There was another vampire attack last night," Willard said.

"Am I investigating it or not?" I thought of my full day's schedule.

"You're not officially on the case, but..." Willard spread her hand in a way that implied she wanted me to look into it. "A janitor that was working late was attacked."

"By a vampire in a ski mask?"

"Someone in a ski mask who tried to bite his neck. That's what he reported. He was cleaning for a dance studio up near Haller Lake. One of the instructors who was working late is missing."

"Haller Lake?" A chill went through me. "That's by Northgate."

"Yes. So?"

"My mom is staying up there." I dug out my phone and plugged in the address of her hotel. "It's just a few blocks from a dance studio." I showed Willard the map.

"That's the same one. I'm sure your mother is fine. So far, these have been targeted attacks on individuals. I wish I knew what the link was. Maybe there's not one, but why would a vampire hop all over North Seattle unless it was for carefully selected prey?"

"Did you go out to the car dealership yourself?" I switched to my camera roll and brought up the shot of the Intelli-Ads screensaver I'd taken the night before in the psychic's office.

"No. Sergeant Banderas went and took a bunch of pictures and poked around."

"Any chance he looked at their computer system and saw this?" I showed her the logo.

"He didn't mention it in his report, but send it to me. I'll check."

I texted her the photo, then called Mom at the number she'd used the night before, presumably the phone in her hotel room. It was a direct line, and she answered promptly.

"Are you up?" I wasn't sure why I asked when I knew she would be.

"At most hours of the night," she said dryly. "I was about to take Rocket for a walk."

Willard mouthed that she had to go, then pointed to Freysha and raised her eyebrows as if to ask if we would be all right. I gave her a thumbs-up, then waved her toward the door.

"Want to walk Rocket over to a dance studio to see if he can smell any vampires?" I asked.

"That's not our usual routine," Mom said, "but I can."

"Good. I'll meet you there."

"When we agreed to meet for breakfast, I was imagining Denny's, not a dance studio."

"Is their food healthy enough for you?"

"I make do when I travel."

"Help me sniff for vampires, and I'll take you to PCC afterward. Everything's organic. You can get eggs plopped out of chickens who've been blissfully roaming sun-drenched meadows dotted with wildflowers and clover."

"Is that on their sign?"

"It's implied."

"I accept your breakfast offering."

I gave her the dance studio address and told her not to go inside until I got there, then hurried to dress.

"Freysha," I said as I returned to the living room, "I've got to go check something out for Willard, and then go to work for my temporary boss. Why don't you settle in here and, uh, do whatever you like?" I waved to the television—did elves watch TV? "Keep the cat company. And your fern."

"I brought that from the park to help clean the air in your apartment." Her nose wrinkled. "Many human vehicles travel past outside. You may need more plants."

"I'm sure of it."

"They can also facilitate you learning magic."

"Potted plants can?"

"All plants. Elves use them as foci and inspiration."

I eyed the fern, not feeling overly inspired. Maggie had climbed out of Freysha's arms and was nibbling on one of the fronds, so maybe she felt differently.

"Call me if you need anything." I realized there wasn't a phone in the apartment and Freysha didn't have a cell phone. "Telepathically or whatever." I waved at my temple, though I had no idea what her range was.

"When do you wish to begin your training?"

"Right away, but I don't have time to start today." I headed for the door, knowing my mom was already on her way to the dance studio, but paused, feeling guilty about abandoning my guest minutes after her arrival. Should I invite her along? If she had magic, she could be useful, but based on what she was working on for Willard—checking translations on ancient tomes—I had suspected Freysha was more of an office type than a field agent. Did elves have offices?

"I will prepare lesson plans," Freysha told me, maybe sensing my reluctance to leave her. "And fix up your home so it will be healthier for those with elven blood."

"I hope that doesn't mean you're going to fill my fridge with wheatgrass."

Her blonde eyebrows drifted upward.

"Never mind. Thanks. I appreciate the help." I hesitated again. Was it wise to leave Freysha alone in my apartment? Willard must have decided she was all right—though her decision to let someone cat sit seemed to have more to do with their willingness to take on the task than having her absolute trust.

"Are you certain you do not wish to start your instruction now?" Freysha asked.

"There's no time. I was just… Look, don't take this the wrong way, but I got majorly burned by the last elf who befriended me, and even though my—uh, our—father vouched for you, I barely know him."

It took Freysha a moment to unravel my ramble. "You are concerned that I will betray you?"

"I've had a lot of people wanting to use me lately, and I don't know if I can trust you yet."

"That is understandable. We haven't spoken many times."

"Or gone into battle together. Once someone saves my ass from orcs, I'm more inclined to trust them."

Freysha touched her fingers to the soil of the potted fern. "I am not a warrior, and that is not how trust is formed for most people."

"No?"

She waved for me to come over. "For most, trust must be earned over time. Those I trust are those who have been there for me on small occasions over the years, who have taught me and cared for me and not betrayed confidences or asked me to act in a manner that upsets my values." She pointed for me to put my fingers in the soil on the other side of the fern.

"Is this an elven bonding thing?" Though skeptical, I touched my fingertips to the cool dirt.

"You can feel how the plant sprouts up from the rhizomes in the soil. Imagine that fronds are sprouting from the fertile matter of your brain, acting as a barrier to protect you from the elements—from anyone who wants to dive into your mind and steal your thoughts."

Oh, this was a magic lesson? I doubted I had time to learn anything, but I did my best to obey. Anyasha-sulin, liar that she'd been, had also used nature imagery in her brief instruction. That must mean it was the elven way, so I would have to learn to embrace ferns.

"Can you sense when someone is trying to alter your thoughts or read your mind?" Freysha asked.

"I think so. At least with the dragons, I've known they're doing it. I just couldn't stop them."

"For a dragon, you must place many more fronds between your mind and theirs."

I imagined thrusting some giant Jurassic fern in the face of the next Silverclaw Clan dragon that messed with me.

Freysha's eyebrow twitched, and I wondered if she was reading my thoughts.

"I am going to probe your mind," she said, "and I want you to draw on your power and the peace of the soil to place layers of fronds between us to keep me out."

"The peace of the soil?"

She smiled and tapped her fingertips on the dirt, letting them burrow in slightly. Then I sensed her mental probe, a tickle at the edges of my mind. It was a lot more subtle than anything the dragons had done, so I didn't get too alarmed. The urge to remove my fingers from the soil came over me, and I realized she was responsible for it.

I closed my eyes and envisioned the fern growing larger between us and acting as a barrier. And as goofy as it was, I tried to imagine the *peace of the soil* flowing up into my fingers to help.

A weird little tingle buzzed in the dirt, and I settled my fingers deeper instead of pulling them out. The tingle flowed up my arms and into my body, and somehow made it easier to wrap imaginary fronds around my mind and thrust Freysha's presence out. An unfamiliar calm settled inside of me, and I imagined this was what meditation felt like, for those who could actually do it.

"Good," Freysha said. "I will try again with more force."

I nodded infinitesimally, afraid speaking would break my concentration. This time, her probe felt like a wind battering at my mental fronds, trying to knock them apart or yank them from the soil of my mind. A tingle of magic or whatever this was flowed up my fingers from the real soil, lending me the strength to keep out the wind. Was she providing that magic or was I somehow tapping into it?

The wind faded, and when I opened my eyes, Freysha was smiling again.

"That was good. This will be easy for you to learn."

"It will?" I asked dubiously.

Wouldn't I have already figured out some magic if I had any natural aptitude?

"Dragons will be difficult to deny, but it should not take long for you to learn to keep less powerful species from influencing you. We will practice more when we have time. When you are ready, perhaps your mate will assist us." She lifted her gaze toward the ceiling.

My mate had been so quiet that I suspected he'd fallen back asleep. Either that or he was doing the dragon equivalent of playing games on his phone.

"Right. I've got to go."

"Wait." Freysha lifted a hand. "Take some soil with you."

"What?"

"In case you need to protect your mind. The soil is rich with *suylirana*—

plant matter—and in the beginning, that will help you focus." Freysha carefully scooped some off the top of the pot—hopefully, the fern wouldn't mind—and thrust her hand out to me.

I imagined sticking it in my pocket and dirt flying free when I tussled on the ground with some enemy. "Hang on."

Feeling silly, I retrieved a zip baggie from the kitchen and held it open. She deposited the soil inside, and I fastened the bag and stuck it in my pocket.

"You'll need to open it to touch the soil for it to work," Freysha said.

"Do elves carry pockets full of dirt around or are you messing with me?"

"Elves who are learning magic do. It is a training aid that you won't need later."

Though skeptical, I left the bagged dirt in my pocket as I headed for the door. If nothing else, I could throw it at an enemy's eyes in a tight skirmish.

*You've been quiet,* I thought toward Zav as I entered the hallway. I still sensed him on the rooftop. *Do you want to visit a dance studio and check for vampires?*

*I must leave you. Another dragon has come to Earth.*

I groaned. I knew it had been too peaceful on the dragon front. *Which one? Another old enemy?*

*He has not declared his intentions to me yet. He is being coy.*

Coy? That didn't sound like Shaygor, the irate father of the dragon I'd killed. *When you say he's on Earth, is there any chance he's visiting a mountain range in China instead of lurking anywhere close?*

*He is on the spire in your city.*

*The spire? The Space Needle?*

*Yes.*

I groaned again as I imagined a dragon perched atop the structure, his tail dangling down in front of the windows of the revolving restaurant. Hopefully, he was using his magic to hide himself.

*I will go confront him,* Zav said.

*Don't get hurt. And don't knock down that spire. It's a city landmark.*

*Fear not. I am not a heathen.*

Why didn't that reassure me?

# Chapter 22

Someone called while I was driving up to meet my mother, but traffic was a snarl, and I didn't recognize the number, so I let it drop to voice mail. Only when I pulled into the parking lot of the dance studio, a hexagonal building from the seventies that backed up to tree-filled wetlands, did I check the message.

"Val?" It was Dimitri's voice, a hoarse whisper. "Val, if you're there, now would be a really good time to answer." He sounded breathless and there was a long pause. "I need some help."

I thumped my fist on the steering wheel. Why hadn't I picked up?

"I'm locked up. This crazy scientist is going to use me for—"

Something clanked in the background, followed by a thump.

"For what?" I demanded as if he were still on the line.

The voice mail ended.

Swearing, I dialed the number. It rang and rang. I hung up and tried again. Nobody answered, and there was no voice mail.

"Damn it."

I ran an internet search on the number. Nothing. My only clue was that it was a Seattle area code. At least Dimitri hadn't been dragged off to another state or country. I glared at the phone, willing Dimitri to find a way to call again.

I was in the middle of texting Nin to see if Dimitri had tried her when claws clattered against my window. I almost dropped my phone. For a second, I thought a werewolf was about to tear me out of the seat, but those were golden-furred paws. A lolling tongue hung out of a familiar canine face behind them.

Mom appeared, snapping her fingers and pointing for Rocket to get down. He sat obediently beside her. As soon as I sent my message to Nin, I grabbed my weapons and got out.

"That's the face you wake up to every morning, huh?" I asked.

"It is. There haven't been others for a long time." She lifted a shoulder, her face wistful, but only for a moment before she said, "We've circled the building, and he picked up a suspicious trail in the back."

Eventually, I would tell her I'd met Eireth, but with Dimitri on my mind, all I did was wave for her to show me the trail. Though the idea of finding a lead outside a dance studio seemed like wishful thinking when Dimitri had called from inside a house—or a laboratory?—and mentioned a scientist. I feared I was barking up the wrong tree with this Intelli-Ads thing. But it was all I had.

"I don't have a way to know it was a vampire," Mom said as we left the parking lot and followed a trail through lilac bushes and rhododendrons to the back of the building, "but it agitated Rocket."

"Don't squirrels and raccoons also agitate him?"

"Not like this."

A text came back from Nin. *I have not heard from Dimitri. Please tell me if there is anything I can do to help.*

Rocket barked when he found the spot he liked and swirled around with his nose to the ground. There wasn't an obvious trail other than the one that had brought us around the building, but he wanted to head into the wetlands. A hint of a pond was visible through ferns, deciduous trees, and evergreens. Duck quacks were audible over neighborhood traffic noise.

I almost waved for him to lead us off, but we were close to a back entrance to the building and something amiss caught my eye. Simple wooden steps led up to a door that had been left open. There hadn't been any other cars in the parking lot, so I'd assumed the studio's classes either hadn't started yet or it was closed for the day because of the attack.

"Was that open before?" I pointed to it.

"Yes. Rocket wanted to go in, but I kept him out here."

I touched the feline charm on my thong necklace and summoned Sindari. Rocket backed up and barked suspiciously as silver mist appeared and the great tiger formed in it. But he'd met Sindari before and recovered quickly from this unorthodox appearance. He woofed and wagged his tail.

*Want to track something, Sindari?* I asked silently.

*Not that overly exuberant yellow canine, I trust?*

*No, I know where Rocket is. There was a vampire in the area last night. The dog might have the trail.*

Rocket dropped his forelegs to the ground and wagged more vigorously at Sindari.

*What is this canine doing?* Sindari asked.

I looked at Mom.

"Play bow," she said.

"And that's what?"

"An invitation to play."

"I don't think Sindari plays. He's regal."

"Is that another word for stuffy?"

Sindari squinted at her. *Please inform her that I gnaw the feet off those who insult me.*

"He says yes." I patted Sindari on the back.

He gave me a dark look.

Rocket, perhaps realizing his new companion wouldn't frolic with him, returned to snuffling at the ground.

"Take Sindari and start checking out the trail, please. He'll help if you find any trouble." I doubted they would in this little pocket of nature. There was a busy street on the other side of the pond, and people's yards hemmed it in on the ends. Still, I didn't want to take chances. "I'm going to take a quick peek inside, and then I'll catch up."

*I smell a vampire.* Sindari was examining the ground—more regally than the exuberant Rocket.

*Good. You can compare notes with the dog.*

Sindari eyed the loudly snuffling golden retriever.

*My people do not have a written form of our language. I suspect his don't either.*

*Probably not.* I waved for Sindari to go with Mom and Rocket, then climbed the stairs.

It was dim inside, the copious trees on the property keeping even the large windows out front from letting in a lot of light. This door led into a short back hallway with offices open to either side. I drew Chopper. Willard's people, and probably the police, should have already investigated, so I doubted anyone would jump out at me, but better ready than not.

I found the spot where the janitor had been attacked. An upended coat rack lay on its side, and spatters of blood had dried on the polished wood floorboards. The dance studio itself was open and offered few clues, so I returned to the offices. They were filled with boxes and exercise equipment, desks here and there hunkering between the stacks. Computers rested on the desks, so it didn't look like the open door represented a robbery. Maybe someone had forgotten to lock it, and the wind had blown it open.

I checked the computers, by now expecting evidence of Intelli-Ads. One was turned off, but the other came alive at the wave of the mouse. I checked the browser tabs and found one open to the Intelli-Ads website, a reporting dashboard that showed ad clicks and how much the dance firm had spent that week. Before I got a good look, the website reloaded, and a prompt came up for a password.

"Figures." I poked in the drawers and peered around the computer. A yellow note was stuck under the keyboard. *6969titties*. "Classy."

When I typed it in, access returned. I poked through the website's dashboard, but nothing looked fishy to my non-expert eye. The studio was spending a couple hundred a month on ads and had another open file with a list of leads they'd gained from their landing page.

As I walked out of the building, I called the person I probably should have contacted first about the company.

"Hey, Val," Thad answered. "Everything okay?"

"Not exactly. Two friends have been kidnapped and I'm at a dead end. Do you know anything about an internet advertising company called Intelli-Ads?"

"Who is it?" a woman's voice sounded in the background. That sounded like Shauna. Didn't she ever leave him alone? Like to go to work and be a productive member of society?

I resisted the urge to tell Thad he should have an office somewhere instead of working from home but winced when he told her it was me. Thad wasn't much for lying, but a fib now might have saved him a lecture later. Maybe I should have texted instead of calling.

"I haven't heard of them," he said, "but I can look them up and ask around. You think an internet company would be tied to kidnappings?"

"This one is tied to something. Why, are software developers too elite and sophisticated to be involved in such things?"

"Too puny to throw people over our shoulders. Have you seen my arms lately? I haven't been working out much."

"Ha ha. What do you know about Bernard Weber?"

"That he sold his cybernetics business for a ridiculously overpriced valuation and has since started several internet businesses that have bombed." Thad sniffed. "I don't think he writes any of his own code."

"Is that what passes for an insult in your world?"

"You couldn't tell?"

"I wasn't sure. Any chance he'd have anything to do with Intelli-Ads? Either as a client or as the creator? I saw its logo in his office when I was at his house."

"You were at his *house*?" Thad sounded affronted.

"I'm his bodyguard currently."

"I... don't know what to say to that."

"He's irked people in the magical community." I gazed out into the trees, not seeing Mom, but I sensed Sindari on the other side of the pond. "Defending against irked magical beings is my specialty."

"I'll see if I can dig up anything for you."

"You're doing her a *favor*?" came Shauna's voice—she was probably hovering right by his shoulder.

"Hi, Shauna!" I said with false but loud cheer. "How are you doing? Did you like the cupcakes?"

That earned a haughty sniff and silence.

"I'll text you if I find anything," Thad said dryly.

"Thanks. Bye."

I trotted into the wetlands to catch up with Mom, Sindari, and Rocket. Even though it was August, the earth was muddy around the edges of the pond, and I almost lost my boot to a quagmire hidden by leaves and cattail fluff.

*Were you expecting to find a body out here?* Sindari asked as I drew close enough to see him and Mom looking down at something.

*No.* I remembered Willard mentioning a missing man.

"Val?" Mom peered through the trees at me. "There's a dead man here. With a message."

I puzzled over that until I reached them. Mom was standing back, Rocket's leash on now to keep him from getting too close to the body in the mud. He'd been a twenty-something guy and wore a T-shirt promoting the dance studio. A knife in the chest had taken him down, and there was a note pinned to it. It wasn't a bone knife like the one dark elves had left in my apartment, but this reminded me of that scene. A deadly version of that scene.

Assuming that neither the police nor Willard's people had found this guy, I took a few pictures for them before inching close enough to peel back the paper. It was soggy and limp, and I assumed it and the body had spent the night out here.

*This is the fate of those who deal with Intelli-Ads. Support them and die.*
It wasn't signed.

"Do the tracks smell of vampire?" I waved at two sets of prints in the mud.

Mom spread her hand. "Rocket can't tell me *what* he's tracking, but it's the same suspicious thing that had him agitated by the door."

*The vampire's scent is here along with the man's,* Sindari told me. *No other people have been in the area recently.*

"Where did the vampire go after killing the guy?"

"Out into the water," Mom said. "I'll circle the pond with Rocket and see if we can pick up where he came out."

Sindari also padded off, sniffing the ground and the air liberally.

I stared bleakly at the body, jerking when a thought occurred to me. I called Nin.

"Do you have news on Dimitri?" she asked, concern in her voice.

I didn't want her to worry more than she already was, so I didn't tell her about the phone message he'd left, the message I was kicking myself over since I could have picked up and hadn't. "Not yet, but do you know by chance if he was using a service called Intelli-Ads to promote his yard art? Or the new business?"

"He did not mention it. It would have been premature to promote the coffee shop, but it is possible he was trying to sell some of his yard-art creations online. I know he had Zoltan helping him record videos for the socials."

I shook my head, reminded that Zoltan was also in trouble. Were he and Dimitri in the same place? I'd assumed Dimitri had only been kidnapped because he'd been in the wrong place at the wrong time for his investigation, but now I wondered if he'd been targeted specifically.

"You haven't heard of the ad company, have you?" I asked.

"It sounds familiar. Maybe I have seen a brochure. I will search around and also ask my contacts."

"Good. Thank you."

The more people hunting for information on this company, the more likely I would figure this out.

One thing I knew for sure was that I was going to question Weber this afternoon and find out everything he knew. If he was a target himself, I would learn about it. If he was involved with whoever was behind this... I would learn about that too. I hoped Zav would finish up with the other dragon in time to help me, but one way or another, I was going to get to the bottom of this.

# Chapter 23

Sindari sat in the back of the Jeep with his head out the window as we rolled into Laurelhurst. I'd taken Mom to eat—her appetite had been muted after finding a body, but Rocket had helped himself to her scrambled eggs—and dropped her off at her conference. I was going to arrive early at Weber's, but that was fine. I was eager to have a chat with him.

*I smell orcs,* Sindari announced.

"*Here?*" I threw on the brakes. "In Laurelhurst?"

*Is this neighborhood supposed to be orc-free?*

"Well, I'm sure they can't afford the property taxes." I stretched out with my senses as I peered into the large yards. "I don't sense anything."

*I also do not sense magical beings, but I sense an artifact or something else magical. Continue forward.*

As I followed the road around a bend, the first inkling of what Sindari had mentioned tickled my senses. As he'd said, a magical artifact, not a person. But it was on the move. We weren't far from Weber's house. Maybe someone had made off with one of his security devices.

*Turn right.* Sindari had his nose out the window, nostrils quivering as he sampled the air.

I obeyed, though it would take us off the route to Weber's house. Maybe I wouldn't be early after all.

The new road curved left and right, meandering around the hilly topography toward the water. The aura of the magical artifact grew stronger until it was almost dead ahead.

As we rounded another bend, four cloaked and hooded figures came into view like ringwraiths out of *Lord of the Rings*, except that they weren't half-obscured by mist on a dark night. It was a sunny day, and the big figures threw shadows as they crept off of a perfectly manicured yard and crossed the road toward a wooded area that sloped steeply downhill toward Lake Washington. They were carrying a heavy iron box, one gripping each corner. It was the source of the magical aura.

When I sped up, they glanced at me. Despite the hoods, I glimpsed beady dark eyes, a hint of blue-tinted skin, and short snouts with tusks. Orcs, not ringwraiths, though it was strange that I didn't sense them. They appeared to be full-blooded, so they should have had substantial auras.

One orc's cloak opened enough to show a sword in a belt scabbard, its hilt glowing green. There was no way I shouldn't have sensed a magical blade, but the box continued to be the only thing I felt. Either these guys were wearing camouflaging charms of some sort, or the magic of the box drowned out everything around it.

The orcs hurried up when they saw me, though the heavy box slowed them down. I couldn't imagine how much an iron chest would have to weigh to slow down burly seven-foot-tall orcs. As they hopped the curb to head into the woods, one dropped his corner of the box, and it struck the cement. The orc closest to him punched him and yelled.

I sped up, intending to catch up to them and have a chat. They were heading vaguely in the direction of Weber's house, not away from it, so they hadn't stolen this from him, but whatever they were up to, it looked shady. They recovered the chest and hustled between the trees, maneuvering down the steep slope.

*Careful,* Sindari warned as I braked beside the road. *They have magic, even if we can't sense them. I think they've used a spell to camouflage their magic.*

"Why wouldn't they have hidden themselves from sight as well as magical sense?" I parked, grabbed my weapons, and got out.

*I don't know.*

"And why wouldn't they be hiding the box too?"

*Whatever is in that chest may be so significant that we're sensing it through their spell.*

"Maybe they just don't care about cloaking it. Get around front of the group and see if you can delay them so I can catch up."

Sindari let himself out and bounded down the hill first. As I rushed after him, a flash of light came from the trees. It was bright enough to sting my eyes even on the bright day, and I winced and held my hand up. When it faded, the orcs and the chest were gone.

Sindari had almost been to the group, but he faltered, sniffing at the air. I could see the lake through the trees, sun glinting off the gentle waves, and also the rooftops of the waterfront houses at the bottom of the slope. Nothing stirred in the woods.

Guided by his nose, Sindari angled off to the side, cutting across the hill instead of continuing down it. I jogged after him, ivy hiding roots that threatened to trip me. I'd almost caught up with him when he spun toward me.

*Look out!*

I tore Chopper from its scabbard and sprang to the side. Instincts warned me of the right direction more than any sound or sense, but at the last second, the orc charged close enough that I saw through whatever magic hid him. It was the one with the green glowing sword, the blade now bared as it flashed toward my head.

I parried and also scrambled away from him, certain the big orc would mow me down if all I did was block the blow. Metal screeched as our swords met, Chopper flaring blue to match the green of the enemy blade. The jarring power of the strike almost knocked my weapon from my grip.

With startling agility, the orc whirled to attack again, launching a series of feints and serious thrusts that had me skittering backward. The uneven ivy-covered terrain added to the difficulty level, but that wasn't the only problem. Right away, I realized this was a powerful and skilled opponent, far better trained than most orcs I'd met.

As soon as I found my balance and managed to push back with a series of attacks of my own, he snarled a word in his language, and invisible power slammed into my chest like a locomotive.

It hurled me ten feet up the slope, and I crashed into a tree, my head striking the trunk hard enough that I saw stars. The orc rushed after me, but Sindari flew up the slope and launched himself into the air. He landed on our enemy's broad shoulders, taking him down.

As I scrambled to my feet, blinking away dizzying dots floating through my vision, they rolled on the ground, both roaring, both attacking each other. Sindari bit and clawed while the orc punched and also bit, his tusks as dangerous as a tiger's fangs. He hurled Sindari back as I was charging down to help. Before I reached them, the orc rose to one knee and slashed with that wicked green blade. Sindari twisted away, quick enough to avoid the brunt of the blow, but the tip scoured his flank, and blood flew.

I sliced Chopper at the back of the orc's neck while he was distracted, but he sensed the attack and rolled to the side. My blade sliced uselessly through the air.

The orc leaped to his feet, his hood now down around his shoulders, revealing beads made from rocks in his long white braids and swirling black tattoos on his cheeks and forehead. He spat a string of guttural words at me, but I couldn't take the time to tap my translation charm.

Waiting for Sindari to get back to his feet, I advanced slowly, carefully. With his blade up and ready, the orc backed up so he could keep both of us in his sight. He glanced down the hill. I tensed, expecting more orcs to charge out of their invisibility shroud, but the woods remained quiet in that direction. Maybe he was trying to buy time. Making sure his allies could get away with their prize? The chest's aura had faded, but I could still sense it. Now, it was closer to the waterfront houses.

*Attack together,* Sindari ordered.

We split up, trying to flank the orc, and rushed at him at the same time. His free hand dipped under his cloak, and he flicked something at me before he spun to face Sindari.

No larger than an eraser, the projectile was hard to track. I thought about whipping up Chopper to knock it out of the air, but some instinct warned me that would be a bad idea, so I dove to the side instead.

The projectile clipped the branch of a tree behind me and blew up like a grenade. The tree blew up with it, and even as I was rolling away, using the hill to roll faster, branches and chunks of wood slammed into me with the force of cannonballs. One struck my already bruised skull and smaller pieces bounced off the ground and hit my mouth and cheeks. One almost took my eye out.

"I'm really starting to hate this guy." I shoved myself to my feet as branches and twigs rained down all around me.

## False Security

The orc was battling Sindari, matching fang with his sword, and my ally bled from a dozen gashes in his silver hide. Even though Chopper was a more powerful magical weapon, I was tired of getting close to the cursed orc. I yanked out Fezzik and fired over Sindari's head.

Bullets slammed into the orc's shoulder and neck. The ones that hit his shoulder bounced away, some armor under his tunic deflecting them, but one plunged deep into his neck.

The orc snarled and faced me as blood poured from his flesh. I fired again, hoping to take him in the eye. This time, he managed to get a magical barrier up, and the bullet that should have dove into his skull bounced into a nearby tree.

Damn it, was he an orc or a *dragon*?

While our enemy was busy blocking my bullets, Sindari charged to his side and sank his fangs deep. Ribs crunched, the sound audible even down the hill.

The orc flipped his sword in his hand, trying to drive it down into Sindari's skull. Sindari let go and leaped away, receiving only a glancing blow. I opened fire again. Another bullet slammed into the orc, striking him above the ear, before he got his magical defenses back up.

He snarled, saliva glistening on his tusks, and stepped toward me, but his knee gave in, and his legs buckled. Maybe his bullet-punctured body had realized it was spewing blood.

Sindari lunged in from behind him, jaws aiming for his neck. The orc still had the strength to wield his glowing blade and deflect the attack. Sindari only managed to land a swipe of his claws before backing away, just avoiding another cut from the sword.

Bleeding from several wounds, the orc pitched forward, one hand dropping to the ground, though he kept the sword up. He didn't want to accept yet that he was defeated, but unless his buddies showed back up, it seemed inevitable.

He threw something into his mouth. Not another eraser-sized grenade, I hoped. Would he blow his own head off to avoid being captured? And if so, *why*?

I'd been thinking of walking up, pressing Chopper to his throat, and questioning him, but I stayed back and aimed Fezzik at his eyes. "What are you people up to?"

I touched my translation charm. The orc sneered and clenched his jaw. He didn't speak. It took me a moment to realize he'd bit down on something—the item he'd thrown into his mouth.

"What was in the chest?" I tried, hoping to get something from him.

"I die with honor," he said in his own tongue. "For the clan."

"Can't you do that after you answer a few questions? I don't suppose you know anything about Intelli-Ads?"

His beady eyes rolled back in his head, and he toppled the rest of the way to the ground. His body convulsed, as if he was having a seizure. Belatedly, I realized he *was* having a seizure. One that he wouldn't recover from. When the orc stopped convulsing, he was dead.

I slumped down in the ivy, wanting to go home and sink my battered body into a hot bath. Unfortunately, I still had to report to Weber for the day's work. And find out if that chest had been delivered to his house or if someone else along the waterfront was ordering magical artifacts.

*Those tattoos mark him as from the Way Rovers,* Sindari informed me.

*What does that mean?*

*It is a clan of outcasts and loners who band together and watch out for each other. They are like your highwaymen, but much more powerful. They train obsessively with weapons and magic, and they are capable of creating portals and traveling from world to world.*

I thought about pointing out that highwaymen were a thing of the past here, but that didn't matter. What mattered was that roving orcs who had the power to come and go were here on Earth. *So, they're not refugees?*

*Likely not. Since they are known to be bandits and burglars, we can assume that chest was stolen.*

*Stolen from whom?*

*I do not know.* Sindari sat beside me, alternately looking down the hill—probably making sure the other three orcs weren't sneaking up on us—and eyeing our fallen opponent. *I regret informing you that orcs were in the area.*

*Why? I like to know when orcs are about.* I said that, but I was inclined to agree that our battle had been pointless. If these had been delivery guys bringing Weber another artifact, I would feel stupid for having picked a fight with them. But if Weber was knowingly ordering stolen goods from other worlds, I could end up in a lot of trouble for standing at his side. Why would he do that? Did he think his home's defenses were so good that he could act with impunity? Or that his money would *buy* him impunity?

*Do these Way Rovers typically kill themselves instead of answering questions?* I asked.

*Actually, yes. They have a lot of notions about dying to protect their brethren and not betraying the clan.*

*Hm. Can you tell where the chest is now?*

*I no longer sense it.*

Neither did I. *Think you can follow the orcs' trail? Not the magical one but their footprints or scent or whatever.*

Sindari rose to his feet. *I will try.*

His tone wasn't enthusiastic, and as he walked slowly down the hill, blood dripped from his wounds. I vowed to send him back to his realm right after this.

*We won't get close enough to fight them,* I told him. *I just want to know if they went where I think they went.*

I followed Sindari as he traversed the hill sideways, different roofs coming into view below. We were getting close to Weber's house.

*Val?* Zav spoke into my mind.

*Yes?* I couldn't sense him. Was he still communing with another dragon at the Space Needle?

*There are now three dragons besides myself in the area.*

*Ugh, why?*

*They are looking for something. The coy dragon—he is from the Starsinger Clan—admitted that much and told me this world will be in grave trouble if they don't find what they're looking for.*

*It's not something that would be stored in a big iron box, is it?*

*I do not know. Are you in any trouble right now?* Zav asked. *None of the dragons here are allies to me. If you do not need me, I will return to my home world and ask my mother if she knows what's going on.*

I touched a sore knot rising on the back of my head. Should I tell Zav what had happened? If he could get intel from his family, I would sure like it.

*I'm on my way to work and had a squabble with some Way Rover orcs carrying a magical chest. I'm okay for now, but I have a hunch there might be trouble later. Like when I wrung Weber's neck and demanded to know why he was buying stolen artifacts and what he knew about Intelli-Ads.*

*Do you know where the chest is now?*

*It's disappeared from Sindari's and my senses.*

*I will go quickly to check with my mother and return soon. It is likely she knows what's going on. Unless you fear you are in danger?*

*Not at this moment.* Right now, I wanted information more than I wanted a bodyguard.

*Are you sure? So far, none of these dragons seem interested in finding you, but it is always my concern that one will target you to get to me.*

*You said they're not enemies of yours, right?*

*They're not allies either. They are all from the Starsinger Clan.*

The same clan as the weirdo who had chatted me up—and then some—in the elven forest. I didn't want to run into him again, but he hadn't seemed that dangerous, at least not to me.

*I'll be okay for a few hours.* I hoped I wouldn't regret telling him that. *Go find out why my world has been invaded by dragons, please.*

*Very well. Do not irk anyone when I am not there to see it.*

*I can't make that promise.*

As Zav's presence faded from my mind, Sindari walked out onto a precipice overlooking the lake. I shuffled out and joined him. We gazed down at Weber's side yard, his lawn as immaculate as it had been two days earlier. I didn't *see* any orcs, but that didn't mean much.

"Let me guess. That's where their trail leads."

*Yes.*

# Chapter 24

The gate opened automatically for me when I drove into Weber's driveway. Sindari was sitting in the back of the Jeep, even though I'd suggested he return to his realm to rest and recover. He admitted that his injuries were significant, and he wouldn't be able to stay long, but he didn't want to leave me when there were orcs and dragons about.

*There are always orcs and dragons about these days,* I told him.

*Yes, but we've just freshly annoyed some.*

*Orcs, not dragons, unless you know something I don't.*

*Just that dragons are inordinately drawn to you.*

I hoped that wasn't the case today, since I'd sent Zav away. I hadn't told Sindari about the dragon that had hit on me in Elf Land. Admittedly, that one had seemed more interested in annoying someone from the Stormforge Clan rather than in me personally. He hadn't even come close enough to look at me.

*I will investigate the property and try to tell if those orcs did indeed come to this house and where they are now.*

*Don't confront any more of them.* Battling one had nearly gotten us killed. I hated the thought of challenging the remaining three at once—especially if they blamed us for killing their buddy.

*I will move stealthily and confront not even a mouse with an attitude.*

*Excellent plan.*

After parking next to a catering truck, I stepped out, wincing at what was turning into a splitting headache. As I climbed the steps to the door, I willed my injuries to heal quickly.

The door opened before I rang the bell.

"Val!" Weber smiled, lifting his arms as if he might hug me, but he stopped himself, frowning at my face and then up at my hair. "Did you get in a fight?"

"It's been a rough couple of days."

"There's moss in your hair."

"It's a new trend. Back to nature, you know. Can we talk? About Intelli-Ads?" I watched his face for a reaction.

"Sure. I used them to find magical beings to test my app's ability to track. Want to come to my office? Or, uh, my first-aid room?"

Damn, how bad did I look? My lip was starting to puff up, and my eye felt swollen. I bet he wouldn't want me to play the role of his girlfriend this evening. "You have a first-aid room?"

"Technically, it's one of the guest bathrooms, but there's a first-aid kit in it. And mosquito repellent."

"How about orc repellent?" I asked, testing him again for a response.

He didn't react and only said, "That didn't come in the kit."

Was it possible the orcs *hadn't* come here? Could another waterfront-living homeowner be collecting valuables from the magical community? Maybe it was like Christmas lights, and Weber had inadvertently started a competition for the best display.

"Everything okay here?" I followed him down the wide hallway toward his office. "You seemed happier to see me than usual."

"I just want to know the house and my guests are well protected for my little party this afternoon. Most of them will be potential investors. I wouldn't want vampires or werewolves to storm the premises and attack anyone who's eager to give me money."

"Vampires don't do a lot of storming when the sun is out. And don't you have a ton of security?" I already knew the answer to that was yes, but I kept hoping to get more information out of him. "I remember the dragon alarms going off."

"Yes. Alarms go off for all of those with magical blood who come onto the property. You twang a few of them." Weber quirked his eyebrows as he looked over his shoulder.

"I'm half elven."

"I figured it was something like that. You're not obnoxious enough to be a dragon." He smiled.

Why did I have the sense that he was buttering me up? Maybe he expected trouble at this cocktail party and wanted to make sure I was ready to defend him with my life.

"You've met a lot of dragons, have you?"

"Actually, that black one was my first. I hadn't realized they ever came to Earth."

I thought about telling him that Zav was mellow compared to a lot of dragons, but I was distracted when he led me past the office, through a butler's kitchen, and into a big room without windows. It was full of television screens showing security footage from around the grounds. Numerous trinkets sitting on computer cases hummed with magical power. The hodgepodge included a glowing golden chalice, a silver tuning fork, a blood-red dagger, and no fewer than ten blue and purple geodes.

The mishmash of power signatures clashed and battered at my senses, increasing my already existing headache to an extent that I tried throwing a few mental fern fronds up around my mind as a barrier. Surprisingly, it worked, and the throbbing faded. I thought about opening the baggie in my pocket and fondling some dirt, but I didn't want to explain that to Weber. Besides, I might need that dirt for something more important later.

"Nice collection," I said. "Where'd you get it all?"

"Fernandez."

"Uh, Fernandez?"

"He's my personal shopper."

My first thought was of some grocery driver loading up on toilet paper and asparagus to deliver to his house. The expression on my face must have shown my confusion, because Weber clarified.

"Fernandez goes to auctions and bids on things I might like. In the past, it was antiques in my areas of interest, but after I started receiving death threats, I spoke to him and found out he went to special types of auctions where magical items came up for sale. I gave him close to unlimited funds to gather things to protect my modest home."

Modest, right. A modest ten thousand square feet.

"We've got an hour until the guests start arriving." Weber pointed me toward the trinkets and a chair at a desk looking at the wall of screens. "I'd like you to survey my setup and make sure it's complete and that there aren't any gaps in the perimeter. Also, if any of the artifacts that attack unwelcome guests—you saw those outside when the dragon showed up—could be enhanced to work better, I'd like that to happen. I'm mostly worried about vampires and werewolves, but I'd prefer dragons not get in either. I trust you didn't invite yours to the party today."

"I don't invite him anywhere. He just shows up."

Weber's lips flattened in displeasure.

"He's busy with something else and isn't on Earth right now."

"Good."

"I can take a look at things here, but I don't know anything about enhancing artifacts." I almost pointed out that I had a missing friend who might be able to help and asked Weber if he knew anything about all the kidnappings going on, but it sounded like he was another client of Intelli-Ads, not the guy running the company. Even if my instincts told me not to trust him, he was about to give me access to his entire security system. This could be an easier way to find out tons of stuff about him than by asking questions that would make him suspicious.

"But you know more than I do. I assume you have some innate magic beyond your weapons and charms."

"Some." I didn't go into detail on the fern fronds.

"Good."

"Is your dog here?" I hadn't heard the barking from the upstairs room, and I abruptly worried that the pooch might be out where he would detect and yap at Sindari.

"I took him to the doggie day spa so he wouldn't be here to snap at any of my guests."

A doggie day spa? Who knew such things existed?

Weber tilted his head. "Why do you ask?"

"I'm cat-sitting for my boss, and there's fur all over me. I didn't want to get attacked."

He looked me up and down, hopefully not noticing the lack of fur on me. Freysha, I was sure, was covered, but I hadn't yet interacted with Maggie.

"Never mind." I waved dismissively. "I'll get to work."

He nodded—was he suspicious of me? I couldn't tell.

"I need to direct the caterers and set up a few things." He pointed me toward the monitors. "Holler if you need anything."

*Sindari,* I asked as soon as I was alone, *how are you doing?*

I poked at the computer on the desk, figuring out how to cycle through the displays and bring up different views as well as recordings from the past.

*The orcs were here.*

*Are they* still *here?*

*I do not sense them. They may have made a portal and left. I'm assuming they first delivered that chest, and I am trying to locate a hidden dwelling or entrance. I have already searched all around the house itself. But their scent is muddled, so it's possible I'm missing something. They used obfuscating magic to make it hard to pinpoint their tracks.*

*Forget the orcs. Just sniff around for scents that might have been left by others, anyone who isn't Weber or his lawn mower. I assume there have been other deliveries.* I eyed the geodes. *The guy has been stocking up.*

*That's a good idea. I'm surprised I didn't think of it.*

*You're injured.*

*Yes. And I'm growing weaker from my wounds. I want to stay and help you solve the mystery, but the pull for me to return to my realm is growing stronger. I wish to find where they went before I leave.*

*If you have to go, I understand.*

While he searched, I cycled through the cameras and poked around at the software. A row of displays came up all black save for a label of *Level Z* on the bottoms of the screens. No amount of poking convinced the displays to show up as anything but black. I couldn't tell if it was because cameras were recording dark rooms or if they weren't online.

"Should've brought Thad." How surprised he would have been to be invited on one of my missions.

*I've followed a trail to what may be a cleverly concealed doorway in the grass,* Sindari informed me.

*Whose trail? And where?* I envisioned the expanse of lawn outside and grimaced at the idea of trying to find a hidden door.

*Kobolds. Their scent is faint, but they were here yesterday.*

*Delivering some magical gizmo purchased by Fernandez?*

*I do not know what a Fernandez is, but it's possible they delivered something. Either that or they came and had a picnic on this particular piece of grass and then left.*

I could sense that Sindari was on the back side of the house not far from the dock. *There's probably a nice view from there.*

*I am observing a duck pooping on the bank.*

*For a tiger, that's a nice view, right?*

*I've had worse. I can't tell for certain that there's a door, but the grass is slightly worn down. There is a faint trail to this spot, and it doesn't go beyond it.*

I cycled through the outdoor cameras but didn't see Sindari. *Are you sure? Is it hollow if you thump it? You'd think he would want a camera on a secret door.*

*It is not hollow. But it's possible the door is thick.*

Stay there. I'll come take a look.

*I must return to my realm soon. My grasp here is tenuous.*

*I'll be right there.* Or so I thought. As I got up and headed for the door, Weber walked in, changed out of the khaki shorts and T-shirt he'd been in earlier to a suit that looked far too warm for the summer day.

His eyebrows rose. Apparently, he'd expected to find me with my nose to the computer or rearranging his artifacts for maximum effectiveness.

"I wanted to ask you about Level Z." I pointed my thumb toward the black screens. "Is that something I need to worry about protecting?"

"No. I set up Level Z when I installed the rest of the system, but I haven't built the basement yet. I'm planning to dig it out and put in a big workshop. I got distracted with this other project."

"Ah." I thought of Sindari's hidden door. A hidden door to a Level Z that *had* been installed already?

"The guests will start arriving soon. Have you learned anything to help improve security?" He looked toward the undisturbed artifacts.

"The house looks well protected from beings with minor powers. Like kobolds." I watched his face to see if he would react, but he was a cool cucumber. Nothing confirmed that he knew anything about kobold deliveries—or picnics—to specific points on his lawn. "Stronger beings will be able to break through the perimeter protection. No offense to you and your antiques scout, but geodes are pretty hokey when it comes to holding power. Dark elves or strong werewolves would be able to push through, especially on the side that lines that slope of trees."

That was where I figured the orcs had come in. I hoped he didn't ask for anything more specific because I had no idea what most of the artifacts did. Nin had once mentioned geodes being poor containers for power, and that was the only reason I knew I wasn't lying about them.

"I see. Perhaps I can acquire better hardware in the future." He gazed at me—trying to tell if I was being honest with him?

The urge to shove him up against the wall and question him came over me, but this was a guy with enough money and influence to make it hard for me to ever get a job in this town again. And I still didn't know if we were on opposing sides. Was he up to something? Or was he himself a victim?

He dropped a hand to his pocket. Remembering that he'd carried a gun the other night, I tensed. But he drew out an envelope instead of a weapon and handed it to me.

"Money?" I asked.

"Combat bonus for the other night. Five thousand dollars." He smiled faintly. "Just under five hundred per hound. If you'd caught that vampire—or if he attacks again and you catch him this time—I'll double this."

I almost handed the envelope back to him and said I wasn't interested. If this was for the other night, I'd earned it, but I had a feeling he was trying to cement me to him, that it was more of a bribe for continued protection. But if I rejected it, he would be suspicious of me. He might ask me to leave. If he did, how was I supposed to snoop around and find that chest?

"Thanks for taking a look at the security," Weber said. "Are you ready for the party?"

"Uh." I still hadn't pocketed the envelope.

*Val?* Sindari asked. *I can't stay much longer.*

*Sorry. Roadblock.*

Weber arched his eyebrows.

"Am I still playing the role of your Tinder hottie?" I stuck the envelope in my pocket. "Or openly prowling the premises while fondling my weapons?"

"Brazen weapons fondling may alarm the investors."

"What about subtle stroking?"

"You could be my date if you looked less injured and… thuggish." His gaze shifted to my swollen eye and lip. "Will you allow my maid to do your face?"

*I'm not going to be able to make it, Sindari.*

"Of course." I forced a smile. "I'm dying to learn how she makes injuries disappear with cleaning implements."

"She's from Guatemala. She's gifted." Weber took my arm and led me toward a bathroom while calling for his maid.

An image floated into my mind from Sindari, a patch of grass between the dock and a row of hedges that marked the property line. He looked down at his big silver foot and scratched the earth. The image faded as did Sindari's presence in this world.

I was on my own.

# Chapter 25

Apparently, male software investors outnumber female investors at least ten to one. As the twentieth male guest arrived, I leaned against a wall in the spacious living room with refrains of Flight of the Conchords' "Too Many Dicks on the Dance Floor" playing in my mind. There were two women clumped together for moral support as they admired the view of the lake through floor-to-ceiling windows that ensured wandering naked through the house at night would be a mistake. A few hundred sailboats and kayaks were visible out on the water.

I itched to sneak outside and look for the spot Sindari had marked, but a couple of guys started talking about this being the investment of the millennium, and I started paying more attention. An app to track magical beings wouldn't fall into that category—it was hard to imagine this many people even being interested in investing in such a thing. Maybe I could find out what Weber was *really* building. I still thought he might be lying about his involvement with Intelli-Ads, but ad software also wouldn't be the investment of the millennium.

Weber was chatting with a trio of men on one of several sets of sofas that the huge room required. Maybe I could wander closer to the pair of investors without attracting his notice.

My phone buzzed, distracting me. It was my therapist.

I texted her that I was working and would call her later.

*I've found a wonderful new therapy for you to try!* came the excited return text. *Floating. You'll love it.*

Floating? Like in the freezing cold Puget Sound? I'd done the Polar Plunge one year for charity and had quickly decided that writing checks was a much saner way to donate money.

*Sounds cold,* I texted back.

*Oh no, it's warm. You float for an hour in a sensory-deprivation tank filled with water saturated with Epsom salt. There's no sound and no light, just you all alone in the absolute dark with your thoughts.*

*Sounds horrific.*

*You'll love it. I'll send the link. See you at your next appointment!*

I canceled on her at least twice a month. It was amazing she could maintain such enthusiasm when communicating with me.

As I put away my phone, the two women came over. One wore glasses half the size of her face and looked like the Asian version of Velma from *Scooby Doo*. The other was a blonde woman with features so perfectly carved I suspected a plastic surgeon's knife behind them. I dubbed her Barbie. They both appeared to be in their early thirties. I wondered what people did for a living to accumulate enough money for big-time investing at that age. Not hunting murderous orcs and wyverns, I wagered.

"Excuse me." Barbie lifted a hand to me. "Is it true that you're dating Bernard?"

Velma looked me up and down. Perhaps unwisely, I hadn't opted for one of the dresses Amber had picked out, mostly because the executive assistant hadn't said it was required today. That left me in jeans and a T-shirt with dirt in my pocket.

"We bonded over Tinder." I resisted the urge to smooth my hair—the maid had already pulled the twigs and moss out.

"I'm an investor in that," Barbie said. "Interesting that it found you two compatible."

"I imagine it found her boobs compatible."

They shared fake chuckles and smiles with each other.

"Should've gone with the weapons fondling," I muttered.

"Pardon?"

"Nothing. What do you want?" I had a feeling I'd get further gleaning information from one of the groups of guys. There were plenty to pick from.

"We were curious if you knew anything about Bernard's current project. Is it as promising as he's pretending?" Velma smiled.

I held back a snort, though I was amused that they wanted to pump me for information when I wanted to do the same to them. "I know lots. He talks in his sleep."

Their looks sharpened as they glanced at each other again.

"Do you know if human trials have started?" Barbie asked.

Okay, this was definitely not about software. "Not officially."

"But unofficially?" Velma adjusted her glasses and lowered her voice. "Sub rosa?"

"Yes." Sure, why not? I glanced at Weber to make sure he wasn't watching me. "Does that make you more likely to invest?"

"So far, all we've seen is the outcomes from the very limited mouse trials. It's extremely early to consider investing, but if there's a chance to get in now, before the valuation becomes ridiculous…" Velma eyed Barbie again.

I drummed my fingers on my thigh, more eager than ever to investigate Level Z. What was Weber doing under his lawn that involved mouse—and eventually human—trials?

The words Dimitri had scribbled on his takeout menu in the van popped into my head. *Longevity potion?*

A knowing flutter of nerves taunted my stomach. I didn't have a solid lead to link Weber with Dimitri and the missing vampires, other than that weird attacks were happening to both of them, but—

A dragon flew into range of my senses, derailing my thoughts. It wasn't Zav, nor was it any other dragon I recognized.

A second dragon followed the first into my range.

Damn. I'd hoped these new dragons wouldn't show up until Zav returned—or at all.

My senses told me they were flying in this direction. It was possible they were just following the water and didn't have anything to do with me or Weber, but as an image of that chest filled my mind, I doubted I would be that lucky.

"Excuse me." I slipped away from the women, leaving them whispering about possibilities of secret human trials, and headed for Weber.

What I would say to him, I didn't know, but as his bodyguard, I felt compelled to warn him of a possible threat. Dragons fly fast, however, and they were nearly above the house by the time I tapped his shoulder.

"We have a problem." As I finished the last word, an alarm clanged.

Weber jumped to his feet. "Intruders." He started to rush past me, but paused and grabbed my arm. "Do you know what kind?"

"Two dragons just flew over your house." I kept my voice low, not sure if any of these people knew about the magical world and not wanting to start a stampede if they did.

Anger sparked in Weber's eyes. "Not that pompous one who thinks you're his mate."

"No, but we'd be in a lot better position if he *was* one of them. I can reason with *him*." I lifted my gaze toward the ceiling, as if I could see the dragons flying around up there. My senses told me they were circling the house.

An alarm gonged again. Some kind of proximity detector.

Unlike Zav, these guys didn't barrel straight through it and set off the defenses, but like Zav, I doubted they were worried about Weber's magical doohickeys. I expected one of them to speak to me at any second or to swoop in and try to carry me off for some draconian punishment.

Weber let go of me. "I'm going to check on something. Protect my guests, please."

"Protect your guests from *dragons*? That's beyond my pay grade."

"I'll pay twenty thousand at the end of the day if you don't let anyone get killed." He raised his voice to address everyone. "I've got to attend to someone trying to sneak past my security, but help yourself to more wine. I'll be back as soon as possible."

Weber started for the hall, maybe to check all of his security monitors, but he halted after two steps. A blue dragon—I'd never seen a blue dragon before—flew low over the water and was visible through his big windows. Its yellow eyes regarded us even as Weber and I stared at it.

Since Weber didn't have magical blood, I assumed one of his wrist charms allowed him to see the dragon. He swore under his breath and said something I wouldn't have caught if my half-elven hearing hadn't been better than average.

"They *promised* me it couldn't be tracked."

He ran into the hallway.

I started to charge after him, suspecting my earlier instinct to wring his neck and demand answers had been correct, but an invisible force gripped me and froze me in place.

## False Security

*You are marked by the dragon lord Zavryd'nokquetal,* a voice boomed into my head, reigniting the headache that had started to fade. *Where is he? If he took the egg, we will raze your city while you watch and then we will slay you last.*

Oh, what fresh hell was this?

*He's not here, and I don't know about any eggs.*

The force around me tightened, constricting my lungs and my airway. *We do not believe you.*

# Chapter 26

I couldn't see the dragon attacking me, squeezing my entire body with magical power, but my senses told me he was on the roof. Unfortunately, I couldn't do anything to stop him while frozen in the hallway. It was getting harder and harder to breathe, and picturing ferns protecting my body did nothing to lessen the invisible vise squeezing me like a tube of Colgate.

*Look, I don't know anything about an egg. I promise.* Yeah, that would work. Nothing like mongrel promises to sway dragons. *But if you tell me where you think it is, I'll look for it. I'm a pro at finding things.*

Yeah, right. I hadn't been able to find Zoltan or Dimitri this week.

"Is she okay?" one of the male guests asked.

I was facing the hallway that Weber had disappeared down because I'd been running that direction when the dragon froze me. That meant I couldn't see the investors and didn't know if they were staring at my ass while I was stuck in this ridiculous running stance or not.

"I don't know, but look out there. The dock just collapsed. Like something landed on it."

Something like a dragon. If I could have turned my head to look, I might have seen the blue one out there. I hoped he crushed Weber's yacht the same way Zav crushed my apartment's deck chairs.

*Can you hear me?* I tried to project my thoughts to the dragon holding me. *Tell me what you need. Let me help. There's no need to raze my city because of the actions of one person.*

One person who'd completely disappeared. Where was Weber? Level Z?

*If Zavryd'nokquetal stole our clan's egg,* we will *destroy his mate and the place where she lives.*

*He didn't. He's honorable. If you know his reputation, you should know that.*

*It is true,* a new voice spoke into my mind from a distance. It was familiar.

I hadn't recognized the first two dragons, but this sounded like the one I'd met on the elven home world. Was he also in the city? He wasn't close enough yet for me to sense him.

*Zavryd'nokquetal is a pompous ass, as all Stormforge Clan are,* he continued, *but he is not a thief. And I met this female in Veleshna Var, where the elven king welcomed her. She has a dwarven blade and is a warrior. She may be able to find the egg. We don't even know for certain that it is here.*

*It is here,* the first voice boomed. *We can smell the conniving orcs that stole it from the nest.*

Were they talking about a *real* egg and not some artifact? Oh, man. The memory of the orcs carrying that chest popped into my mind again. If Weber had asked his personal shopper to have a dragon egg stolen, I was going to kick his ass. And then I'd hunt down the shopper and kick his ass too.

Assuming I survived the next two minutes. I couldn't get enough air into my lungs, and my fingers and toes were already going numb. If I'd been able to move, I would have been rubbing Freysha's dirt all over myself and hoping some magical power I hadn't yet learned would save me.

*Yes,* the familiar dragon said. *Orcs took it. I also smell them. Zavryd'nokquetal's female did not take it.*

*If she did not take it, then why is she here where it disappeared? She is guarding it for the coward who ordered it stolen.*

That was uncomfortably close to the truth, however accidental.

*She is not. Female half-elf, are you guarding an egg?*

*No, and the name is Val. Can you guys let me go so I can breathe? I'll go find your egg for you. I promise.* I tried not to think of the envelope of money in my pocket. If these guys found out I'd accepted payment from the guy who'd ordered their egg stolen...

A distant snapping of wood filtered in through the windows.

# False Security

"What is going on out there?" one of the investors whispered.

Yacht smashing, I hoped.

*What do you care about this female, Xilnethgarish? Why should I let her live?*

*Because if you kill a Stormforge's mate, it may start a war with their whole clan. We must worry only about finding the queen's egg and returning it. Also, I plan to claim a human form and seduce her and annoy Zavryd'nokquetal.*

Uh, what? I tried to tune out the chatter—if I didn't do something, I would *die* while they debated if they should let me live—and focus on fern fronds wrapping around not just my mind but my entire body. Escape, escape... I had to escape.

*You don't think* that *will prompt a war?*

*No, it will humiliate him. It will be fabulous, Myrozelnik. It's counting coup to the extreme. I adore this plan!*

*You are a fool.*

*But still your favorite cousin.*

*Not even remotely.*

The pressure lessened slightly, enough for me to inhale small shaky breaths. I still couldn't move my limbs, but it was something. I thought my meager magic might have actually worked, but then the dragon—Myroz-whatever—released me completely. Only a heroic feat of balance kept me from pitching nose-first onto the floor.

*Find the egg, female,* Myroz growled into my mind, *or you will watch your city fall before I slay you. I disagree with my cousin, and I believe your presence here means you were at least partially responsible for this affront. Given your reputation, the Dragon Justice Court will back any decision I make. You have thirty minutes to find the egg and place it in my talons.*

Though I wondered why they couldn't find it themselves, I hurried down the hall. Weber wasn't in the security room or his office, and I ran for the front door instead of searching the rest of the house. It was time to find Sindari's secret entrance in the lawn and hope the egg was down there. And that a thousand deadly booby traps weren't.

Warm sun beat on my head as I ran outside and across the lawn. A blue dragon was indeed sitting on and crushing the dock. That one hadn't spoken to me yet, but he watched with icy silver eyes as I tried to find the spot Sindari had shown me through our link. My new enemy Myroz perched at the apex of the roof. He was more aquamarine than blue, and even Weber's huge house couldn't make him look anything but massive. His tail dangled off the side, tapping agitatedly at a thrashed rose trellis as he watched me even more intently than the other dragon.

I could now sense Xilneth across the water, flying back and forth over the city, maybe searching for the missing egg instead of expecting someone else to find it for them.

As I hunted for the spot Sindari had marked in the grass, I attempted to project my thoughts toward Xilneth. He was the most reasonable and most likely to answer my questions.

*Is this an actual egg I'm looking for? Like with a baby dragon in it?*

*Yes. It was taken this morning from our queen's lair while she ruled over the clan council nearby. A most brazen theft. Our kind are not fecund and eggs are rare. Our people were turning several worlds upside down looking for it until someone turned in one of the thieves, and he was interrogated.*

*A Way Rover orc?*

*Yes.*

Certain I was close to Sindari's spot—did that look like a claw mark in the dirt?—I prodded at the earth with Chopper, hoping to hear it thunk at a hidden door. I apologized to the long-dead dwarven master who'd crafted it to be a weapon, not a stake.

*I saw the orcs and the chest that might have held the egg,* I told Xilneth. *I think there's a bunker or something under the lawn. Want to come help me invade it and look for your egg?*

If I'd learned one thing by working with Zav it was that enemy lairs were much easier to storm with a dragon at one's side.

Chopper's tip slid through the turf and thunked against something hard. I probed around. There were more thunks. And yes, this looked like the spot Sindari had shared with me through our link.

"Found you," I whispered, dropping to my knees and patting around. If there was a door, there had to be a latch, right?

*I do not sense it yet, but I will most certainly come help you look for the egg.*

Xilneth flew into view, a large green dragon flapping his leathery wings as he arrowed across the water toward me. Before he reached land, he banked hard and faced to the west. The dragons on the roof and the remains of the dock sprang into the air and also turned in that direction.

What new threat was coming?

After a few seconds of not finding a latch or handle or anything but grass, I gave up and turned Chopper into a spade. The tip thunked again and again on something that sounded like metal as I tore away pieces of sod. Finally, I chanced across something—a release button, maybe—and a trapdoor opened upward in front of me. It was more like the hatch to a submarine than the door I'd envisioned. The cement shaft underneath had ladder rungs on one side that descended into pitch blackness.

I sensed Zav fly into my range, and I almost whooped—was he the reason the Starsinger dragons had all sprung into the air?—but then I detected his sister Zondia coming right behind him. As far as I knew, she still hated me and thought I was a conniving wench hanging out with Zav for status. Nothing good could come from her arrival.

Then *more* dragons flew into my range, and I began to fear that my city truly was in danger of being razed. Especially when I recognized two of them. Shaygor and one of the gold dragons—one of his kin— who'd tried to have me dragged back to the Dragon Justice Court for punishment and rehabilitation. Were they *all* here because of this egg?

I peered into the cylindrical shaft, expecting to sense a flood of magical artifacts now that I'd opened the hatch. Surprisingly, I didn't sense anything. I'd thought the hatch door might have been muting the powerful magical artifacts on the other side, much like that vault door under the house in Bothell had, but that didn't seem to be the case.

"Just a weird door in the lawn that descends into hell." I swung my legs down, my boots finding one of the ladder rungs bolted to the cement wall.

*Are you safe, Val?* Zav spoke into my mind.

*For the moment.* I paused, debating whether to pull the hatch shut after me.

*There's about to be a battle*, he warned. *Something was stolen from a clan of dragons, and our enemies the Silverclaw Clan have claimed we were responsible.*

Ah, I'd wondered how Zav's clan had been implicated. Now it made sense. Lies and political maneuvering from enemies taking advantage of an opportunity.

*It has nothing to do with you,* Zav continued, *so stay out of the way.*

*I already know about the egg. And I've been threatened if I don't find it.*

*Who threatened you?* Zav's voice went from a calm if terse tone to booming in my mind like an angry gong.

*A blue dragon named Myroz-something. He thinks I'm working with you and that you sent me to take their egg.*

*I will take his life, the arrogant bastard.*

*Not necessary, but you could come help me infiltrate Level Z and look for it.*

A roar sounded in the sky overhead, and I looked up in time to see a blue and a black dragon crash together in the air, talons raking each other. A third dragon that I couldn't see breathed fire at the other two.

*I will help when we've settled this matter,* Zav said firmly.

He wasn't among the three fighting, but I sensed him arrowing toward them. I had a feeling Weber's house wouldn't be left standing after this. If he'd purchased a stolen dragon egg, then he deserved that, especially if this turned into the spark that lit the wildfire that was dragon politics. The last thing humanity wanted, whether it knew it or not, was to have that wildfire raging here on Earth.

I left the hatch open and climbed down the ladder. Hopefully, if I found the egg, I could put a stop to this war before it got serious.

The shaft descended far deeper than I expected, especially given that the yard and the house weren't much higher than the level of the lake. The two dragons that had been tangling crashed to the ground above me. I couldn't see them, but I could sense them, and I grimaced and gripped the rungs tightly when they tumbled across the lawn hard enough to make the walls around me tremble. They crashed into the raised hatch, and it thudded shut, leaving me in blackness.

Maybe that was for the best. I would have liked Zav's help, but he was busy, and the last thing I wanted was for one of the other dragons to come down and get in the way.

Since it was completely dark, I activated my night-vision charm. That was easier than climbing with Chopper in hand. The world turned to an indistinct slightly blurry green.

I passed through a faint buzzing field—it was like walking under high-voltage power lines—and I could suddenly sense an intense amount of magic. Not directly under me but farther inland. About where that slope and the trees would be.

As my boot reached the ground, a textured cement floor, I realized I could no longer sense the dragons up above. That hadn't been an electrical field but some kind of magic-dampening field. Which would explain why the dragons couldn't sense their egg, assuming it was down here. There were so many kinds of magic that I couldn't pick out any one thing or identify the objects.

Surprisingly, I identified one faint but familiar aura, not of an object but of a person. Dimitri.

I was surprised but only for a moment. I'd thought this would all come together, and it had. If Weber had kidnapped my friend, that would give me another reason to kick his ass—but not until I rescued Dimitri. I drew Fezzik *and* Chopper, ready for trouble.

A wide tunnel opened up in one direction from the ladder well, leading inland—in the direction I sensed the magic—rather than toward the house. I'd only taken a few steps when lights flooded on. My night-vision charm went off automatically, but not before the light scorched my retinas.

Gasping and wincing, I had to blink several times and wait for my eyes to clear. When they did, I found myself staring at a body on the floor. A man wearing a ski mask.

I crept forward and nudged him with the sword. He didn't move. His chest wasn't riddled with bullet holes, nor was his throat sliced open, but he wasn't breathing. Was this the vampire who'd been attacking people who used Intelli-Ads? And if so, how had he gotten here?

As I inched closer to pry the mask up with the tip of my sword, a burst of intense red beams came from both side walls. I sprang back but not before they touched me.

Expecting intense pain, I scrambled back to the ladder. Until I realized they hadn't done anything to me. They bit into the supine form on the floor, but the man—the vampire?—didn't react. Maybe they'd already gotten him. But why hadn't they hurt me?

I'd only managed to reveal part of his face, but his skin was blanched white, and his mouth was open in a silent scream, fangs just visible.

Maybe the beams were a vampire security system. Something that specifically attacked undead intruders. Now that the beams were on, I could feel magic behind the walls.

The beams winked out, and the magic faded. They'd covered about ten feet of the wide tunnel when they'd been on. I ran and dove through, hoping to make it to the other side without being touched.

They sprang to life again, red beams flashing across the tunnel, but once again, they didn't hurt me. I came up in a crouch on the far side. If this place had been designed to take out vampires instead of people, maybe I could walk right in and find Dimitri and the egg.

A *clink-clink-clink* sounded somewhere up ahead, reminding me of a portcullis being raised. Snarls and growls floated toward me—a *lot* of them. I suspected the next security measure wasn't going to let me past unscathed.

# Chapter 27

I activated my cloaking charm, hoping I hadn't waited too long—and hoping whatever was ahead of me couldn't see through it.

The tunnel was lit where I was but not up ahead, and I struggled to pick out the growling, snarling creatures milling in the darkness. All I could tell was that they were large. They didn't sound quite like the hounds I had encountered earlier in the week, but as with them, my senses didn't pick them up as magical.

I touched my feline charm and breathed Sindari's name, but I feared he wouldn't yet be recovered enough to make the journey back to Earth. The charm was cool under my finger and nothing happened. I was on my own.

Staying near the wall, I crept forward, careful not to make a sound or even breathe too heavily. The underground structure, despite looking like recent construction, had a dank mildewy odor. I hoped my lungs wouldn't tighten up—wheezing would lead an enemy creature right to me.

Reluctantly, I paused to dig out my inhaler and use it. Just in case.

The lights ended as the wide tunnel opened into a larger room—no, more of a laboratory. A few LEDs on panels and equipment provided faint illumination, enough to see that work stations and counters filled the area. What looked like cells lined a side wall, and I sensed Dimitri in that direction. But I couldn't head straight for him because huge bears hulked through the area, snapping at each other and sniffing the air. There had to be at least ten of them, a mix of grizzlies and black bears.

What a strange security force. Or was it possible they were part of some experiment?

One grizzly bumped a black bear, eliciting a snarl and a swipe with a forelimb. When it connected with the grizzly, the great brown creature flew through the air as if it had been struck by a train, not a paw. It crashed into a counter that would have been torn out of the floor if it hadn't been made from sturdy metal and cement.

Were these shifters? I checked again but still didn't sense magical auras from them, nor magic of any kind. The hounds had worn magical collars to cloak them and give them commands, but these bears weren't wearing anything that I could pick out in the dim light.

The one that had been struck didn't return to start a fight, nor did any others jump in. They went back to growling and sniffing, as if they'd been promised that a dinner was hidden somewhere in the vast laboratory. Me?

Still following the wall, I crept toward the cells and Dimitri's aura. I wanted to call out to him, but the bears would hear it. I would prefer to sneak in and out without them spotting me, especially after seeing that blow. These weren't just bears but *super* bears.

A thought crept into my mind. Were they perhaps cybernetically enhanced bears?

Just because Weber had sold that company didn't mean he hadn't kept some of the tech for himself. And that would explain why they didn't register as magical to my senses.

I drew close enough to the first cell to see inside it. A man—no, I could sense that this was a vampire—lay bound to a waist-high platform by magical shackles. A huge light dangled down from the ceiling on an articulating arm, reminding me of something a dentist would shine in one's mouth, but it was off. The cell was too dark for me to see the prisoner's face.

Was this Zoltan? The vampire was absolutely naked, pasty white skin like that of a corpse, with surgical cut marks in his neck and chest. He seemed larger than Zoltan, but it was hard to be sure.

I thought about trying to free the guy—my senses told me he was only undead and not truly dead—but an energy barrier that reminded me of a force field out of *Star Trek* hummed at the front of the cell. A sophisticated panel vaguely reminiscent of an iPad, but without any of the familiar icons, was mounted to the wall. It glowed slightly, enough for me to see that the icons had no handy labels.

I rested my hand on the narrow strip of wall between the force field and the control panel and willed my lock-picking charm to open it. Even if a force field wasn't a lock, the charm had opened everything from magical bonds to enchanted doorways. Unfortunately, it didn't seem to know what to do with something so high-tech.

If the laboratory hadn't been full of bears, I might have slammed Chopper against the control panel to see if that opened the cell. As it was, I risked poking the field with the tip of my blade. Maybe if magic met technology, magic would win.

The field buzzed angrily and sparked yellow. Claws clacked on the floor behind me, and I sprang to the side.

Two bears crashed into the field, and yellow sparks exploded as they bounced off. One swiped at the air in my direction, and I backed farther away, Chopper up to defend if the animals saw through my camouflage. The other bear took out its frustrations on its buddy. A swat sent it into the field again, sparks flying once more. They ended up wrestling and tearing each other apart on the floor, blood spattering the cement wall behind them as they battled with unparalleled power.

A clank came from a doorway deeper in the lab. The bears might not be the only ones down here. Someone had let them out, after all, and I hadn't seen Weber since he left the living room.

I put Fezzik away, deciding against opening fire. It was possible nobody knew I was down here, and I wanted to keep it that way.

More growls and snarls came from the rest of the bears, and a few headed toward the fight. One veered right toward me.

I couldn't back up since the wall of cells—and force fields—was behind me, but I scooted sideways. A bear swiped at the air where I'd been. The fight stopped, but the bears didn't calm. They joined their buddies in sniffing and trying to find me.

A groan came from the end of the cells, a groan that sounded human.

I kept scooting in that direction, doing my best to avoid the bears. But one either saw through my camouflage or guessed right. It charged at me, a thousand pounds of muscle and mass on enhanced legs, and it came so quickly that I almost didn't jump out of the way in time. Somehow, it guessed which way I would dodge and lashed out with a huge paw.

I swept Chopper at it, slicing off the tips of the bear's claws. It roared, pivoted, and lunged. I sprang straight up in the air, finding a light fixture to grab onto with one hand.

The metal rectangle, with long bulbs mounted inside, hung on chains and swayed alarmingly under my weight. I held on as the bear charged past underneath me, even managing to twist and slash at its back with my blade. It yowled and whirled, but it swiped at the air under me instead of guessing that I was above it.

Four bears rushed into the area, sniffing and growling at the floor right under me. I pulled my legs up higher, and the chain holding the light fixture creaked ominously.

"Uh," came a confused utterance from the closest cell.

Dimitri sat against the wall in the back, his legs curled to his chest. He was naked with magical metal shackles clasping his ankles. His eyes were wild and his face gaunt, as if he'd been in there for weeks, not days. Racks holding IV bags and tables of needles and surgical implements were off to the side of his cell, out of his reach. He wasn't hooked up to anything other than the chains, but there were parallel cuts in his chest and a bandage around his neck. What the hell?

*I'm working on getting you out,* I thought to him, wishing there had been time for Freysha to teach me telepathy.

Dimitri's eyes widened. Had he heard my thoughts? Or could he tell from the swinging light fixture that someone nutty was here?

I kept waiting for the bears to look up and figure out where their prey had gone. The ceiling was high, but if one of the big grizzlies stood on its back legs, it could take a chunk out of my butt.

The lights came on, almost startling me into letting go. It wasn't only the fixture I clung to but all of them, and they were red lights rather than the fluorescent bulbs I'd expected. Infrared lights? Like in Zoltan's lab? Something that wouldn't harm vampires?

A strange whistle blew, and the bears under me stopped slashing and sniffing. I wished they would scatter so I could jump down—my arm was starting to get tired—but they stood right under me.

Two people walked into the laboratory through that back doorway, a wispy-haired man in a white lab coat and... Weber.

The bears growled and shifted, glaring at the men, but they didn't advance. Maybe they'd been trained with shock therapy to avoid whoever blew that whistle. I wished I could overpower their training and convince them to attack the two men. As long as I dangled from the light fixture, I couldn't run over and do the job myself, though I wanted to.

"They've been fighting again." The scientist waved at the bears—and at me, but I trusted my cloaking charm hid me, so long as they didn't notice the odd cant to my light fixture. "They're dumb as shit. You should have let me put some computer chips in their brains when we were making their muscles stronger."

"Our company didn't make chips. They can probably sense the dragons." Weber looked toward the cement ceiling. "Did you get the sample you needed from the embryo? I think my house is going to be toast if I don't throw that egg up there to them."

"You sure they won't kill you even if you *do* throw it up there?"

"No." Weber pushed a hand through his hair. "Why'd I let you suggest this? We were doing *fine* with the vampires."

"*You* were the one who said there are dragons on Earth now, so there might be a way to get an egg."

My forearm quivered from the effort of holding my weight by my fingers. If I could sheathe Chopper, I could at least hold on with two hands, but I was afraid to move. The light fixture kept creaking faintly, and I worried it would break.

"I only took that risk because you said dragons live for thousands of years and studying them would be so much more likely to yield the results we want than taking cells from walking dead people." Weber tapped an earbud and stalked away from his scientist, talking under his breath.

My ears picked up most of it.

"What do you *mean* a dragon is searching the house? Did you get the guests out? Where's my bodyguard?"

One of the chains gave part way, a quick jerk dropping me an inch. Shit.

A grizzly looked up, beady black eyes focusing on me. In that moment, I knew I was close enough to them that they could see through my charm's camouflage.

It rose onto its hind legs, arm lifting for a mighty swing. I jerked my legs out of the way and swung Chopper with all the speed and strength I could muster from the awkward position.

The sharp blade sliced through the bear's paw before it would have clawed my entire backside open. The grizzly yelped and dropped to the ground.

The chain that had shifted gave way entirely. Still hanging from the light fixture, I plummeted downward as half of it dropped from the ceiling.

A bear snapped at my leg. I kicked it in the face, then twisted and leaped, trying to land away from them and with my back to the cells.

Both Weber and the scientist were staring in my direction. From across the laboratory, they couldn't see me, but—

"Someone's in here," the scientist barked.

"It's Thorvald. It has to be."

"I thought she was on our side."

"So did I," Weber said grimly, then lowered his voice, so it was barely audible over the snaps and snarls. "I bet she's someone else's spy and has been all along."

"I'll take care of her." The scientist pulled a pistol out of a pocket in his lab coat and opened fire as the bears lunged for me.

Weber lifted a hand to stop him.

The scientist jerked away from the grab. "You're just the investor. I'm daily operations, remember? Let me deal with this."

As he fired again, I ducked low, hoping the bullets would hit the bears instead of me, but that didn't do much to keep me safe. My furry foes swarmed me with jaws snapping and claws slashing. Using Chopper, I kept them back—but barely. There were too many of them, and they were showing the scientist exactly where I was, even if he couldn't see me.

"Don't *kill* anyone," Weber said. "Just lock her in here with the others for now. We've got a bigger problem to deal with."

Yeah, an angry pile of dragons swarming the area.

Weber ran deeper into the facility while the scientist stayed behind with the gun. The bears attacked as if they were pack animals, shoulder to shoulder as they surged at me. I backed into the corner, whipping Chopper across and down as quickly as I could, blocking the barrage of attacks.

A bullet slammed into the cement wall to the side of Dimitri's cell—inches from my head. The scientist had climbed onto a counter so he could shoot over the bears. So much for not killing anyone.

I shifted to one-handed defense with Chopper and pulled Fezzik from its holster. Weber's ally fired at me again—what kind of sci-fi scientist kept a gun in his lab coat?

Though I was sorely tempted to pound rounds right into his chest, I aimed at the chains of the light fixture hanging over his counter. Two precise shots, and it collapsed onto his head. He pitched off the counter, and I heard the gun clatter onto the cement. I hoped it slid under a counter where he couldn't get it.

"Val?" came Dimitri's voice, weak and scared. "Is that you?"

"Yeah." I ducked lower than the bears to stay out of the scientist's sights in case he got the gun again, and kept defending myself. Two of my furry assailants were too injured to keep going, but the rest were driven by some crazy desire to thrash me. "At least until they get me and I'm as dead as your vampire friends."

I fired directly into a grizzly's chest as I deflected a paw strike from another one trying to get at my side. The bullets slammed in, but the bear kept fighting. Chopper was doing more damage, lopping off paws with its magical edge, but that also didn't always stop these guys.

"Let me out to help," Dimitri croaked. It sounded like he hadn't been given any water for days. "No, let Zoltan out. He's next to me. And all the other vampires."

"I'll get right on that with one of the key rings the deputy bears are wearing."

One of the big black bears snarled and rushed in after I shot him in the chest—hurting these guys was making them angrier and stronger. Even though I dodged the main attack, he clipped me with a paw, and it felt like a sledgehammer smashing into my ribs.

Only mad flailing kept me from losing my balance, and I had to spring over another bear to keep from being smashed into the wall. I landed on his head. Not much better. He roared and reared up.

As I ran down his back like a rider trying to stay on a bucking mechanical bull, I spotted the door panel for the cell next to Dimitri's cell. I still had no idea how to open it, but I tried my earlier idea and slammed Chopper's blade into it.

Glass shattered and sparks flew. I leaped off the bear's back as another grizzly rushed toward me, but I landed on a paw and lost my balance for a second, just enough to pitch toward the cell. I winced as I caught myself, expecting to hit the force field and get electrocuted, but there was nothing there. My brute-force tactic had worked, and it was down.

The naked vampire inside—that *did* look like Zoltan—was chained to a slab, the same as the first one, but he lifted his head at my unexpected entrance. The bears had surged forward, and now I couldn't get *out* of the cell. At least there were walls to either side so they couldn't flank me easily.

"Dear robber," Zoltan said, either seeing through my charm or having heard Dimitri. "Free me."

"That's the plan." I ducked under a swipe from a roaring black bear and stabbed the creature in the chest.

In other circumstances, I would have felt bad about hurting innocent animals, but I didn't have the luxury of regret right now. And something more sinister than Mother Nature was compelling these guys to attack me.

"Cut my shackles. They're steel enhanced with magic, so I'm powerless against them. Quite frustrating."

"I can imagine." It took me a moment before I dared take a swipe to the side to hack into one of the shackles, and Zoltan shrieked, almost destroying my aim. "What was that?" I demanded after I'd cleaved through it and faced the bears again.

I ran around the head of his slab to the other side.

"You looked like dear logger instead of dear robber. I thought you were going to free me by lopping my arm off."

"My aim is excellent and precise." I slashed a bear's ear off, and it landed on Zoltan's naked chest.

"And horrific. *Really.*"

The next cut took off Zoltan's other shackle. His first act was to sit bolt upright on the table, grab the ear, flick it off, and wipe his hands vigorously.

"I can tell that freeing you is going to help piles with getting out of here," I grumbled, sweat streaming down my face as I debated how to push the bears back and get out of the cell so I could free more vampires. Or maybe I could reach that scientist and find the whistle he'd used to drive back the bears.

"Do not underestimate me."

One of the bears plowed toward me, not caring that five of my bullets were in its chest and I'd taken its ear off.

I leaped up onto the slab with Zoltan, slashing the bear as it passed. From my elevated position, I could see the scientist climbing to his feet with his gun again. This time, I fired at his hand, my bullet passing clean through. He screamed and dropped the weapon. For good this time, I hoped.

"If you try to shoot me one more time," I yelled, "the next one goes in your eye!"

"Barbarian!" he cried and ran for the back door.

There went the bear whistle.

I spotted an opening and leaped over the bears crowding the cell, using the slab like a diving board and somersaulting over them. By the time I landed, the scientist was gone. I thought about racing after him, but I would have all the bears chasing after me. Instead, I rushed to the next cell and slashed into the control panel before my attackers figured out what I was doing.

Not wanting to get trapped in a cell again, I ran to the next one instead of pausing to free the vampire. With another blow, I cleaved another control panel.

"Go behind me and let out your buddies," I called to Zoltan over my shoulder.

"With what tools, dear robber? Those shackles are imbued with anti-vampire magic."

I managed to break one more control panel before the bears caught up with me. Surprisingly, only two had followed. I looked back in time to see Zoltan hurl a bear across the laboratory. Several had stayed back to battle him, but he wasn't as helpless as I'd imagined. He hurled another bear away. I had known vampires had superior strength, but somehow, I'd never lumped Zoltan in with other vampires.

"Uh, never mind. You handle the bears, and I'll free your buddies."

"Excellent. Away, foul furry beast, away!" He shoved a bear into a counter. "Their breath is odious."

"Yeah, their breath has been my biggest concern too." I ran into the nearest cell.

Another naked vampire was sitting up, and I cleaved his shackles open. This one didn't shriek, though that was probably less because of faith in my abilities and more because he looked so out of it. What exactly had Weber's scientist been doing to these guys?

The vampire recovered enough to lumber out and help Zoltan with the bears. Soon, five vampires were knocking the creatures back, and I was able to run unimpeded back to Dimitri's corner.

"Let's lock them up in a cell," Zoltan called to his buddies.

"Someone broke all the panels."

"The half-elf is a brute."

I made it to Dimitri's cell and bashed open his panel too. Brutishly.

"There's an empty one," one of the vampires said. "Thrust them inside."

Trusting them to handle the bears, I rushed to Dimitri's side and unchained him.

"Are you all right?"

"No," he rasped. "I've been in this loon's basement since Monday. I don't even know what day it is. They've been stabbing me and injecting me with God knows what." He gripped the side of his neck. "Like a guinea pig."

"More like a mouse." I thought of the investor women's questions about clinical trials. "Can you stand?" Not waiting for an answer, I hoisted him to his feet. "And do you have clothes?"

"They took them. They took *everybody's* clothes."

"Yes, I saw. Vampires are alarmingly pasty. Have you seen any dragon eggs?" I maneuvered him out of the cell.

Dimitri leaned heavily on me and grimaced with each step. Bruises I hadn't noticed before darkened his ribs on one side.

"No. Is that a problem?"

"Only in that a bunch of dragons are going to raze all of Seattle starting with Weber's house if we can't produce their missing egg."

"The bastard had me kidnapped just because I tried to keep his thugs from getting the blacksmith vampire. I'd be okay with his house being razed."

"Me too, but I'm partial to the rest of the city."

The vampires had succeeded in locking up the bears and stood outside Dimitri's cell.

"He took the egg because he believes dragons are immortal and would be key in succeeding with his longevity formula," Zoltan said.

"They were seeking to create something capable of making humans much more long-lived. He had his scientist studying our kind originally, since we are immortal once we are undead, but apparently progress was slow. They thought they could leapfrog ahead by taking cells from a dragon embryo."

"Well, the dragon's mother and the entire rest of her clan found out."

The laboratory quaked, as if one of those angry dragons had slammed to the ground right above us. The lights creaked and swayed on their chains.

"He has made many enemies," another vampire said. "That foolish human will not survive the day."

Neither would we if we didn't get out of here before fighting dragons collapsed the ceiling on us.

I pointed toward the door leading deeper into the underground complex, trying not to be concerned that Weber and the scientist had gone that way. "Let's see if we can find the egg. A dragon told me I had thirty minutes to bring it to him."

"How long ago was that?" Dimitri asked.

"Forty minutes ago."

"Great."

"Lead the way, dear robber." Zoltan bowed and waved for me to go ahead. "We shall be your legions and back you up against whatever enemies impede you. So long as we can stay in the dark."

I eyed him. "In the past, when I've envisioned having legions, they were never naked."

"How unimaginative your mind is."

So long as the vampires could hurl enemies aside, I would take them.

But as I jogged toward the door, two loud thunks reverberated through the structure. Big metal vault-like doors had swung shut on both ends of the laboratory. We were trapped.

# Chapter 28

I went to the door the scientist and Weber had used to run deeper into the underground complex. As far as I knew, the way I'd come in only led to that ladder back up to the lawn. There weren't any eggs in that direction. All of the magic I sensed was either in the laboratory with us or deeper under the hillside. It remained hard to pick anything specific out of the jumble, but I was sure the iron chest wasn't in here with us. I thought I detected its signature beyond this very solid metal door.

It lacked a knob or latch, but there was a control panel similar to the ones beside the cells. I bashed it mercilessly with Chopper. Somewhere, a dwarven blacksmith was crying in outrage at this unacceptable use of a fine magical sword.

"The Ruin Bringer is as much of a savage as I imagined," one of the vampires said.

"Indeed," Zoltan said. "We first met when she broke into my domicile and destroyed my guard tarantula."

"A guard tarantula? That doesn't sound very ferocious."

"It was almost eight feet tall. I'd built it its own room. Now I've been forced to convert that into a study."

I gave them an exasperated look as I lowered the sword, more because my savage bashing wasn't working than because I cared about the conversation.

"That's Jimmy," Dimitri said. "The blacksmith I was visiting when we were both captured."

*Jimmy?* What kind of vampire was named Jimmy?

"I saw the rental sign out in front of his house and thought you'd gone to apply." I sheathed Chopper, gripped my lock-picking charm, and rested my hand on the door. This wasn't a force field. Maybe the magic could figure out how to unlock it.

"I would if I could. That's a fabulous location, but a house is out of my price range. I believe Jimmy is a squatter rather than a tenant."

"I moved in shortly after the house was built," Jimmy said. "A dwarven master put my magical anvil in, back when one could still find dwarves in the world. It would be inconvenient to move, though I have considered it lately."

"Do you find it invigorating to live in the city?" Zoltan asked as I focused on the door, willing my charm to unlock it.

"I would prefer your estate in the country for my smithing work. The lake has grown very busy with noisy people and vehicle traffic. It is difficult to sleep during the day."

"Humanity has also increased in the area where I live. Ugly houses sprout up like mushrooms after a rain. It used to be very private."

"But it is less crowded than the city," Jimmy said.

"True." Zoltan raised his voice. "Dear robber, do you sense that there are orcs on the other side of that door?"

"What?" I jerked my hand back, but the charm had finished the job and the door unlocked with a thunk.

I drew Chopper again, ready for orcs as the door slid aside to reveal another wide hallway. It was dark and empty.

"Not immediately on the other side but farther back," Zoltan said.

I stretched out with my senses. Everything above—including whatever the dragons were doing—was blocked to me, but I still sensed myriad artifacts up ahead. With so many magical objects, it took me a moment to pick out three beings with magical blood.

And I groaned. Not only were they orcs, but they were the orcs that had carried the big iron chest. It had taken everything Sindari and I had to defeat one. And now I didn't have Sindari, just a bunch of naked vampires.

"Maybe they'll be open to negotiating." I tapped my translation charm though if I'd been alone, I would have opted for my cloaking charm.

"What do we have to negotiate with?" Naked Jimmy waved down his body and pointed at Zoltan's similarly unclad state.

"Our services?" Zoltan suggested. "Had our captors any brains, they would have consulted me about their plans to create a longevity potion instead of chaining me to a cold slab and stealing tissue samples. My brain was a completely wasted resource. Humans are such ignorant heathens."

"You don't consider yourself human?" Dimitri asked him.

"Not any longer, thankfully," Zoltan said. "I was quite pleased to shed my mortal flesh and give up the pursuit of hedonistic pleasures."

"Could we cut the chitchat?" I felt like a beacon as I advanced down the hallway, more thanks to nattering vampires trailing after me than the glowing sword in my hand. "Actually, I take that back. New plan." I stopped and looked at Dimitri. "You and your friends go ahead and try to negotiate with the orcs for the egg. On the chance they haven't sensed me yet, I'm going to fade out and try to work my way around to it while you're talking to them. Distracting them."

"You don't think you're in a better position to negotiate?" Dimitri asked quietly.

"They'll see me as more of a threat because I'm armed. And clothed. Also, I killed their buddy, and I'm sure they know it." I waved for Dimitri to go ahead and activated my cloaking charm. "Just run if they attack you. I'll do my best to deal with them."

"I'm immensely comforted." Dimitri stretched a hand toward the hall. "When you stealthed yourself, your glowing sword disappeared. I can't see anything anymore."

"We shall lead you." Zoltan stepped into the lead. "The dark is so blessedly soothing."

One of the vampires put Dimitri's hand on his shoulder, and they moved forward together. This was the weirdest group of stalwart adventurers I'd ever seen. I wondered what Amber would think if I later talked about this adventure in a public place.

I scooted around the side of the group and trotted ahead of them, wanting to see what we were dealing with before we reached the orcs. The tunnel continued farther back than I expected—we had to be far beyond Weber's property borders by now and maybe beyond that slope of trees as well. I imagined an epic battle taking place under somebody's hilltop mansion.

A chamber came into view, a faint green glow illuminating it. I thought of the glowing sword of the orc I'd killed. It had been the same hue of green.

The smell of mildew and mold grew stronger, and I knew my lungs would be tightening if I hadn't taken my medicine. They still might. Memories of fighting the dark elves in that gas-filled volcano hell sprang to my mind, memories of how I'd struggled to get enough air to breathe.

I shook my head as I neared the chamber. This wasn't anything like that. It would be fine.

As I reached the end of the hallway, my skin tingled with the power of so much magic nearby. I paused to survey what turned out to be more of a storage chamber than a laboratory, with massive stainless-steel refrigerators and chemistry equipment lining the walls. In the back, rows and rows of shelves and racks held vials and petri dishes and other containers I couldn't name.

Closer to me, magical artifacts were stacked in a pile in the middle of the cement floor like some dragon's treasure hoard. The iron chest was there, the lid tilted open, and a golden glow came from the interior. The curve of something that might have been a giant egg was visible behind two of the orcs. They were staring straight at me. No, they were staring straight at the hallway the vampires were coming up. Their eyes weren't focused on me, so I trusted my charm was working. A third orc was prowling the perimeter of the room with a green glowing sword on his shoulder.

"We demand to be paid!" one of the two by the egg shouted to the advancing vampires, my translation charm turning the guttural language into words I could understand.

"What did he say?" Jimmy asked.

"They wish to be paid," Zoltan translated, his words floating out of the hallway.

"Does he think we're carrying wallets? Because it should be quite obvious that we aren't."

"Nor am I inclined to pay anyone in this bunker of torture and iniquity," another vampire said.

I sneaked around the outside of the room, wanting to get to the egg in case the orcs decided to do something crazy like destroy it because they hadn't been paid.

"It's the vampires," one orc said.

"Weren't they locked up a minute ago?" his buddy asked.

The first orc shrugged indifferently. "They escaped."

"Where'd the vermin in white go? He was supposed to get our gold."

Where *was* the scientist? And Weber for that matter. There hadn't been any doors off the hallway, at least not obvious ones, so they should have come this way.

Avoiding the prowling perimeter guard, I circled and sneaked closer to the chest, coming up from behind the other two orcs. There were several weapons on the heap of magical artifacts—Weber's buyer had been putting in overtime. Maybe if I could arm my vampires, they would be more intimidating.

"Ah, there they are." Zoltan stepped into the chamber and looked at the orcs. "The bounteous flesh we were promised."

"Are tattooed orcs from other worlds tasty?" Jimmy asked. "I've only sampled the feral ones that wander within the sphere of my influence."

"I don't know, but these have big tusks. You know what they say about the blood of those beings with big tusks."

"What are they babbling about?" one orc asked the others.

I had a feeling I was the only one here with a translation charm. The orcs couldn't understand the vampires, and only Zoltan seemed to know the orcs' language.

It didn't matter. The orcs were paying attention to them, and that was what I needed. Carefully, I grabbed a couple of magical crossbows and two swords off the pile of artifacts.

The power of so much magic in one place crackled over my skin similarly to Zav's aura, though without the harmonious allure that came from his energy. This was clashing and chaotic—unpleasant. And very noticeable. If Weber hadn't had someone cast a spell to shield his underground structure so the auras of these goodies didn't seep out, he would have had nightly treasure hunters sneaking in to steal from his stash.

"Come no closer." One of the orcs pushed aside his cloak and pulled out a crossbow of his own. "We will guard our prize until we've been paid for it."

"What are they saying?" one vampire asked.

They'd all stepped out of the hallway now. Only Dimitri remained behind them, thankfully staying within the relative cover of the walls.

"They want gold," Zoltan said.

"You're an alchemist. Can't you make them some?"

"That's not any more possible than creating longevity formulas, information that I would have shared with the geniuses here if they'd consulted me."

The orcs growled to each other, maybe annoyed that Zoltan wasn't replying in their language.

My naked legions weren't as helpful as I'd hoped. Since the vampires couldn't see me any more than the orcs could, I couldn't wave to Zoltan to negotiate.

I tried to will him to understand my desire, mentally thinking, *Barter with them*, into his mind.

"I can make elixirs far more valuable than gold." Zoltan stepped forward and raised his arms. He'd switched to their language. Had he heard me? "Large blue visitors to this world, you must hand over the dragon egg if you wish to get out of here alive. Perhaps we can find a way to pay you with something, but I warn you for your own sake. I've learned that there are a dozen dragons here who want that egg back, and they'll find this place and come down here at any moment."

The orcs glanced at each other. They understood him. Good.

With my arms full of weapons, I was debating whether to carry them back to the vampires or toss them over the orcs' heads to my allies, allies who couldn't see me and would be startled to have weapons raining down on them. Before I'd decided, one of the orcs whirled toward me, nostrils flaring. His unfocused stare said he didn't see me, but he sensed something.

Zoltan stepped forward again, drawing their attention back to him. "Will you not heed my warning?"

"We will flatten you like the vermin you are, blood sucker."

The vampires were all looking at the orcs, and I was behind those orcs, so I tossed the weapons over their heads, trusting that my allies would see them. Zoltan blinked in surprise, but he caught the crossbow. Two other vampires stepped forward and caught the swords by the hilts with practiced ease. Another crossbow I threw hit the floor and skidded into the hallway where Dimitri crouched.

The orcs roared. One whirled in my direction, and the other two rushed at the vampires.

The closest orc lunged for the chest. I didn't know if he intended to use it for a bargaining chip or just keep me from getting to it, but I also sprang for it. As I landed atop it, kicking the lid shut, a current of raw magical energy surged up my legs. Pain lanced through my body like fireworks lit under my feet, and it startled me so badly that I reacted too slowly when the orc attacked again.

His big two-handed sword swept toward me from the side. I threw myself back off the chest, an inch from being eviscerated—or completely cut in half—and landed in an ungainly roll.

As I jumped to my feet, certain the orc would be on me before I could recover fully, a great boom rang out from the back of the chamber. A baseball-sized round slammed into the orc's face and exploded. It blew his head off, and pieces of skull and brain matter struck me, spattering against my cheeks.

As the vampires and Dimitri engaged with the two other orcs, I whirled to face this new threat and spotted Weber standing in the shadows between two refrigerators, an unfamiliar magical gun in his hand. It looked like a small cannon, and if it had fired that round, it was deadly as hell.

He'd been aiming it at the orc, but he shifted it toward my chest, having no trouble seeing through the magic of my cloaking charm. Cursing, I yanked out Fezzik and pointed it at him as I prepared to spring aside and do my best to dodge. But he didn't fire. His face was grim and determined but also hesitant. My gun now pointed at his chest, but I was also hesitant and well aware that he could have shot me in the back instead of the orc in the face. And he'd had another opportunity to fire in the second that I'd been drawing Fezzik.

"I thought you were on my side," Weber said as the clangs and bangs of the other battle rang out behind us. "I didn't think you were on *their* side."

His cannon of a gun didn't waver as he jerked his chin to indicate the vampires.

"You hunt them. You *kill* them. That's your reputation." Frustration laced his words, almost anguish.

"I know." I lowered Fezzik, returning it to my thigh holster, and lifted a hand. "I hunt the bad guys."

"Vampires *are* bad guys. They kill people and suck their blood."

"Most of them don't bother that many people. How did you even find them all?" My eyes narrowed as the pieces clicked together. "It's something to do with Intelli-Ads, isn't it? You're not a client. You started it, didn't you?"

"As a way to crowd-source finding magical beings through businesses in the community, yes. But I only wanted to know about the vampires. Nobody was supposed to miss *vampires*." He shook his head with disbelief in his eyes. Disbelief and betrayal. He was looking at me like it was my fault this was falling apart for him.

"You didn't just take vampires. You took Dimitri."

"The orcs only did so because he was there and in the way. And then Bollinger said we could use him for a few tests. I didn't want to, but we couldn't let him go. He knew everything."

"You can't just run tests on people."

"We thought he was a bad guy. He was hanging out with vampires! And we're trying to help all of humanity, to come up with a formula to extend lives. Isn't that worth sacrificing some vile vampires? We didn't even kill them! We just took samples from them. We're not the bad guys here." Weber's earlier equanimity was gone, and his hand shook on the gun.

That bothered me more than a little, but I didn't want to shoot him. If I could disarm him, maybe I still had time to get the egg to the dragons before this escalated too far to stop.

"Hey, we all make mistakes now and then when choosing friends." I tried a smile, my hand still up, and took a couple of slow steps toward Weber. "Like I don't think Bollinger was the best buddy you could have chosen."

Weber didn't smile.

"Let me help you get out of this." I pointed upward. "You must know about the dragons." I was sure that was why he was freaked out. "The vampires were one thing, but you can't keep their egg."

"I know that. I want to give it back and say it was a mistake, but they're destroying everything up there, and they'll *kill* me if I try to hand it back to them." Weber licked his lips. "We screwed up. I know. But—"

The bangs of a gun echoed from the hallway. I dropped into a crouch, expecting Weber to freak out and fire, and was ready to leap away.

Out of the corner of my eye, I saw Dimitri fling himself out of the hallway and into the chamber, landing on the hard cement floor. He gripped his shoulder and hissed in pain as blood streamed from his fingers.

"The madman!" one of the vampires cried. "Get him!"

Two vampires charged into the hallway as Zoltan and Jimmy continued to battle one of the orcs. The *last* orc. The others were dead on the floor.

Weber's hand was still shaking, that gun still pointing at me.

"Put it down," I said, trying to make my voice gentle and trying not to sound worried. I wasn't good at it. Talking guys off ledges wasn't my specialty.

He firmed his grip, and the gun steadied, unwavering as the huge barrel pointed at my chest. "You'll take the egg up there. And protect me from the dragons."

I hesitated. I wanted the egg and to return it to them, but I doubted I could protect Weber from even Zav at this point. He'd want to drag him to the Dragon Justice Court, and the others would want to kill him outright.

The hesitation was a mistake—I saw it right away in the wild look that came to Weber's eyes. Before I could open my mouth to agree to his terms, glass shattered right behind me.

I skittered to the side, trying to see what it was and keep an eye on Weber at the same time. The remaining orc was down on one knee, but he'd hurled something. Green smoke oozing magical power came from shards of glass on the floor and flowed out into the chamber, filling it rapidly.

Still bleeding, Dimitri fired his crossbow into the orc's chest.

Weber backed up, and a hidden door opened behind him.

"Wait!" I tried to croak, wanting to tell him I'd help with returning the egg, but the smoke filling the chamber got into my mouth and nose and curled down my throat. The word turned into a strangled cough—dozens of them as my lungs spasmed under the influence of the noxious stuff.

Feeling like a band was tightening around my chest, I ran to the farthest corner and yanked my shirt up, holding it uselessly over my nose and mouth. Dimitri's pained coughs filled the room. Only the vampires were unaffected—and the orc, if he was still alive.

Belatedly, with tears streaming from my eyes, I remembered the charm Zoltan had made for me weeks ago, the charm I still wore. It had been designed to stop another gas, but I activated it, hoping it would help with this.

As seconds passed, I finally got control of my coughs. My eyes kept watering, tears streaming down my cheeks, but the smoky chamber stopped affecting me as badly. My lungs were tight, but they didn't get any worse.

"Dimitri?" I managed to call. "Are you all right?"

His coughs had grown more distant—he must have run back into the hallway. But the scientist or whoever else had been shooting at us had been in that direction. Had the vampires taken him out?

"That asshole shot me," Dimitri called, his voice hoarse.

"So, you're not all right?"

"No." After a pause, he added, "But I did shoot him back."

"The scientist? Is he dead?"

"I don't know. He ran away."

What about Weber? I hurried to where I'd last seen him, but he was gone. And I couldn't find whatever he'd pressed to open that hidden door.

"The orcs are most certainly dead," Zoltan reported. "And I am fine, not that you asked after my welfare, dear robber."

"I knew *you'd* be fine. It's not like you can die."

"I do not believe she values us sufficiently." Now, Zoltan sounded like he was speaking to someone else. Jimmy, perhaps. The smoke was still too thick to see much. "Given that we volunteered to be her trusted legions and were instrumental in the defeat of her enemies."

"They were our enemies too," Jimmy pointed out.

"This is true."

I rested my hand on the wall where I thought the hidden door was, thinking of using my lock-picking charm, but I stopped. Did it matter if Weber got away? Even if I found him, I didn't want to drag him out to be punished by the dragons. All I really needed was to get that egg.

Assuming it was still there. The image of someone sneaking in under the cover of smoke and dragging away the chest surged into my mind, and I sprinted back to the pile of artifacts and weapons. The chest was still there. I opened the lid, releasing a shaky breath of relief at the sight of the glowing egg.

I closed the lid, afraid to risk any damage to it. "Now we just have to figure out how to get this out of here and back into the hands—talons—of its rightful owners."

And hope we weren't too late to keep the dragons from destroying the city.

# Chapter 29

The good news was that between Dimitri, me, and the vampires, our group could carry the extremely heavy iron chest back to and through the laboratory. The bad news was that I hadn't figured out how we would get it up the ladder and up onto the lawn so that the proper dragon could collect it. The vampires couldn't go outside in daylight, and Dimitri was bleeding from the bullet that had grazed his shoulder. The idea of removing the egg and risking breaking it while we climbed terrified me, but it was the only thing I could imagine working.

Maybe I could get Zav to come down and help. Assuming he wasn't in the middle of getting his butt kicked up there. I hadn't been able to communicate with him since passing through that field on the ladder, and I didn't have any reception on my phone. Being cut off from the outside world made me uneasy, and I worried about what we would find when we came out.

"What happened to the scientist?" I asked when we didn't see sign of him in the laboratory.

"We chased him off, but he got away when that smoke bomb went off," one of the vampires said.

I'd been hoping they would say he was dead. If Weber survived, I wouldn't mind that, but the scientist had been trying to kill me.

The cement structure trembled again as we reached the first hallway.

"We will not be able to leave this place until night falls and it is safe to travel," one of the vampires said.

"Quite true," Zoltan said. "Dear robber, you and Dimitri will have to carry this box out by yourselves."

"I know," I said. "I'm working on a plan."

"Did you bring a block and tackle?" Dimitri asked.

"There's a winch on the Jeep and rope in the back, but I'm skeptical about walking across a battlefield to get to them. I was thinking more along the lines of climbing the ladder and yelling for the right dragons to come and get their egg."

"I prefer to disappear into the bowels of this establishment before dragons are invited in," one of the vampires said.

"You can go back and hang out with the bears."

We reached the place in the hallway with the beams, and I swore. I'd forgotten about them and, if not for the body on the floor, I might have kept on forgetting about them.

"What is this?" Zoltan waved at the wall and pointed at the fallen vampire.

"That's Zephryn," one of the others said in a grim tone. "He's a friend of mine. A good friend. I had thought he might come searching for me when I didn't show up for our last meeting. Now I wish he hadn't. He's dead. All the way dead."

The vampires looked at me.

"He was like that when I came in," I said. "Beams shoot out of the walls. They didn't hurt me, so I'm guessing they were designed to keep vampires out."

Zoltan lifted his chin. "Because the vile villains behind this scheme knew our comrades would come looking for us."

"This vampire was attacking people around town." I waved at the body. "Not random people. People using Weber's ad company."

"Maybe Zephryn thought these kidnappings and experiments would stop if he scared away all of Weber's customers," Zoltan said.

"I don't know how Intelli-Ads worked, but a psychic implied the ads targeted people in the magical community or those with partially magical blood to bring her customers interested in her services. Weber might have used the data the ad network collected to locate vampires for his experiments." If I was right, Intelli-Ads hadn't existed to put money in Weber's pocket, and this Zephryn had been attacking the users of the service pointlessly.

"Val," Dimitri groaned. "Can we set this down?"

"Yeah, sorry." I'd forgotten he was injured in addition to carrying the heavy chest.

We lowered it to the floor, and I waved Chopper in front of the wall where the beams had shot out earlier. They flared to life again, crisscrossing the hallway and making it impossible to pass without touching them. Nothing happened to my sword. I risked waving my hand through a beam to show the vampires that nothing happened to me. Zoltan tapped a fingertip to a beam, then jerked it out.

"Definitely anti-vampire," he said.

"With time, we can figure out how to deactivate it," one of the vampires said, "or we can find another way out. They brought us in another way, I believe. I had a bag over my head, so it's hard to know."

"If necessary, I will *make* another way out," Jimmy said.

"Give a vampire a metalsmith's hammer," Zoltan said, "and he'll solve every problem with brute force."

"I suppose you would prefer to create some alchemical concoction to eat through layers of cement."

"Most certainly. Alchemy is a mature and sophisticated way to solve problems."

"Dimitri." I pointed for him to grab the end of the chest again as I maneuvered to the front. "We're on our own. We just have to get it to the ladder."

"What about them?" He pointed toward the vampires.

"They'll find a way out. And the sooner we get this egg out, the more likely Seattle is going to survive those dragons." I hoped.

The chest was a lot heavier without our legion of vampire porters, but we pushed and pulled it through the beams and to the bottom of the ladder.

"Stay here." I climbed up, hoping it would be easy to open the hatch from below. "I'll try to get Zav's attention."

*Val!* Zav boomed into my mind as soon as I climbed through that buzzy field. *You are alive.*

*Yes, I am.*

*You disappeared completely from my senses.*

*Yeah, I'm guessing Weber didn't want anyone to find this place. Dimitri and I have the egg, but it's in a chest that's too heavy for us to carry out.*

When I reached the top, I patted around for a switch or lever. Nothing. I tried putting my shoulder against the hatch and shoving. That also didn't work. That dragon that had knocked it shut better not have collapsed injured on top of it.

*Did you hear me, Zav?* I asked when long seconds passed without a response.

Maybe he was too busy to monitor my mind. I patted around again. There *had* to be a switch.

*Yes. We are doing battle. It is demanding my attention.*

*Why? Because they blame you for their lost egg? Will me showing up with the egg stop the fight?*

*Possibly, if it can be proven that my clan wasn't responsible for taking it in the first place.*

*Just find Weber and get those charms off his wrists so you can read his mind. That'll prove it.*

*He is dead.*

*What?* It hadn't been ten minutes since I'd spoken to him.

*He popped out of a secret door in the rocks on that slope and ran for his domicile. He wasn't a target, but one of the Silverclaws' gouts of fire caught him full on.*

My hand brushed an indentation, and the hatch lifted, hazy sunlight streaming in with a *lot* of smoke.

Screeches and roars that I hadn't heard underground now battered at my ears. My lungs were already on edge from the unnatural smoke of the orc's weapon, and this new smoke flowed into my airway, prompting a fresh round of coughs.

Outside, a black dragon struck what had been a lush grassy lawn and was now scorched earth. He rolled past, head over tail as he tumbled toward the water. A blast of fire from the sky above bathed him, the flames close enough to heat my cheeks.

I thought about grabbing the hatch and yanking it back shut, but if all this was because of the egg, I needed to get it out there and hope the right dragon snatched it up. Skipping the rungs, I slid back down to the bottom like a fireman on a pole.

"That doesn't sound good." Dimitri was peering up the ladder well at the smoky opening.

"Nope. Help me get this egg out of here."

The vampires had disappeared back into the complex. As flames engulfed the open hatch, momentarily blotting out the sunlight and shadowing the shaft in dim orange light, I decided I envied them.

Dimitri and I opened the chest, and I debated how I would carry the glowing egg up the ladder. I thought I could wrap my arm around it and keep it from falling, but it would be tenuous, especially if that left me climbing the ladder one-handed.

"We're going to have to do it together. I'll wrap my arm around the middle, and you come after me on the ladder and make sure it can't fall out of my grip." I was tempted to reverse that and make him go first, since I trusted my reflexes more than his if one of us fumbled, but I didn't want to see him get scorched by dragon fire if another gout hit the ground as we came out. With luck, my fire-resisting charm would keep me alive if that happened.

A roar echoed down from above, followed by a reptilian shriek of pain. I couldn't tell one dragon's cry from another, but concern for Zav made me tense as I carefully levered the egg out of the chest. As far as I knew, he'd only brought his sister along to back him up. What if Shaygor and his relative sided with the Starsinger Clan against them?

The dragon egg reminded me of a green-tinted ostrich egg, except much bigger. It wasn't heavy, but it was awkwardly large, and an unpleasant threatening tingle of electricity crawled over my skin as I gripped it. I didn't want to think about what would happen if we dropped it.

"We won't," I vowed.

"I'm ready," Dimitri said grimly as smoke filtered down to us.

As we started up the ladder, advancing together in awkward stages, I had to fight off visions of dropping the egg twenty feet onto the cement. That *wasn't* going to happen.

We passed through the magical barrier, and the dragons came onto my senses again. And we came onto theirs. I could tell because the roars and screeches halted, and the world fell silent save for the crackle of flames and the distant thrum of helicopter blades. A fire engine siren wailed from somewhere in the neighborhood.

Thanks to the fires above us, the shaft had grown hot, and sweat dripped from my brow and dampened my palms. I climbed more carefully than I ever had before.

As I neared the top, I sensed two dragons flying toward me. I didn't recognize either of them. Zav and Zondia were within my range but farther up on the hillside.

*Are these two dragons coming at me from the right clan?* I asked, focusing on Zav. *Do I give it to them?*

*They are from the right clan, but they are angry.* Zav leaped into the air and flew toward me.

He wouldn't make it in time to intercept the other two dragons.

"Stop here," I told Dimitri while we were still below the lip of the shaft and partially protected by the open hatch. *Does that mean I should thrust the egg up to give it to them, or not?*

*Look out!*

There was nowhere for me to go with Dimitri right under me on the ladder, but I ducked my head down, expecting a burst of flames. Instead, a great wrenching sound tore into my eardrums as talons wrapped around the open hatch and tore it off.

Dirt tumbled down onto us as more sunlight streamed into the ladder well. A distant splash sounded—the hatch being hurled all the way to the lake?

Magical power wrapped around me and tried to levitate me and the egg upward. I squawked a protest and tried to hang on, but then I realized Zav had gotten closer and the magic had his familiar aura to it. Trusting him, I let go and held the egg with both arms. As I was lifted from the ladder, I glanced down to see Dimitri's wide terrified eyes staring after me.

Zav levitated me out onto charred earth and to a scene much different from what it had been when I first went down. Weber's house was on fire, and the house on the other side of it had been flattened. The yacht and the dock were burning, as were many of the trees on the slope above the house. Several large trees had been knocked down and tumbled into the yard where the grass was completely gone, leaving dirt and blackened soil behind. Ashes and smoke mingled in the air, and I struggled not to start coughing again.

*Give us the egg, you thieves. You bring it out now only to save yourselves.*

I didn't recognize the voice in my mind, but it came from a great blue dragon on the ground with his wings spread as he faced me. His eyes glowed like something out of a nightmare, and he was crouched, as if to spring at any second.

Thankfully, Zav had landed right beside me, just as large and fierce as the other dragon. One of his wings came down to shelter me from the angry dragon. Surprisingly, Zondia settled to the ground on the other side of me. Lending her support to Zav, I decided, not me.

"We're not the ones who took it." I lifted the egg into the air. "Some orcs that are now dead did. They stole it for the guy that lives—or lived—in that flaming castle there. You can have it back. I just went down to get it for you."

As I glanced toward the house, my gaze snagged on a blackened corpse on the ground near the driveway. Most of the body was burned beyond recognition, but I sensed magical trinkets on the charred wrist and knew it was Weber. All his planning and all his money, and he'd died simply because he'd gotten in the way of a dragon battle.

A dragon battle that had started because of a choice he'd made. I tried to tell myself he'd deserved his fate, but I wasn't sure. He'd absolutely made a mistake, but maybe I was the crazy case for siding with vampires and dragons. The rest of humanity might not agree that he'd been wrong. I didn't know.

*We will give you the egg,* Zav said, *but we insist that you agree to leave our clan alone. We had nothing to do with this, and the only reason we're being implicated is because I've been working here on this planet where your egg was brought.*

*You are implicated because your mate was working with the one who stole it!*

I winced. How had these guys learned that? And what was I supposed to say? That I hadn't known about the egg? I hadn't, but they would never believe me.

"Get up there," came a firm voice from down in the complex. Zoltan?

I was close enough to glance back down the shaft. Dimitri was still on the ladder, and he was looking down too.

"Go up or I'll shoot you now, you vampire-slaying miscreant," Zoltan said.

*My mate took employment without knowing the heinous nature of her employer,* Zav replied to the other dragon. He didn't give me the dark I-told-you-so glance that he could have, and I appreciated that, but I was worried he was going to get in trouble because of me. Again, damn it.

*Your mate does as you say.* That was Shaygor's smug voice. He was flying lazy circles high above, looking down upon us with eyes gleaming with delight. *Admit it. This was a Stormforge plan all along.*

*Why would my family steal the egg of another clan's queen?* Zav demanded. *Your accusation is as ludicrous as you are. If you wish to challenge my honor, come down here and fight me face to face.*

"No need for fighting," I called. "Just come get your egg and go back to your world. It's perfectly fine now, but if you idio—venerable dragons keep fighting, you might break it."

"Nice save." Dimitri scrambled off the ladder and into a crouch behind me. He slung the crossbow off his back. "Should I point this at someone?" he whispered.

"No. Better if the dragons don't notice you exist. Trust me."

I wanted to tell him that he should have gone back down where it was relatively safe, but someone else was coming up the ladder. The scientist. He kept glancing back down nervously, and he slipped twice on his way up, managing to get his lab coat caught under his sneakers. He stopped before coming all the way out and hooked his arm over one of the rungs as if he meant to hang out there.

He looked up at us. "They can't come close to the sunlight, right? One of the bastards shot at me."

"You were experimenting on them, and you don't even know their physiology?" I asked.

"He was taking samples from them. He was experimenting on *me*." Dimitri pressed a hand to his scarred chest, then grimaced as the gesture no doubt hurt his injured shoulder.

Shaygor banked and swooped down close, as if he would try to take out Zav, me, *and* the egg. I set it down on the ground, drew Chopper, and glared defiantly up at him.

Zav should have been glaring defiantly up at Shaygor as well, but his long neck craned over me, and he peered into the ladder well.

*Is this the one who ordered the egg stolen?* Zav asked me silently.

*You guys fried the one who ordered the egg stolen, but this guy was in on it and probably knows everything.*

Before I finished the words, Zav was levitating the scientist out of the shaft.

A new dragon swooped down toward us—I recognized Xilneth's aura. He landed to the side of the two groups facing each other. Zondia hissed at him and ruffled her wings, as if she might pounce.

*I have met Zavryd'nokquetal's female,* Xilneth told everyone. *She is an*

## False Security

*honorable warrior and would not have knowingly worked for thieves. And as I said before, the pompous Stormforge Clan dragons are not thieves either. It is time to relax and take back our queen's egg, not to start a war on this backward benighted world.*

I stared at Xilneth, surprised by his defense. It wasn't as if we'd bonded during that brief chat in the elven forest. He looked over at me and one of his eyelids flickered. It wasn't exactly a wink, but it was some kind of message or at least acknowledgment.

Zav wasn't paying attention to him. His focus was on the scientist.

*His blood is full human, and he has no idea he is surrounded by dragons, but my sister and I are allowing him to see us,* Zav said as the terrified scientist flailed and tried vainly to escape. *All of us will read his thoughts and see the truth. The other human was protected by trinkets. This one is not.*

"What's happening?" Dimitri hunkered down beside me.

"All these dragons are going to read his mind, I think."

The fire engine arrived in the street outside of Weber's driveway and started deploying people with hoses toward the house. As far as I could tell, they couldn't see the dragons. They only saw the fire.

A helicopter brought a tanker of water and dumped it on the trees. The dragons paid no attention to them. They focused on Zav's prisoner.

"I don't know!" the scientist screamed.

Zav had deposited him between the two groups of dragons, and he'd dropped to his knees and gripped the sides of his head. Were they doing that mind-scouring thing? I almost felt bad for the man, but then I remembered that he'd shot at me. *Numerous* times.

The cries stopped abruptly, and I worried he'd been killed. But the man scrambled to his feet and sprinted toward the fire truck.

*See?* Zondia spoke to the other dragons. *The Stormforge Clan had nothing to do with it. Some arrogant vermin thought to use our kind in an experiment.*

*Appalling!* The egg floated away from me, heading toward one of the Starsinger Clan dragons. *All vermin on the entire planet should be exterminated.*

*Yes! If one thought to enact this scheme, another one will try it again one day. Their kind have grown too clever, and there are too many of them. It will be safer for the entire Cosmic Realms if they are eliminated.*

"Uh." I lifted a finger, though I had no idea what to say to stop this train of thought.

*It is not the way of the Dragon Justice Court to eliminate intelligent species,* Zav boomed.

*What is important now is that we take the queen's egg back to her,* Xilneth said. *The denizens of this world are too weak to do anything to harm us. It was only the greed of the orcs that made any of this possible. Their clan must be punished.*

*The orcs will absolutely be punished,* one of his clan mates agreed.

Silver light flashed, filling the area as a great portal opened up. Two dragons floating the egg between them flew through it. Shaygor and his allies glared at Zav and Zondia a little longer, but they also took off through the portal. More dragons followed until only Zav, Zondia, and Xilneth remained.

Xilneth did the eyelid shiver again for me and shook the tip of his tail. *I told you we would meet again. Perhaps you would like to go with me to my home world for a time.* He glanced at Zav, as if to gauge his reaction.

*What are you doing, Xilnethgarish?* Zav demanded, fury igniting in his violet eyes. *You presume to flirt with my* Tlavar'vareous sha?

I had no idea what to make of Xilneth. He'd helped—sort of—but surely for his own agenda.

*I am a presumptuous dragon, but have I not just assisted you in avoiding a war?* Xilneth asked. *If your female wishes to come with me, you should allow it without a duel. Let her choose the dragon she wishes for herself.*

Zav shifted at my side, his tail going out rigid and straight. Zondia eyed him but didn't comment, at least not so that I could hear it.

As he had on the elf world, Xilneth put thoughts of smooches with himself as a human in my thoughts. *Come to me,* he whispered into my mind, magical compulsion lacing the words, and I took a step forward before I caught myself.

I tightened my grip on Chopper, but the pull was powerful as he gazed into my eyes. My legs took a few more steps. Zav and Zondia both looked at me as if I was betraying them. They had to realize he was using magic on me. Couldn't they tell?

Growling, I willed Chopper to help me resist. Would Freysha's lesson help with this? As I envisioned protecting my mind with the fern fronds, I stuck my hand into my pocket and opened the bag to stick my fingers in the dirt. The magical compulsion lessened ever so slightly. In my mind, I built a fern the size of the Space Needle between me and Xilneth.

Teeth gritted, I turned my back on him and returned to Zav's side. I was tempted to stand defiantly with my arms crossed to show that I was my own person, but the dragons probably wouldn't grasp that. So I made a show of choosing Zav by wrapping my arm around his powerful foreleg. That ought to make a point they would understand.

*You choose that boring boulder over me, half-elfling?* Xilneth shook out his tail. *Very disappointing, but I shall accept your choice. For now.* He gave me the eyelid shiver again, then formed a new portal and flew into it.

*That one is angling for something politically,* Zondia said to Zav, though she included me. *He wants your female so he can embarrass you and perhaps embarrass our mother.*

*He will not have her. She is too strong to be fooled by such an imbecile.* Zav sounded pleased as he looked down at me.

Zondia eyed me, and I expected a more scathing comment from her. She'd made it clear her last time on Earth that she did not trust me and did not approve of Zav's choice. I braced myself.

*So it would seem,* she said. *And she risked much to retrieve their egg, as we saw in the puny vermin's mind.*

*Yes,* Zav purred. *She is a worthy mate and ally.*

I didn't know how to feel with the two dragons staring down at me. Dimitri had scooted back at some point. I was surprised he hadn't fled altogether, though I didn't know where he would go without any clothing. He was injured, and it was a long walk back to where he'd parked his van.

*For a mongrel,* Zondia allowed. *I still believe you should have a dragon mate. But you will tell our mother that Val is a great warrior who fought to protect our clan.*

I was still bracing myself, still expecting scorn from Zondia.

She tilted her head, then the scales around her shoulders rippled. The dragon equivalent of a shrug?

*I will tell her she fought to retrieve the egg. We must both go see our mother and report all that occurred so she will be prepared in case there is any fallout.*

*Yes.* Zav sounded reluctant, and he touched the tip of his tail to my shoulder. *I will return, but I must go for now. Will you be all right?*

*Yes.* I looked around at the fires burning—there was no sign of the scientist—and wondered how I would explain all of this in the report Willard would doubtless demand.

*Keep practicing to resist dragon compulsions.*

*Oh, I will.* I patted his tail.

Zav sprang into the air, and he and Zondia disappeared through another portal.

That left Dimitri and me standing in the scorched yard alone with smoke blanketing the area. The firefighters working on the house ignored us in favor of their more pressing task.

I walked over to Weber's body, a tangle of emotions warring inside of me as I questioned if I'd failed him. If I hadn't taken his money, I could have accepted that he'd done the equivalent of chasing tornados and this end wasn't surprising. But I'd agreed to be his bodyguard, and now he was dead.

Practicality overrode my mixed feelings, and I bent and removed the charms around his wrists. I would keep practicing magic with Freysha, but I had a feeling dragons would return to Earth again before long, and I had to be ready with as many tools as I could find.

"Can I get a ride home, Val?" Dimitri asked.

"I don't know." I pushed aside the grim thoughts and forced a smile. "I don't usually let naked guys ride in my Jeep."

"You let Sindari ride in there. He's naked."

"He rides in the back, and his fur covers all of his indelicate bits."

Dimitri looked down. I'd been making a point of *not* looking down and continued to not look down now.

"I have some coverage," he said.

"Gross."

"Right now, I'm a little unkempt, but I was imprisoned for weeks."

"It was barely days. And I never thought I would discuss *kemptness* with a business partner." I waved for him to follow me to the driveway, hoping there would be room to slip out around the fire engines. The catering van and all the cars of the investors had already disappeared. Hopefully, that meant everyone had gotten out before the house burst into flames.

"Well," Dimitri said, "our business is kind of weird."

"This is true."

# Epilogue

Dimitri was beaming when I joined him on the sidewalk in front of the Victorian vampire house I hadn't expected to see again. The For Rent sign was still dangling out front, glistening with droplets from a recent rain. The house was more noticeably rundown by the light of day.

"Did you actually ask the landlord to meet you here?" I thought he'd been joking when he'd asked for my help with negotiations.

"I did."

Dimitri grinned and bounced on the balls of his feet, a startling gesture from a six-and-a-half-foot-tall linebacker of a man. At least he didn't look any worse for wear after his time incarcerated in Level Z. His black Alice in Chains T-shirt hid the shoulder wound, but I trusted it was healing.

I also trusted that Zoltan and the rest of the vampires had made a safe escape. By the time Willard had made it back from her training exercise and sent someone to take possession of the contents of Weber's underground laboratory—specifically, the piles of magical artifacts—they had been gone. Maybe Jimmy the vampire blacksmith had already moved back into the basement here.

"Your business has only been open, officially open, for three days," I said. "You can't afford this."

"That's why you're here. I plan to bargain, and you're going to help by looking intimidating and rubbing your weapons."

"If that worked, I wouldn't be paying sixteen hundred a month for my current place." I tapped the app that showed the rent for this house. It was still listed at twenty-eight hundred. Incredibly inexpensive for the area, but I highly doubted Dimitri had that much money. He wouldn't be living in a van if he did. I showed him the app.

"We'll get it down." Dimitri nodded confidently. "It's been on the market for months, and they were trying to sell it for *years* before that. There are all kinds of rumors in the neighborhood about it being haunted. And the landlord knows about the vampire living and working in the basement. That's probably why people think it's haunted. The late-night banging of hammer on anvil."

"Why would you want to move into a house with a vampire banging on things in the basement all night?"

"It's better than living in a van. It has upscale amenities. Like a refrigerator. And a toilet."

"Upscale." I rubbed my face.

"Besides, Zoltan and Jimmy got to be buddies while they were locked up together."

"So?"

"Jimmy has been looking for a more peaceful area where the houses aren't so close together, and Zoltan said he wouldn't mind being closer to his new business in town."

"They're swapping places?"

"They're talking about it."

"Does either of these vampires pay rent? You said the landlord knows about Jimmy?"

"Jimmy didn't pay rent, but the landlord found that it's difficult to evict a vampire. They're very strong, you know."

"I've heard that."

"Few people are willing to challenge them. That Weber guy was a loon."

"I think his scientist was the bigger loon." Too bad he'd been the one to get away—unless one of those dragons had swept him up when I hadn't been watching and taken him to visit the Dragon Justice Court. I wouldn't object to that guy receiving years of punishment and rehabilitation. "It's crazy that they almost got away with their scheme. If they hadn't added the dragon egg to the mix, and if some meddling kids hadn't come along, they might have."

"Meddling kids? Is that us?"

"Yeah." I decided Dimitri was too young to have watched a lot of *Scooby Doo* as a kid.

His brow crinkled, but he shrugged away any confusion. "Zoltan said he would kick in a few hundred a month for rent if I promised to wall in the basement windows so no pesky light gets into his area. And I can manage a few hundred. Maybe more once the business gets rolling, but a few hundred for sure."

"That leaves you eighteen hundred short by my reckoning."

"I think I can get the landlord down to twenty-six hundred."

"Fine. That leaves you sixteen hundred short."

"Didn't you say that's what you pay for your rent? And that your lease is up?" Dimitri raised his eyebrows.

I stared at him. "You can't be serious."

"Nin said you're looking. It's a huge house. We wouldn't even have to see each other. Did you look inside?"

"Only the part where the wiring and furnace hadn't been updated since the nineteen-thirties, and there was a vampire coffin in the basement."

"There are three levels. It's huge. I could take the rooms in the back on the ground floor. You could have the turret upstairs. It's perfect for a princess. Didn't you say you're a princess now?"

"No. Freysha is a princess."

"Oh, right. She's staying with you now too, isn't she? How much can she chip in for rent?"

"Nothing. She's teaching me in exchange for the poshness that is my couch."

"I've slept on your couch. It's not posh."

"Only because you didn't bother to put the cushions back on before crashing. It's not my fault the apartment had been ransacked that night."

"She could have her own room here. And the conservatory in the back. You could grow all kinds of plants. Elves are into plants, right?"

I grimaced—how had he known? It had been less than a week since Freysha moved in, and the potted fern had turned into two more ferns, orchids, aloe vera, chrysanthemums, and some kind of vining plant that was already crawling up the side of the refrigerator. Maggie had found the plant infestation delightful, batting and nibbling at the leaves until

Willard had picked her up. I, on the other hand, was less certain of the new foliage and earth scents permeating the apartment. Freysha *did* need a conservatory. But...

"We're not renting a house together, Dimitri. It's not safe for anyone to live with me. My place gets ransacked and shot up all the time."

Maybe if I moved, it would take a while for the magical community to figure out where I'd gone. I eyed the turret a little wistfully, though the roof had moss all over it and probably leaked. A princess tower it was not. Still, those windows were amazing. I bet they had a nice view of the lake.

I shook my head. No. All those windows would only make that room vulnerable. It would be easy for someone to drive by and lob a grenade through one.

"I could make it a lot safer." Dimitri wriggled his fingers. "I do have some talents. I thought up a lot of new defensive designs while I was chained to the wall with nothing better to do. And I got a few ideas from the magical artifacts Weber had around his house. I might not be able to keep out dragons, but I could build stuff to keep out less powerful beings. There's a nice big lawn. Plenty of room for highly functional yard art."

Was it insane that I was considering this? I'd lived alone since Thad and I had gotten divorced. More than ten years. It was hard to imagine having a roommate—roommates—now, but I'd already committed to Freysha. I had imagined her stay would be temporary, but it *would* be nice if she didn't have to sleep on the couch. And if I had a room for visitors, my mom wouldn't have to stay in a hotel when she came up to Seattle.

If Dimitri truly could install some alarms and other devices to protect the place from enemies, maybe it wouldn't be that horrible of an idea. I'd been avoiding getting close to people for so long that it was habit, and my first thought was to recoil, but if our domicile could be turned into a nearly impenetrable castle, maybe it could work. And even if the idea of having a vampire in the basement was nuts, it would keep out the casual riffraff. Like a Rottweiler slathering at a chain-link fence.

"Where would my dragon land? He uses the roof of my current apartment building. If he did that here—" I waved to the chimney and pointed roofline of the Victorian, "—he'd end up with a spire up his butt."

"Is he not into that?"

"We haven't gone over his sexual preferences yet."

"Really? I thought— Well, I think everybody thought…" Dimitri spread his hand.

"Who's everybody?" I scowled at him.

"Nobody."

My scowl might have grown more vocal, but a bandy-legged man ambled up to us with a briefcase.

"You Mr. Plotnikov?" He looked Dimitri up and down and frowned, then turned the frown on me.

What was this guy's problem?

"Yes, sir. Are you Mr. Scott?"

"That's right. You said you have a new business in the area and are a serious renter. I was expecting somebody older."

"She's older." Dimitri pointed a thumb at me.

Was this the part where I looked intimidating and rubbed my weapons? I wasn't good at negotiations. Dimitri should have invited Nin.

"Not much," Scott grumbled. "Are you sure you can afford this place? I'm not going any lower on the rent."

"There's a vampire in the basement."

"The rent is already reduced to allow for that. There's a Craftsman a few blocks away that's the same square footage and bedrooms as this and rents for almost six thousand a month."

"Is it vampire free?" I asked.

Scott scowled at me.

"Vampires lower property values a *lot*," I said. "It takes special renters to be willing to put up with that."

"So I trust. If you qualify, I'm going to have you sign a number of papers promising you won't hold me responsible if he drinks your blood, damages your belongings, or otherwise maims you or your visitors."

"Jimmy sounds rough," I told Dimitri.

"Yeah…" Dimitri gripped his chin pensively as if he were having second thoughts. "Maybe this isn't a good idea after all."

Scott, who'd been hesitant to consider us worthy prospects, changed his tune and lifted a placating hand. "Look, if you've got the deposit and first month's rent, we can make something happen."

Dimitri looked at me, and I nodded infinitesimally. Even though

I hadn't made as much from the Weber gig as I'd originally thought I would, he'd given me a good chunk of money. I'd mailed off most of it to pay down the auto loan, but I had some left and could come up with rent and a deposit. *If* I decided this was a good idea.

"I won't even run a credit check if you'll sign the papers," Scott added. "But you know the place is reputedly haunted too, right?"

"Are you always so forthright about your house's potential flaws?" I asked.

"I've learned I have to be, otherwise the tenants stop paying, and the courts always side with them." His lips twisted. "Because this house has a reputation."

"A reputation in the judicial system?"

"Just a reputation. Period."

"We're interested if you can rent it to us for twenty-six hundred a month," Dimitri said. "We can work with reputations. We're a little quirky too."

Scott eyed me. "She doesn't look quirky."

I was debating whether to feel pleased by this unbiased assessment—especially given how many people had called me odd lately—when Dimitri said, "She dates a dragon and has a magical tiger."

Scott must have been dealing with magical beings for a while, because he didn't bat an eye at this. "Maybe you can handle the vampire then."

"It's the wiring I'm more concerned with." I imagined Dimitri plugging in a power tool to work on a project and the whole place going up in flames. "Can we do home improvements?"

"You want to improve my property?" Scott stared at me as if I'd grown dragon scales and horns.

"Do renters not usually do that?"

"No. It typically goes the other way."

"Dimitri is a landscaper, and I… have replaced a lot of doors." More accurately, I'd replaced one door that had been broken down many times.

Scott opened his briefcase. "Here's the contract."

"How long is the lease for?" I hadn't even seen the inside yet, other than the basement. What if it was even more of a pit than I imagined?

"A year. I'll knock two hundred off the monthly rent if you sign up for two years." Scott's eyes gleamed.

Why did I have a feeling nobody even stayed for six months?

"Twenty-four hundred?" Dimitri reached for the pen.

"Can you afford to pay the mortgage and everything on that?" I wasn't as quick to sign. What if the place was slathered with mold on the inside, and I couldn't breathe? I'd end up sleeping on a cot in the back yard.

"I own the house outright," Scott said. "It's been in the family for a long time. The insurance and the property taxes are the main expenses. King County doesn't factor vampires into its land valuation considerations."

"Weird."

"I've spoken with them about it. The first clerk said vampires don't exist. The second said to remove the vampire. As if I haven't tried. It's not like you can just call pest control."

The powerful aura of a dragon came onto my radar, not the dragon I wanted to see. Zondia.

She was very slightly better than Shaygor and his kin, but she could crush me with her mind as easily as they could—and probably still wanted to. Fortunately, Zav came into my range a few seconds later. I breathed out a relieved sigh. Hopefully, he'd recovered from his injuries, settled everything with the egg, and life could return to normal. As normal as someone like me could hope for, anyway.

Dimitri was cheerfully skimming and signing and initialing page after page of a contract far longer than any lease agreement I'd ever seen. He didn't notice the dragons flying in over Green Lake.

"You're reading that before you sign, right?" I asked.

"It's all about us agreeing not to sue him for accidents around the house, attacks, or break-ins."

"You can't expect a haunted house to be free from quirks," Scott said.

"Is it actually haunted, or can the quirks be attributed to the vampire blacksmith clanging away at night?" I asked as Zav and Zondia landed in the street, barely managing not to crush a Volkswagen Beetle.

"I really can't say," Scott said. "I haven't spent the night there since I was dared to as a boy. I heard strange noises and left hastily before midnight."

"Great." I envisioned something akin to Zoltan's haunted carriage house.

The dragons shifted into their human forms, Zav in his usual black robe and back in slippers today, and Zondia in black leather pants and a leather jacket decorated with heavy zippers and metal grommets. Her hair was the same shade of lilac she was as a dragon. Nobody would have guessed they were related.

Dimitri must have finally noticed their powerful auras for he handed the papers and pen to me and stared at them. As far as I knew, he'd never encountered Zondia before.

"Are we going to have trouble?" he murmured.

"I hope not. I'm planning to ask Zav how he feels about landing on a spire."

"He seemed to do okay landing in the street."

"Yeah, but there's a street outside of my apartment building, and he always opts for the roof instead. Maybe roofs are superior landing pads."

"Maybe they don't like hot tarmac on bare feet on a summer day."

"Maybe." I took the papers and pen and headed toward the dragons.

Scott lifted a finger in protest, but Dimitri distracted him by leading him onto the yard and asking if it was all right to trim rhododendrons that were so overgrown they obscured the windows of several ground-floor rooms.

"Greetings, my mate," Zav said, his aura flowing around me as he approached and spread his arms.

I had time to see Zondia roll her eyes in a very human manner before Zav wrapped me in an embrace punctuated by a kiss that made me forget about spires, vampires, and rental agreements, and also that there were other people around. Even though I had a vague sense that I should pull him behind one of the rhododendrons for this, it was hard to want to do anything except lean into his hard body and bask in the tingling warmth of his aura as it crackled around me. Little zings of pleasure ran through my veins, and I hoped he was here to stay for a while.

"Such randiness is unseemly from one of your stature, brother," Zondia said tartly.

*It is proper for a powerful dragon to let all know that he claims his mate not only with magic but with his body, and woe to the enemy who gets between them.* Zav responded telepathically, not taking his lips from mine as he ran his hand down my back and squeezed my ass. I let my hands do a little squeezing of their own and thought about how much more appealing it would be if I could get him out of that robe one day.

*I sense that you're pleased to see me,* I thought. *Does that mean everything went well at home?*

*Things are a mess at home, but I* am *pleased to see you. And that you are continuing to learn magical lessons to defend yourself from annoying, irresponsible, juvenile dragons.*

*You're more pleased that I knocked aside Xilneth's pass than that I got that egg and was willing to fight Shaygor, aren't you?*

*What is a pass?*

*His attempt to woo me away for sex.*

*He will* not *woo you away, and you will* not *mate with anyone but myself. You are mine. Forever.* He growled as he kissed me harder, and I wondered if he wanted to mate right now.

The primal part of me that was enjoying the hell out of the kiss and the hungry caresses almost thought that sounded like a good idea. But the grass was wet, the sidewalk was hard, and there were witnesses. Besides, I refused to set a positive precedent after he said stupid possessive things like *you are mine.* I planted my hands on his chest and drew my mouth back.

"Cool your jets, dragon boy. I'm my own person, and we're not promising forever before we've even had sex or spent the night together." Maybe I should have stuck with telepathy because the words came out breathless, and Zav looked a little smug as he saw his effect on me.

His violet eyes flared with inner light. "This will be soon now that you are learning to use your power. You please me, and I will have you every night."

"Good to know." I patted him on the chest.

He captured my hand as he gazed into my eyes. We stood still, and his power continued to curl about me, thrumming at my nerves.

"Is it normal for this species to have feelings of nausea when listening to horny drivel like this?" Zondia asked.

"Yes," Dimitri said from behind us—he must have finished commenting on the landscape. "Val, can you sign that stuff and wait until you're in your tower to have sex with him?"

Zav's gaze shifted from my face past my shoulder, and he narrowed his eyes at Dimitri.

Dimitri lifted his hands defensively and bent his knees, as if he expected to have to spring away from laser beams shooting out of Zav's eyes. I stepped back out of his embrace in case I needed to stop that.

"What tower?" Zav asked.

Dimitri pointed to the turret rising up from the second story of the house. Calling it a tower was a touch optimistic, though I did hope the room inside with all the windows was as fabulous as it looked like it might be.

"I figure that can be Val's room after we move in," Dimitri said, his hands still up. "She's paying the majority of the rent—or she will be once she signs the lease—so she can have the whole upper level. I just need a room for myself, and Zoltan and Jimmy are working out the details on a basement exchange."

"You are acquiring a new domicile?" Zav looked from the turret back to me.

Dimitri stayed back, but he pointed at the pen and papers.

"It does seem that way." I stepped a little farther from Zav to skim through the pages and sign and initial. "There's more room. Freysha wouldn't have to sleep on the couch."

"But you will also live with the vampire and that one?" Zav pointed at Dimitri.

"His name is Dimitri and yes. This was all his idea."

"It was his idea that you have a tower?"

"It's a turret, and yes. The person paying the majority of the rent gets the turret. The person paying the majority of the rent also has the others carry her furniture when it's time to move in." I smiled at Dimitri and handed him the signed papers back.

"Uh. Can't your dragon move it with his magic?"

"From what I've seen, Zav's magic is for hurling enemies into walls. I don't think he should be responsible for moving my bedroom set."

Zav frowned at me as Dimitri trotted the papers back to Scott. "My magic is sublime."

Zondia cleared her throat. "Are you going to tell her sometime today, brother?"

I eyed her warily. "There's something to tell?"

Zav sighed. "My mother suggested that I ask you to warn your world leaders that more of our kind are now aware that this planet exists and has species sophisticated enough to arrange thefts from dragons. What should be done is being debated in the Dragon Justice Court. Your people may receive a more official visit than they have before. It is possible dragons will vote to assert authority here to keep it from being a wild planet where criminals hide."

Warn my world leaders? "Sure, I'll call up the president and the secretary-general of the UN tomorrow."

"Excellent."

Ugh. I would warn Willard. She could figure out how to get the message to the higher-ups. I wasn't sure whether to be horrified or amused at the idea of a dragon flying into the White House. Probably horrified.

"Is there any way to convince your people to leave Earth alone?" I asked.

"I will continue to round up criminals here, but it may already be too late." Zav stepped close and wrapped an arm around my shoulders.

I leaned against him, wondering if his presence would make me safe if dragon trouble came to Earth or more of a target. Given past incidents, I feared the latter. But I still leaned against him.

"You will continue your training with the elven princess?" he asked.

"Yes. You think I'll need it?"

"Yes."

## THE END

## CONNECT WITH THE AUTHOR

Have a comment? Question? Just want to say hi? Find me online at:
http://www.lindsayburoker.com
http://www.facebook.com/LindsayBuroker
http://twitter.com/GoblinWriter
Thanks for reading!

Made in the USA
Las Vegas, NV
11 April 2025